EVERY LITTLE PIECE OF MY HEART

Non PRATT

WALKER
BOOKS

First published 2020 by Walker Books Ltd
87 Vauxhall Walk, London SE11 5HJ

2 4 6 8 10 9 7 5 3 1

Text © 2020 Leonie Parish
Cover illustration © 2020 Helen Crawford-White

The right of Leonie Parish to be identified as author of
this work has been asserted by her in accordance with
the Copyright, Designs and Patents Act 1988

This book has been typeset in Fairfield and Avenir

Printed and bound by CPI Group (UK) Ltd, Croydon CR0 4YY

British Library Cataloguing in Publication Data:
a catalogue record for this book is available from the British Library

ISBN 978-1-4063-6694-5

www.walker.co.uk

MIX
Paper from
responsible sources
FSC® C020471
FSC www.fsc.org

For Teesside, where I left a piece of my heart

FOREWORD

There's something of me in every character in this book, but there are key differences too: I have not been diagnosed with a chronic illness; I've never been Chinese and gay; my upbringing was firmly middle class.

I've listened to people who understand these characters' lives better than me and I've tried to avoid anything too misleading or harmfully ignorant and just let the characters exist as (fictional) humans on the page.

However. A range of characters is no substitute for a range of storytellers. Readers deserve more stories from more people. Stories where disabled characters have the same adventures as abled ones and characters of colour aren't viewed against a white default. Stories where poverty is understood, not leveraged for pity, where religious beliefs aren't sensationalised for plot, where a character's gender or sexuality doesn't preclude a happy beginning, middle and end. Stories that spring from creative authenticity, where the writer felt free to write anything they wanted and the reward is an audience.

Please write those stories, please believe they'll get published and please read those that exist. If you're writing already and would like support, I'm on Twitter and Tumblr and have a website with a contact form. I'd like to elevate other people's voices, not drown them out with my own.

FRIDAY

SOPHIE

Sophie woke with her phone in her hand, pain screaming down her fingers, into her wrist, loud enough to echo in her elbow.

Every morning, pain came first – feeling it, locating it, processing it. Today's was both sharp and dull, all the muscles and joints of her left hand objecting to the mistake of falling asleep still holding her phone. But that was the worst of it. Nothing else hurt any more than it had when she'd gone to sleep.

Hope came second.

Switching hands, Sophie pulled her phone free from the charging cable snaking across her pillow to check her messages.

There were a lot. Notifications from friends who'd stayed up beyond the time she'd dropped off, emails with discount codes, and alerts for new content from channels and accounts that she'd subscribed to.

Nothing important. Nothing from Freya.

Still, Sophie kept on checking – after she'd brushed her teeth, once she'd got dressed, before feeding the cat, after feeding the cat, while feeding herself...

"No phones at the breakfast table."

Keeping her head down so Mum couldn't see her eye roll, Sophie flipped her phone over and picked up her spoon to prod the contents of her bowl. Her Weetabix had already dissolved into mush, the cranberries and raisins swollen with milk. Breakfast was often a struggle, but eating wasn't optional: Sophie needed meds. Meds needed food. Sophie needed food.

Doggedly, she spooned up the mush, eyes fixed on Friday's compartment of the pill box next to her glass of water. Mum was in constant motion in the background, emptying the dishwasher, opening the back door to let the cat out, preparing coffee for the school run.

"I'll make sure we've something nice in for breakfast tomorrow." Mum talked as she breezed across the kitchen, every step fizzing with the energy of someone who'd woken with 100% charge and wasn't permanently operating on low power mode. "What sort of thing do you fancy?"

The truthful answer was "a lie-in", but it wasn't the one Mum wanted to hear.

"I don't have anything in mind." It was all Sophie could do to finish what was in her bowl – thinking of eating anything more was beyond her.

"Hmm … something high in protein, get that GCSE revision off to a good start…"

"Don't forget I'm going out tonight," Sophie said. The way Mum was talking made it sound like she'd forgotten.

"We'll see how you feel after school."

"I'll feel fine."

"We've talked about this, Soph—"

"And we agreed that for one day I get to live the life I'm supposed to have." Her spoon clattered on the side of her bowl as she stared across the table.

"It's just you've been doing so well this week…"

For Mum, "doing well" meant behaving well and taking

care of herself in a way that Sophie loathed. She'd eaten every breakfast without grumbling, promised to let her friends carry her school bag between lessons and stayed out of sun that she longed to be able to bask in. Every evening had been a quiet one – do very little and get very bored and go to bed at a parentally pleasing hour.

All of it so she'd be able to go out tonight.

Not that there were rewards for good behaviour. Being chronically ill meant only ever trusting what was happening *now*.

And right now, Sophie felt hopeful.

Mum wasn't going to take that away.

"You don't need to keep me sealed in a bubble. I'm not contagious."

Mum sighed, her lower lip tucking itself away: a habit Sophie had inherited to stop herself from saying something she shouldn't.

"I know, darling," Mum said eventually. "It's my daughter I'm worried about, not other people. *But*" – she stressed as Sophie took breath to object – "you're right, we agreed."

There was more to come, but then the doorbell went and, like a particularly thirsty Pavlov's dog, Mum perked up and disappeared out into the hall. Nothing in the furthest reaches of heaven or hell could stop her mother from seizing a chance to flirt with the postman.

Sophie idly flipped her phone back over.

Instagram opened on a post she'd looked at more times than was healthy since 1 January.

Freya standing by a door, looking back over her shoulder

as she pushed it open to reveal a sliver of dark beyond. Even in an outfit as unremarkable as the white shirt and black skirt she wore for work, Sophie's best friend managed to look special. The gleam of golden light on her pale blonde hair and the tilt of her chin, the confidence in her smile because she knew someone was watching.

The caption below was classic Freya: *January. Named for the god of doorways. Let's see where this one leads…*

A many-layered comment that multiplied in meaning when the teacher skipped over the name "Freya Newmarch" the first day back at school. An above-average amount of likes spiralled into hundreds, and the first flurry of compliments from the usual suspects turned into increasingly urgent demands to know where Freya was as speculation broke out in little sub-chats.

Are you OK? We're worried!
Why aren't you replying to any of the comments?!
Where u gone?
 I saw her mum last night!!!
  You saw someone you *thought* was her mum.
  You calling me a liar?
Were you on the number 678 this morning? I waved but I'm not sure you saw me…
 Duh. She was not on the bus.

The highlight came when someone typed the first line to "Rehab", and the rest of the comments were people writing the lyrics line for line with a few pill and needle emojis thrown in for good measure – a bout of mild hysteria brought on by boredom and intrigue. Once the song reached its conclusion, Freya returned to her feed for an encore.

You guys are SO WEIRD. (I love it.) No rehab. No kidnapping. I moved to Manchester! Followed by a string of cry-laughing emojis.

Sophie stared into the screen.

The photo had been tagged at Rabscuttle Hall, Freya leaving through the main doors for the drama of a good Insta post – framed by heavy wood and brass panels, bathed in a warm and comforting glow before she stepped into the night.

She'd been dreading that shift. Sophie had sent a message asking how it was going, and Freya had answered with a brief. *I survived xxx*

Not knowing how to take such a short answer, Sophie had done what she always did and replied with something light and breezy – a sign that she was happy to listen if Freya wanted to talk.

Only she hadn't wanted to talk.

At all.

130 days since that photo was posted and Sophie hadn't heard a word.

Today was the last day before GCSEs began, a day of stupid awards in assembly and messing around in lessons, of signed shirts and pranks the school had strictly forbidden. Stuff she and Freya should be doing together, not a hundred miles apart.

The sound of Mum returning had Sophie popping her

phone into the pocket of her school skirt, ready to stand up and clear away what was left of her cereal.

"That man." Mum fanned herself with the parcel she was holding. "I'd take a special delivery from him any day of the week and twice on Sundays. Make sure you thank whoever sent this."

She held out a parcel bound in plain brown paper. Sophie's name, Sophie's address…

Freya's handwriting.

WIN

Buckthorn sixth form common room was filled with break-time buzz and the rustle of crisp packets circulating round the group sprawled over the comfy chairs.

"Win! Someone looking for you!"

Win looked up from where she'd been sitting alone in the corner, Converse resting on the edge of the coffee table, phone propped on her thighs as she paused the video her friend Felix had sent.

The lad who'd called her name pointed to the door.

The someone looking for her was a girl yet to graduate from the Buckthorn green-and-white-and-gold into the heady uniform-free life of a sixth former. She crossed the room, ignoring the way she caught the attention of Sam Baker and his mates as she passed, and came to a standstill in front of Win.

"Hi. So, this is weird, but I'm Sophie." Then she added, "Charbonneau."

Win already knew Sophie Charbonneau as a pretty face in a crowded corridor, freckles blurring the surface of her skin, the most elegant arch at the apex of her eyebrows, and cascading flames of red hair. A girl for whom Win's breath hitched, even as she squashed any notion of something more.

"I would say I'm Win, but we already established that." Win raised her eyebrows, not quite sure what to expect. "And I can help you … how?"

"So long as you're Winnie Su?" Win nodded. Win was,

17

indeed, short for Winnie. "I've to give you this."

Sophie swung her bag round to get something out. Win had never been close enough to notice the line of slightly darker freckles that sat along Sophie Charbonneau's top lip or the bump on the bridge of her nose. A second later she produced a brown paper parcel from inside her bag – only she held it close a moment, giving Win one last, wary look.

"You *did* know Freya Newmarch, right?"

"I did." This made a little more sense. Sort of. "She lived next door."

"Well, this is from her." And Sophie held out a parcel with the name "Winnie Su" written in smooth strokes of black pen across the front. It was a satisfying size, lighter than it looked and slightly squishy.

A beat after she'd handed it over, Sophie sat on the coffee table, leaning forward, brown eyes melting to amber in the sun filtering in from the window.

Win's breath did the thing.

"It arrived this morning at my house," Sophie said. "The first layer was addressed to me, but when I opened it, there was one for you inside – and a note."

Win had already noticed the thin, grey fingerless gloves Sophie was wearing – odd for this time of year – but she made no comment as Sophie reached inside the palm of her right glove and produced a piece of paper that she then handed over.

Hey Soph, pass this along would you? There's treasure at the end, promise. F x

Same writing as on the front of Win's parcel.

"Treasure?" Win looked again at the parcel, then back at Sophie, who took the note and shrugged.

"In pass the parcel the biggest prize is the one in the middle, right?"

"Was that all there was? A note and another layer to unwrap?"

"Biggest prize" made it sound like there might be others, and Win preferred to have all her information up front.

Sophie pressed her lips together a second, then looked down as she tucked a finger beneath the wrist of her left glove.

"There was this too," she said, and she hooked out a fine silver bracelet, each link so delicate that the chain moved like a trickle of water against the inside of Sophie's wrist. "It used to belong to Freya."

Win recognised the arrow-shaped clasp that formed the only detail on the chain. She'd once asked Freya if she could have a closer look at how it worked – that had been the only time Win had seen her take it off.

Sophie might not have noticed that Win was Freya's neighbour, but Win had walked ten paces behind those two on enough Fridays after school to remember the way they laughed and gossiped. She'd seen Freya loop her arm in Sophie's and rest her head on her shoulder as they walked, years of comfort in one single gesture.

"That's a really lovely thing to send you," she said.

"Yeah, well…" Sophie trailed off, before sitting up a little straighter, the confidence with which she'd come over returning as she looked at the parcel. "Aren't you going to open it?"

"Not right now." If there was a present beneath this paper as personal as that bracelet, Win didn't want to find out what it was in front of an audience. "I'll open it later."

There was an air of thwarted expectation in the way Sophie looked at the parcel in Win's hand, a pinch of her brows and tightening in her jaw.

"In that case…" Sophie pulled out a permanent marker from the front pocket of her bag – standard issue for Year 11 shirt-signing the last day before exams. Leaning over, Sophie's hair fell forward, profile pale against the curtain of curls as she wrote her number on the paper of Freya's parcel.

Capping the pen, she stood, saying, "If there's treasure in the middle, I want in."

She shouldered her bag and held up a hand, waving as she left. Everything about her, from the tilt of her chin to the way she spoke, exuded the kind of confidence that came from never having to make an effort. She expected people to do what she wanted because that's what they always did.

Same as Freya.

April – 245 days before Freya left

The first person Win had come out to in person was her sister – 88 minutes into what must have been their fifth viewing of *Thor: Ragnarok*. They were on Win's bed, her laptop balanced on a pile of GCSE revision guides she had no intention of opening. It was February and mocks had finished the week before; revision for the real thing could wait. Just for a day.

"Is it wrong to have a crush on the Hulk?" Sunny had said.

"You mean Bruce Banner?" Win asked. If so: definitely wrong. Mark Ruffalo was older than their dad.

"I mean Hulk. Big, green. Kinda grumpy. Kinda sexy."

"Well, he's not to my taste, but you do you."

Sunny never did anything else. She scooped up a handful of the popcorn sitting between them and then said, "So who is? To your taste, I mean."

A question Win had spent most of her life evading with a change of conversation, or a supple little lie that slipped out before it could be stopped.

But that day, with her sister, she wanted to tell the truth. It wasn't easy

"Valkyrie," she managed. More croak than word. "Definitely more my type."

"Yeah, she's hot." Except Sunny's tone suggested the point had failed to strike.

"And Hela." There was still a distinct shake in Win's syllables as she said it. "Particularly when she's not all antlered up. And, y'know, I'd take Topaz over Thor."

Sunny was nodding, slowly, like she'd shifted from appreciating an aesthetic to understanding there was something more going on. She didn't say anything though. On Sunny, silence meant that she was trying to listen, which meant Win had to talk.

Win cleared her throat and kept her eyes on the screen. "Are you sensing a theme?"

"Yes." The word burst out of her and Sunny wrapped Win in a hug that lasted until the end of the film. As the credits rolled, she shuffled up straighter and added, "Just to check. That was you telling me you're a lesbian, right?"

Win would never have guessed that three months later she'd be telling the girl who lived next door.

The day should have been perfect. In many ways it had been – Win had caught the train to Leeds, the journey there an exquisite agony of anticipation, her phone out as she and Riley sent each other a barrage of updates. Selfies from the train, the view from the window, Riley's walk from her house into the centre of town, Win poring over the pictures, barely able to believe she was finally going to see her girlfriend in person. Her whole soul was nerves, leaving no room for any other thought or feeling that didn't relate to Riley, until she was speed-walking through the barriers at the station and then they were together, arms wrapped round each other in delight, breathing each other in and finally relaxing in relief.

No kisses.

No hand holding.

That would come later, when they were both ready. For now, being close, hearing her, seeing her – that was enough.

The plan was to head to the cafe Riley's sister worked at – nestled between a barber and a dentist on the same road as the gay bars that came to life long after Win would go home – then they'd catch whatever was showing at the Queer Film Festival. A holiday into Win's future, with the girl she wanted to kiss in the present.

Like any holiday, Win became more aware of herself, of the confidence that she usually held close, the side of her that only her sister and her friends online got to see, because they were the only ones who knew how to look.

That day, with Riley, Win *glowed*.

"I can't believe I get to do this." Riley squeezed Win's hand, their fingers fused together as they left the cafe.

"Me neither."

And because she felt bold, because she felt brave, because she was feeling so utterly herself, Win lifted their hands and pressed a single kiss to Riley's knuckles, delighting in the grin she got for it – the promise of a kiss that crept closer with every second.

As the two of them stepped onto the pavement, Win turned to look for the bus stop.

And saw her next-door neighbour.

When Win looked back at that moment – which she did, a lot – she wasn't sure what really happened. She knew she let go of Riley's hand. Knew that she'd had a moment of hope in which she thought she might have gone unnoticed, because that was, after all, Win's superpower.

Except it wasn't. She was only human and she was standing right in front of Freya Newmarch, outside a cafe called Bi Artisan Bakes, whose menu was a list of gay puns.

"Winnie!" Freya didn't know Win well enough to realise that only her parents and teachers called her that. The searing blue of Freya's gaze shifted to Riley in a less-than-subtle question that Win was not prepared to answer.

"Freya. Hi," Win said. "We're in a bit of a rush, so…"

"Of course." Freya half-turned to the man behind, who was frowning down at his phone and muttering something about this not being the viaduct he'd been thinking of, before she gave Win a superficial, "I'll see you around."

Post-date, Win's head should have been nothing but endorphin clouds and memories of kissing Riley round the back of the community centre where they'd just watched a series of shorts, the slight hint of salt from the popcorn and the warmth of another mouth on hers, lips as much smile as kiss.

But Win's joy came tempered by worry about Freya. Most of what she knew came from neighbourly interactions – invitations to the occasional barbecue or that one time Freya's mum invited everyone over for drinks at New Year – and a little from attending the same school, one year apart. Freya didn't inhabit the same corners of the internet as Win, but her profiles were public and nothing Freya did went undocumented – or unnoticed. Everyone at Buckthorn knew who she'd kissed on the French trip, who her friends were and where they would be...

An existence that was the antithesis of Win's.

That night, between a stream of wistful messages to Riley and excitable updates on the group chat, Win scrolled through Freya's feed, filling colour into familiar outlines, building a more detailed picture of someone who used her own secrets as currency for attention, who didn't shy away from asking public questions of things better kept private, and who (it appeared) knew every single person in the entire school one way or another.

Including Sarah Evans, who'd been seeing Win's cousin Gen since the two of them battled it out in the final of a regional debating competition, and Andy Ho, whose parents were friends with Win's.

On the day of the date, confidence had come from feeling in control and Freya had wrenched the wheel from Win's hands without even wanting to drive: the only option was to wrench it back.

Her hand was remarkably steady as she reached to knock on the door the following morning.

Freya opened it, bare limbs and feet, hair wild, eyes narrowed against the sunshine. She was pretty and slender and sleepy, like a pedigree cat woken from a nap.

"Oh. Hello again."

Win couldn't gauge anything from that.

"Hi." A breath, then, "Sorry for running off yesterday. I thought maybe we could have a chat about that."

"I mean, it's fine. You were with your friend and I was with my dad…"

Friend. A word to give Win a way out. But she was here now. She had prepared. And that word still held wriggle room that would give Freya power over a narrative that belonged to Win.

"I'd still like to talk. If you're free?"

Instinctively she slipped out of her Converse and followed Freya barefoot across cold stone tiles and into the hollowed-out belly of a house that only resembled Win's from the outside. Inside was chillier, less homey, with one enormous room doing the work of three – kitchen, dining room and lounge all wrapped as one around the hall.

Freya padded across the kitchen to a row of artfully mismatched tins.

"What would you like?" What Win would like was to know if she could trust her. If Freya could keep Win's secrets better than she kept her own. "We've got PG Tips, Earl Grey, one of these is mint, I think, or there's coffee?"

"Mint's fine, thanks."

Coming out to Sunny had been terrifying – the same vertigo as standing at the edge of the highest board at the pool, staring at the blue below. But underneath the fear there had been faith that Win could make the leap, break the surface and come back up for air. Nothing like the persistent prickle of doubt crackling like static as she watched Freya fill the kettle and flick it on, fetching the mugs...

Win gripped the edge of the worktop, feeling the pressure of truth about to come out.

"I'm going to tell you something because I think I have to." She might have been the one who'd written the lines, rehearsed them in her mind, but her voice sounded like it had come from someone else – the sound of a song playing through her headphones before she'd had chance to put them on.

Freya stopped what she was doing. Set the mugs down and turned to lean back against the sink, the span of the breakfast bar between the two of them.

"OK, I'm listening."

"I wasn't with a friend yesterday." Win swallowed, held her nerve. "Riley's my girlfriend. We were on a date." Then, just to be clear, "I'm gay."

A statement Win accompanied with a very good impression of the Elmo shrug GIF because she wasn't sure what to do with her hands.

Then she made herself look at Freya.

She wasn't laughing, like she thought this was a joke, or recoiling like she didn't approve. She was just nodding, looking serious and thoughtful, like she'd actually heard what Win had to say.

"That's cool," Freya said, lifting her eyebrows a touch before she said, "Do you still want a mint tea?"

Win did.

They talked then. A bit about yesterday – Freya asked how she knew Riley, how the date went – and Win tried to get her head around the fact that she was talking to someone other than her sister about this, veering wildly between being glad to have said something and terrified that she'd not yet said enough.

"How come you were there – in Leeds?" Win asked.

"With Dad." Freya pushed over the punnet of raspberries she'd been picking from and Win took one as Freya carried on. "He's in Manchester, Mum and me live here – and Leeds is halfway. It's a good place to meet during term time when Mum thinks I've too much on to go all the way to Manchester."

"I didn't know your dad lived in Manchester," Win said. She didn't know much about Freya's family life beyond how much she argued with her mum. Neither of them seemed to realise that the louder they shouted the further it carried

27

and that Win's window was nearly always open because of how hot Mama set the central heating.

"Why would you?" Freya said with a shrug. "It's not like I talk about it."

Win realised then that she'd assumed Freya's online life was a full measure of her real one because that was how Win measured her own. That there were parts of Freya's life she kept private was reassuring.

Time to finish what she'd come here to say.

"About that. Talking, I mean…"

She sensed Freya straighten, knew that she had switched back to a more attentive mood than the one they'd relaxed into.

"I'm not out at school and I've not told my parents yet. Although I will, soon." She picked her mug up, took a tiny sip, put it down. Knew she was delaying. "Sunny knows and I'm out online."

Freya frowned then.

"If you're out online then wouldn't your mates know?"

"My mates do know." Win's frown matched Freya's.

"But you said you weren't out at school—"

"Oh." Win laughed and shook her head. "Yeah. When I say 'mates' I mean my online crowd, not the people I go to school with."

To Win, being someone's friend meant knowing that bad days required pictures of Chris Evans and his dog, or that the best way to make someone feel part of a con they couldn't go to was to take a photo of their face on a stick to hold up in all the official photos with the actors. Friends were people who didn't flinch at a stream of all caps in an argument and understood that *Thor: Ragnarok* could be someone's favourite film even if it didn't pass the Bechdel test. Win's friends might have been made behind the anonymity of a quippy username and a fan art avatar, but they were the people she trusted the most in the world.

The other end of a direct message was as good as sitting next to each other at school.

"So," Win said, drawing in a breath and meeting Freya's eye, "I came over because you saw me with Riley, and I feel safer telling you the truth, making it clear it's not something to talk about, than leaving it for you to guess, or ask someone else—"

"I wouldn't. I *won't*." Freya's face, so carefree in all the pictures she posted, held conviction. "I understand. This is your life; you get to choose who you tell. Not me."

SOPHIE

Last period had descended into chaos. The whole of Year 11 swarmed the grounds, ties knotted around limbs and heads, fists bristling with marker pens as students wrote all over each other – shirts, skin, whatever was on offer. The world had become a hurricane of movement and noise that left Sophie feeling besieged. Trying to write something meaningful on everyone's shirt was a challenge for someone whose brain wasn't willing to play along. Although at least if someone's name dropped out of her head she could scan their shirt for an answer.

Her hand hurt though – her right this time. The compression gloves helped with her joints, but something about the angle, the need to press her pen into the material, made things worse.

Stepping back from the storm and swapping pen for phone, Sophie checked for any messages from the mysterious Winnie – *Win* – Su.

Nothing.

Not exactly a surprise. Giving Win her number had been a long shot – desperate curiosity disguised as an offer of help. Not that Win looked like someone who needed help. Sitting on her own, she'd not looked as if she needed anyone else's approval, with that super-short fringe and a black-and-grey aesthetic that didn't ask for attention. And the way she'd looked at Sophie… Only people who believed in themselves made eye contact like that.

"Sophie?"

"Mm?" She'd not noticed anyone was talking to her.

"You OK?" The corners of Morgan's mouth tucked themselves away into her soft, round cheeks. The Sympathetic Look.

"I'm fine," Sophie said, sliding her arm through her friend's to rest her head on Morgan's shoulder. She was one of those people who was always warm and Sophie sank into the feeling of having someone else take a little of the weight. "Just recharging a moment."

"Same."

They both knew it wasn't.

Lupus was an invisible illness, which meant Sophie had the option of keeping it that way around people who didn't look too closely. For a while, she'd not wanted to tell anyone else at school. Dealing with other people's reactions was hard when she was still struggling to get a handle on her own. But without Freya around, Sophie had needed at least *some* support, and Morgan and Georgia had been her best options.

But best didn't mean perfect.

"You going to be OK for the party later?"

Sophie resisted the urge to tell Morgan she sounded *exactly* like her mum.

"I'll be fine."

"Is there anything—"

"I said I'll be fine." Sophie regretted the edge in her voice. Being nice never used to be this hard, but then, she didn't use to be in a constant state of pain and/or exhaustion. No one had warned her how much other people's concern could drain her, how she'd always have to accept it or risk being rude. Looking for a change of subject, she went with, "Where's Georgia got to?"

"Over there, getting signed by Ewan Moore."

Sophie followed Morgan's gaze to where Georgia – whose tiny frame and innocent little face would see her ID-ed for life – fluttered like an amorous hummingbird at a boy standing half a head taller than his friends, most of it hair.

"That's my girl," Sophie said, grinning as she reached up to tuck her hair back behind her ear.

"This is nice." Morgan touched a finger to the bracelet that rolled down from beneath her glove. "Didn't Freya use to have one like it?"

Panic lanced through Sophie's heart. This bracelet was so definitively Freya that when it had slithered out of the first layer of the parcel, silver links pooling on the kitchen table, Sophie had burst into tears. Ambushed by her emotions, she'd put it on without thinking.

"I guess she did," she said with a non-committal shrug.

"How is she?" Morgan had the same soft tone for asking about Freya as she had for asking about lupus.

"Sad to be missing out, obvs." Sophie tried a smile copy and pasted from her past. "Even sadder once she finds out that Georgia has *actually* made contact with Ewan after two years of long-distance pining."

"Better send her a photo as evidence."

"Good plan…" Sophie let go of Morgan to reach for her phone, the promise of sending Freya a photo yet another lie inched out from the Jenga stack for Sophie to set atop an increasingly precarious tower. No one knew the truth. They *never* could. Not after five months of lies.

She'd not meant for it to get like this.

That first day, when everyone at Buckthorn learned that Freya had left, Sophie was the person they'd turned to for an answer. And she had given a tight-lipped smile and gently shaken her head like there were things she knew not to give away. Like everyone else, she'd believed that even if Freya ghosted everyone else in this town, the bonds of best friendship were strong enough to transcend the metaphorical afterlife.

She'd never thought that first impression would turn into a barefaced lie that kept on growing, making her more anxious, more miserable and more lonely.

When Georgia came buzzing over from the Ewan Moore encounter, Sophie's hug was as much to keep her from taking off as it was to congratulate her. After a few seconds, she released her friend so she could take a photo.

"Hang on a sec, let me just…" Phone in hand, Sophie switched to her camera and—

"Too tempting!" Came a voice Sophie knew all too well, as a hand flashed out and knocked the phone up out of her hand to catch it – except Ryan Krikler fumbled the catch so badly that her phone clattered straight onto the concrete.

"Ryan you absolute *shit!*" Sophie yelled, angry at how the knock had hurt – angrier about her phone.

"Oops."

Buckthorn's biggest gobshite stood there, concern dialled

down below zero as he watched Sophie crouch to collect her phone.

Anger ballooned into rage at the sight of her screen.

"You *broke* my phone."

Ryan's attention darted down to her phone, then back up to her face, eyes shifty beneath perma-scowl brows. "Come off it, your phone's fine."

"It's chipped!"

A crowd had gathered. People always liked a bit of drama and Joe T, one of the decent ones, elbowed Ryan in the side and nodded towards Sophie.

"Just say sorry, you dick."

Ryan rolled his eyes. "Whatever, lighten up. Her phone still works. No harm no foul."

"That's not much of an apology." Sophie tucked her phone into her pocket, fingers brushing against her pen.

"Because I'm not fucking sorry."

"You should be."

"And you're going to make me?" Ryan's voice was steeped in sarcasm, but Sophie's hand closed round her pen – the wonky moustache inked on one of the lads behind Ryan giving her an idea.

"Maybe if Joe could hold you still a minute…" She pulled the cap from her pen with her teeth, and as Ryan made to get away, the lads held him back.

And because it was hold still or risk getting stabbed in the eye with the point of a Sharpie, Ryan stayed where he was, teeth grinding as Sophie put her pen to his forehead; her friends, his friends – anyone close enough to be curious – crowded round, someone letting out a strangled, "Oh, that's class," in contrast to Georgia's scandalised, "Sophie!"

Ryan wasn't worth her remorse. Not today. Not ever.

Stepping back, Sophie studied her handiwork and enjoyed the slow-burn glow of satisfaction.

"What? What have you drawn?" Ryan reached up to touch his forehead like she'd embossed it.

"A masterpiece."

She didn't need to take a picture of her own. Everyone else was too busy shouting Ryan's name, getting him to turn so they could marvel at the penis she'd drawn on his head, hairy balls and all.

As he glared at her through the crowd, Sophie blew a kiss.

"Sorry yet?"

June – 206 days before Freya left

On Fridays Sophie went to Freya's. On *sunny* Fridays, they got off the bus in town, bought something cold and went to sit on the bench outside the bakery to scope out anyone interesting. Lately "interesting" just meant fit. The Year 10 French trip had been and gone and both of them had kissed someone. Two someones in Freya's case. Both boys: one French and pretty; one English and rough but, as Freya had put it, sexy as hell.

Sophie had kissed her first girl. Pretty. English. Just the once under the safety of a dare.

There were only two things Sophie remembered from that trip: the day she was too wiped to go to the cheese factory and spent all day huddled in her bunk bed switching between Pokémon Go and Two Dots on her phone – and the rise of excitement that tingled through her body after that kiss. A tingle of *knowing*.

None of their conquests went to Buckthorn, but ever since, both Freya and Sophie had felt an awakening of interest, as if sexy humans had only now started to exist as *options* rather than hypotheticals.

"No, no, no, maybe, no, no, mmm … no…" Freya sighed into her can of Diet Coke and scanned the high street. "Where *is* he?"

She was looking for the boy they'd code-named the Campion Prince. They'd seen him a few times now – mostly from the bus, although apparently Freya had passed him on the high street when she was out with her mum a couple of weeks ago and he looked even better up close. When it came to taste in boys, there wasn't much overlap between Sophie and her best friend. Freya's crushes had that narrow, suspicious look about them, like a cartoon weasel. Boys who looked like they couldn't be trusted.

The Campion Prince was a rare exception.

"Hey, I got the job." Freya only had two modes: butterfly brain and hyperfocus. Today had been flit-ful.

"That's good!" Sophie raised her can to tap it against Freya's, but her friend's response wasn't enthusiastic.

"Is it?" Freya slumped back onto the bench, head tipped to the sky. Given that two days ago all she'd talked about was getting a job up at Rabscuttle Hall, Sophie was inclined to say yes. But she knew Freya better than to answer questions her friend hadn't intended to ask.

"It's just…" Freya sighed. "It's another way to be trapped, you know?"

But Sophie didn't know.

"Think of the money," she said, trying to find something positive. "And not having to spend as much time at home with your mum."

A smile touched Freya's lips at that, before she noticed Sophie pressing her can to the top of her right arm to stop herself from scratching. A rash had blossomed there and heat made it worse.

Freya nodded at her arm. "I thought you'd been to the doctor about that?"

"I have. She now thinks it's eczema."

Freya did the Pet Lip of Pity and gave Sophie's shoulder a gentle squeeze. "At least they can treat that."

Which was the same thing she'd said before, when they'd thought it was ringworm. Optimism wasn't always the answer, but it was all Freya ever offered when it came to health stuff. And there'd been a lot of it that year – enough for the school to call her mum in about how many sick days she had. Not that there was anything either of them could do – it wasn't like she was faking. Sophie might pretend to enjoy re-watching *Sam and Cat* so many times she dreamed in sarcasm, but really, she'd prefer to be at school. Which was sad.

"Ladies…" Ryan emerged from the bakery behind and hopped over the back of the bench, forcing Sophie to scoot over so he could sit between them.

Historically, Ryan Krikler was nothing more than someone who made a nuisance of himself from the back of whatever classes they had in common. Lately, though, Freya had been reacting to his piss-taking and general ass-hattery in a way that seemed to be giving him ideas.

"Doughnut?"

Ryan held out a box of them – three chocolate ring doughnuts, the fourth already stuffed in his mouth. Freya took one, but Sophie turned him down. She preferred it when the only thing Ryan offered was the opportunity to start an argument.

"Carbs? You sure?"

"Please don't call me that." Charbonneau was a last name that could be butchered any number of ways, each cut as ugly as the last: Chardonnay, Carbonara, Carbs… *Bonbon*. Sophie hated them all.

Sophie leaned even further away to stop Ryan knocking her with his elbows. "Why are you here?"

"Waiting for someone."

When Ryan ate it was cartoon-sized bites that had him chewing with every muscle in his face, the scar that ran from his jaw and across his ear lobe accentuating every move.

She glanced down at her phone.

"We need to head if we want the next bus," she said, standing up and looking at Freya, then giving Ryan a dismissive "… guess we'll see you next week."

"You guess? We're in half the same classes, you spleen." The insult came round a mouthful of icing and half-chewed dough as he leaned round to look at the cobbled parking bay behind. "My ride's here anyway."

Sophie turned with Freya to see a black BMW pull up. Freya tensed a second as the passenger door swung open and a boy got out to push the seat forward. It was him. Freya's *objet d'amour*. Blue Campion uniform, tie off and shirt unbuttoned at the collar, sleeves rolled up to the elbow. His dark hair was brushed back from a face that was handsome in a way that looked more rebel than regal and, when he glanced towards them, the way he squinted against the sun only added to the appeal.

"Ry, you coming?" he called.

Freya whipped round to look at Ryan. "You know him?"

Ryan closed the lid on the last of his doughnuts and frowned. "What? You mean 'do I know the person who just called my name out and is waving me into the back of his car'?" Ryan smirked. "You concerned about stranger danger?"

She punched him on the arm hard enough that he winced. "I'm serious. Who is he?"

Rubbing his arm, Ryan scowled at Freya, then at the boy next to the car. "That's my cousin, Kellan."

WIN

Had Sophie given this parcel to Win's sister, she'd have torn it open the second she saw it, too desperate to know what was inside to care who was there to see it.

Win waited.

The parcel remained in her bag, unopened, through Physics, then lunch, then a particularly torturous Mechanics lesson going over momentum calculations. It wasn't until last period, after she'd returned a university prospectus to the Careers room, that Win finally had the peace and quiet she wanted.

Alone, sitting in the driver's seat of the car she shared with Mama, Win scored down the seam of the tape with her thumbnail and unfolded the paper.

She'd been right to wait.

Under the paper was a rainbow flag. Big and bright and bold – the one that she'd worn round her shoulders like a cape last July, Pride fever giving her even greater confidence than she'd felt in Leeds.

The day had been planned around Riley – tickets to London booked and paid for, a perfect opportunity to introduce her to her friends IRL – until Riley and Win broke up during a particularly tearful FaceTime right in the middle of Win's exams.

Rather than go alone, Win had offered the train ticket to Freya. (Sunny had sulked for the whole week and several days after, but fourteen was too young for her to go to London without their parents wanting a lot more detail than Win was prepared to fabricate.) Freya had embraced her role as straight ally to the fullest, making a playlist – "No, no … a *gay* list!" – for the journey, and had wowed Win's friends so much that Felix still referred to her as his "Favourite Flirtatious Straight". Then, on the journey home, tired and smudged and glitter-coated, she'd accepted the flag that Win had held out across the table. But only for safe-keeping, she'd said, until Win wanted it back.

Returning it like this was the opposite of keeping it safe. Of keeping *Win* safe. One of the lads in her year was a homophobe – the kind that didn't feel ashamed enough to keep his opinions to himself. Waving a rainbow flag on the streets of London during a parade was a long way, in every possible sense, from pulling it out of a parcel like a magician in the middle of Buckthorn sixth form.

Win sighed and folded her arms over the top of the wheel, resting her chin on them and staring out at the Year 11s starting to leak out of the school gates.

What if she'd opened this in front of Sophie, like Freya had so clearly been hoping? Freya might have assumed it would be fine. But that hadn't been her decision to make. She *knew* that. Or she had, once.

If it weren't for the fact that she'd find someone else's name under the flag, Win would have shoved the whole lot back in her bag and forgotten about it.

Taking a breath, she removed the rest of the paper, then the flag. Then, finally, she read the next name.

Lucas Antoniou

"Great," Win muttered. She had absolutely no idea who that was.

But she knew someone who would.

Win watched as her sister said farewell to her friends with all the intensity of an astronaut scheduled for six months aboard the ISS. She'd never cope with friendships like Win's, where hugs were conveyed with one of the many GIFs she had saved of the MCU cast and crew, or where concern was expressed with a worried-looking selfie.

Once she finally tore herself away from the rest of Year 10, Sunny bounded across the car park and folded herself into the passenger seat with all the elegance of a half-drunk giraffe. Whereas Win was stocky like their father, Sunny was all gangle: long legs, scrawny arms and an annoying inch and a half extra height. On days when her sister had been particularly annoying on the way to school, Win liked to move the passenger seat a notch further forward for the return.

Today she'd moved it forward two.

Irritating or not, Win needed Sunny's encyclopaedic knowledge of the boys of Buckthorn, which wasn't something she'd ever considered utilising before.

"I need your help," she said, putting the parcel on Sunny's lap and pointing at the name. "Do you know Lucas Antoniou?"

Sunny immediately began listing candidates.

"There's a Luke Partridge in my form. Plays guitar and never shuts up about it. Or Anthony McGrath in the year above – he used to have really nice hair but then he shaved it all off and has a weird-shaped skull—"

Sunny had never had a thought that didn't come out of her mouth, but Win wasn't that interested in the phrenology of Anthony McGrath.

"Lucas. Antoniou." Win tapped the parcel to get Sunny to refocus. "Those two names, in that order."

"Why? What is this?"

"Answer my question and I'll answer yours. Is there a Lucas Antoniou at our school?"

"No," Sunny said with absolute certainty.

"You're sure?"

Sunny shot her down with nothing more than a look.

"My turn." She pointed at the parcel. "Explain this."

"You remember Freya?"

Sunny rolled her eyes. Freya had been too cool for her to warm to. "Of course."

"She sent a parcel to her friend Sophie this morning" – Sunny twitched with interest but managed not to interrupt – "and inside Sophie's parcel was another parcel. For me. And inside mine, there was this one for Lucas Antoniou."

Sunny looked at the parcel, then at Win, lip curling up a second before she said, "You what?"

"Basically, it seems to be a very prescriptive game of pass the parcel. Unwrap a layer, pass it on."

She left out the bit about the note and the treasure, distracted by the way Sunny was squeezing and shaking and – weirdly – sniffing the parcel.

43

"Stop that."

"I'm trying to work out what's in the middle." Sunny squashed it and frowned. "It's too squishy to just be infinite layers of names."

Win sighed. Keeping things from Sunny had always been a challenge.

"There might be stuff between the names. There was a flag sandwiched between my layer and this one." She knew Sunny had guessed what kind by the way her eyes flared wide in outrage. "The one from Pride."

"Freya Newmarch asked her friend to hand over a parcel with a rainbow flag *at school*?" Sunny's voice had risen almost as high as her over-pencilled eyebrows.

"She couldn't have known it would be at school – and I opened it in here."

The Freya who'd tasked Sophie with hand-delivering a parcel that could have been sent safely to Win's house might have annoyed her, but Win still felt a need to defend the Freya who'd been a decent friend when she'd needed one.

"Look, can we skip over all this and focus on Lucas? Whoever he is."

"Alternatively, we could just open it?"

"Sunny, *no*. That's not the point."

Sunny rolled her eyes and reset herself with a breath, then, "Checked her Instagram?"

"Done it."

"Facebook?"

"Tick."

"Does she have a TikTok? Snapchat?"

"Obviously I've already tried those—"

"I dunno … *ask* her?"

"She ghosted me months ago, same as everyone else—"

"Everyone?" Sunny asked, holding up the parcel. "Even her best mate?"

Win conceded the point. "She wrote Sophie a note asking her to pass it along, promising treasure at the end."

"What a weird thing to make your friends do."

"You're a weird thing." The insult came automatically as Win frowned at where her phone rested in its holder next to the wheel. "She *did* give me her number."

"Who? Freya?"

"Sophie."

"Well duh." Sunny snatched the phone up and shoved it so hard at Win that it nearly smacked her in the chin. "Ask Sophie who he is. If he's Freya's pal, he'll be hers too, right?"

SOPHIE

Like half the people at Buckthorn, Sophie, Morgan and Georgia were queuing up for the self-serve at the Tesco over the road, buying supplies for the walk (or bus ride) into town: one Cherry Coke, one Tango – and a can of Red Bull from the back of the chiller for Sophie. She'd found a study somewhere that suggested caffeine could help with pain – a theory Mum has dismissed because it didn't fit with what she wanted to help. Sophie was willing to conduct her own entirely unscientific study without her mum knowing. Even if it didn't help with the pain, Sophie could use a little help with the pep.

The three of them had made it as far as the till when a message buzzed through and Sophie slid her free hand into her skirt pocket, heart leaping at the sight of an unknown number.

Hi Sophie. This is Win.

Then a photo of the next layer of Freya's parcel with the caption: *Friend of yours? I'm drawing a blank.*

This was her chance. Sophie stared so hard at the screen that her eyes started to water – but that didn't make the name any more familiar.

Sophie waited until they'd paid and were heading for the exit.

"Do either of you remember Freya talking about a guy called Lucas Antoniou?" Sophie watched Morgan for a reaction. Whereas Sophie struggled to recall what she had for breakfast and Georgia lived in a rose-tinted cloud of oblivion, Morgan's brain hoarded titbits like this. The kind of witness that wouldn't just tell you it was Professor Plum in the library with a lead pipe; she'd know if there was a book missing from the shelf, which hand he'd used to strike the killing blow and what scandalous secret gave Plum the motive.

"Boy from work." Morgan clicked her fingers with a decisive snap.

"Whose work?" Georgia frowned.

"Freya's work, you noodle." Morgan gave her a gentle nudge as they stepped out into the sunshine. "The good-looking pot washer who started after she did. Definitely called Lucas. Not sure about the Anthony part."

"Antoniou," Sophie corrected.

"Why d'you ask?"

"Oh, you know when you get a name stuck in your head on a loop?" Sophie deflected so neatly that Georgia was nodding already.

"*Yes!* Like an earworm…" And Georgia was off talking with enthusiasm about the *Danger Mouse* theme tune because her sister had been watching it over breakfast. As she burst into song, Sophie sent Win a reply.

Think he used to work with Freya. Something that gave the impression it was Sophie who'd done the thinking.

Up at Rabscuttle Hall?

Sophie replied with a tick. Of course Win would know where her neighbour worked. Once she'd started work at the restaurant, Freya had been happy to tell anyone who'd listen all her hilarious/gross/outrageous anecdotes, but the harder Sophie pushed to try and recall any mention of a Lucas among them, the faster the fog rolled into her brain.

Another message popped up from Win.

Right. Guess I'm driving up there to deliver it.

She could drive? That was news.

Now?

As soon as I stop messaging you and actually leave the car park.

Sophie glanced back the way they'd come. The only route from Buckthorn to Rabscuttle would take Win straight past the end of this road. Without hesitation, she hammered out a message.

If you stop by the end of Fell Avenue, you can pick me up on the way.

Her friends were sympathetic about her saying she'd rather hitch a lift than wait for the bus, though a bit ruffled by how insistent Sophie was that if they hurried they could catch up with the crowd who were walking. She needed them gone so that there was no one to ask any awkward questions about who Win was or how Sophie knew her.

They were far enough away that Sophie was alone, sitting on someone's garden wall, when a small silver car pulled over and a Chinese girl – all limbs and long hair, broad smile studded with braces – flung herself out of the passenger side.

Most Year 10s weren't memorable enough to leave an impression, but Sophie recognised this one. She belonged to a clique that always looked like they were having fun, whether they were messing around in the queue for lunch or being shushed on the way into the hall for school-wide assemblies.

"Hi. I'm Sunny – Win's sister."

"I'm Sophie."

The two measured each other with a similar look, then Sunny said, "Apparently we're giving you a lift." She held a fist up. "Rock, paper, scissors for who goes in the back."

Before Sophie could respond, Win called out from inside the car, "Whoever wins, Sunny loses. Sophie, you're in the front!"

Sunny gave a good-natured eye roll and clambered into the back, scooting all the way across until she was behind the driver. As Sophie got in and shut the door, Sunny was saying, "Oh no. So little leg room. I shall just see if I can *get comfortable*," while kicking the back of Win's seat.

When Sophie glanced across, Win pressed her lips together in a secretive smile. The next second, her seat ratcheted back as far as it would go, squashing Sunny with a squeal.

"Don't test me, sunshine." Win directed the comment to her rear-view mirror and Sophie smiled her approval into her own lap. Before her brother left for university, the two of them had fought for the front seat on every school journey. The stunt Sunny pulled was *exactly* the sort of thing Christopher would do.

"So is Sunny short for Sunshine?" Sophie asked.

"Absolutely not," Sunny said as she rubbed her knees.

"Her English name is actually—"

"*Don't you dare,*" Sunny hissed, thumping the back of Win's seat before turning to Sophie. "You get a choice between Sunny or Xiaohui and there is literally no one outside my family who uses my Chinese name, so…"

Being squashed didn't have any effect on Sunny's mood as she lunged forward between the seats.

"Anyway. Enough about me. We'll find our mystery man up at Rabscuttle. That right?"

Win's eyebrows twitched in apology as she met Sophie's eye. "I could make her walk home if you want?"

"No need." Being in the passenger seat of a car had lifted Sophie's concerns about saving her energy for the next few hours, and the less she had to worry about her lupus, the more brain space she had for other people. Even ones with as much relentless energy as Win's sister. "Do you have the parcel?"

Win took it from the side pocket of the driver's door and handed it over. Same brown paper, same bold black writing, different name.

"Nothing else? No clue? No note?" *No gift?* But Win was already shaking her head saying there was only another layer. Relief needled at the edges of Sophie's heart as her hand went to the bracelet around her wrist.

Maybe it was selfish, but it felt good to feel special. Good enough to blow away the clouds of jealousy that had been gathering on the horizon at the thought of sharing Freya's parcel with another stranger.

They'd merged with the traffic when Sunny started up again. That she'd been quiet for so long was a personal record.

"I have some questions."

"When do you not?" But when Win looked across at Sophie, expecting to share an exasperated smile, her passenger was frowning down at her phone in her lap.

"So," Sunny carried on, "talk to me about this Lucas."

"Not much to say," Sophie said. "He worked with Freya up at Rabscuttle. That's all I've got."

"Well … why don't you ask her for more intel?" Sunny persisted. "Have you tried messaging her? Win said she wrote you a note and you still talk to her, right?"

"Right." Sophie's reply was quiet and she was still looking at her phone. "She's not replying to any today though – kind of busy celebrating the end of school."

"Shouldn't you be doing the same?"

"You'd think."

"Maybe if you just called her—"

But Sophie had the measure of her and was already holding up her phone so that Win caught a flash of Freya laughing on the screen before the car filled with her voice.

"Hey there, it's me. Not answering right now. Don't bother with a message, I never check them."

As Freya finished with a kiss, Sophie arched her eyebrows at Sunny and ended the call.

"I already tried," Sophie said. "She's set this up as a game and if you want to play, you're going to have to get over

51

the fact that all we've got to go on is a name and a vague promise of treasure."

Win bit her lips together to hide how much she wanted to smile at the idea of Sunny getting over anything that didn't suit her.

It was strange, hearing Freya's voice through the phone when all Win's interaction with her had been in person. Considering how much time she spent messaging her other friends, leaving them voice notes or having FaceTime on so she could chat to Felix while she coloured up her webcomic, Win could easily have kept up with Freya once she'd moved.

Clearly that wasn't what Freya had wanted. Back in January, Win had sent her a message saying that she hoped Manchester was treating her well and she looked forward to catching up next time Freya was back at her mum's, but Freya never replied. Win had figured that was that. She'd been ghosted the same as everyone else.

Everyone except Sophie, who had turned to look out of the window, hair swept over her far shoulder, exposing a heavily studded lobe, a single steel hoop through the tragus. Sophie's best friend had always been the one people made a fuss over – Win had seen the comments beneath Freya's selfies, been there when Freya would check for them mid-conversation – but Sophie's face was a striking kind of beauty that Win wished she could compliment her on.

But only the Sunnys of this world got to blurt out admiration like it was effortless.

Suspicious of the silence, Win watched her sister in the rear-view mirror. She was scrolling through something on her phone, brow furrowed in a frown.

"Are you looking for Freya online?"

"No… I'm looking for *clues*."

Sophie's weary expression matched Win's, as if she was only now realising they should have made Sunny walk.

"There's no point," Sophie said, twisting to look over her shoulder as the car slowed to join the queue of traffic waiting to cross the bridge into town. "She's not posted anything since January. Unless this parcel got very delayed in the post, there won't be anything useful."

"Why though?" Sunny punctuated her question with a tut. "I'd be all about the updates if I'd moved."

"Hard to make new friends when all you're thinking about are the old ones," Sophie said. "She's deleted all her apps to take away the temptation. Gone cold turkey until she's settled in for real."

"It's been five months…"

"It takes time, Sunny," Win said. Maybe her sister couldn't see it, but Sophie's patience had been watered down so far it was practically homeopathic.

"I'm just saying –"

Win closed her eyes for longer than a blink. "You really don't have to."

"– that I'd find it ridiculously hard. I'd want to keep in touch with everyone. Not just my best mate… No offence, Sophie."

"None taken," Sophie murmured, head down as she

checked her phone, as if she nursed hope that Freya might call her up right now. If Freya could see the sadness that shadowed Sophie's face, she might have done.

Win would have.

June – 203 days before Freya left

Things with Riley had fizzled out before they had dissolved into tears. Win wouldn't have said she was heartbroken, but she was sad – and she needed somewhere other than her own home to feel it. Crying alone in her room in the middle of her GCSEs was behaviour that would worry her parents on a cellular level.

So when she could, Win escaped to Freya's, armed with revision notes as cover – and for something to do when Freya got distracted by her phone.

Where Win's home buzzed with the feel of family – the murmur of the TV in the lounge and singing in the kitchen; the smell of cooking; conversations shouted between rooms and up the stairwell – Freya's did not. Even on the rare occasions her mum was there, the two of them weren't enough to fill the space inside.

Maybe that was why Win valued peace and privacy and Freya preferred to live out loud. Win could have taken an extra GCSE in Freya Drama and been confident of getting top marks. And there was *a lot* of drama. Everything was a big deal for her – there was the war of attrition between Freya and her mum; her concerns over what her teachers thought, or said, or how they'd given her unfairly bad marks; some boy she fancied (or maybe she didn't); what her friends were doing and the many ways in which they were amazing, but also the worst…

Then she'd ask how Win was feeling, and Win would get halfway towards actually talking about it before the irresistible dog whistle of another message would light Freya's screen. For Win, who was selective about who she shared her number with and only answered messages when she had time to talk, Freya's way of life looked exhausting.

"Are you going to your prom?" Freya had just finished typing something when she looked up from her phone to where Win was sitting at the opposite end of the sofa, Physics folder open on her lap, pen poised over a page of formulae she'd been over so often she could have scribed it from memory. Which was exactly the idea.

"I am." Win had bought a plain black dress from TK Maxx and had every intention of noping out of the official photos, but she had a few people she wanted to party with.

"Now that you're not with Riley, are you planning on taking a date?"

"Obviously not." Win hadn't been planning on taking Riley, either.

"Do you want one?"

"Ha!" Freya was straighter than a spirit level. "Thanks, but you're not my type."

"I meant I could find you one…" Freya looked at her phone speculatively and, for one moment, the word *Who?*

threatened to leap from the tip of Win's tongue so that she had to clamp her teeth tight to stop it.

"I told you," she said, hoping her self-control wouldn't go unnoticed from whatever god-like being was watching. "I'm not out at school. And I don't want to be."

"I thought that was a not-yet thing, not a not-ever thing?"

This wasn't the first time this had come up, but Freya had a bad habit of only remembering the things she wanted to be true.

"Not-yet might be not-till-university."

"*What?* I'd die."

Win blinked for a little longer than necessary. That wasn't a great thing to say.

"Is it because of your parents?"

Also not great, but again, Win didn't say so.

"No," Win said, with a certainty she wished she felt. She couldn't *know* how they would react, only guess. "I'm going to talk to them after we come back from Dom and Liu's wedding."

Telling them before would be unnecessary stress for everyone, her parents having to figure out how to behave around family they only saw every couple of years, while they might not know how to behave around *her*. After gave them time.

"So…?" Freya was in one of her inquisitive moods, and Win capped her pen, knowing that revision was done for now.

Sometimes being with Freya felt like being interrogated; on other occasions Win was appointed casting director as Freya read for the part of "Friend", her interest more performative than real.

Nothing like the conversations she had online, or with Sunny. But then, most of Win's online crowd were queer, and her sister was Chinese. Freya was neither and sometimes that showed.

This conversation was exactly the kind that dropped down the gap between the two.

"At school, and around the people my family know, I'm this Win." She waved a hand at herself. "And I like her. I don't feel like I'm lying or hiding. But if I come out, that changes who I am to other people and that takes effort. It wouldn't be easy."

"You did it with me," Freya said.

"Yes." Win nodded. She didn't add that it wasn't always easy with her, either, that even talking like this was work. "But you're only one person."

"I get that," Freya said, nodding. "People already have an idea of who you are around here. When you're with them it's hard to remember how to be anyone else." Which wasn't exactly what Win had been getting at, but when Freya meandered down a tangent, Win let her. "Like, change is so much easier when there's no mould for you to break. Otherwise you have to find twice the strength, enough to push through other people's expectations and enough to make yourself new."

"Maybe…" Win considered how important it was for Freya to understand. Decided it was worth a shot. "I suppose it's that there's all these different pieces of me. There's

School Win and Home Win and Online Win and they're all just fine. I know them, I like them. I'm happy being them. But one day there's going to be University Win and I think she's like the *Endgame* Iron Man version of me."

"Dead?"

Win laughed and shoved Freya with her foot. "The one that's assimilated all the lessons of my earlier films to come back as a total badass. Familiar but fundamentally different in the best possible way – being that Win'll be easier. I think."

"Does that work?" Freya said. "Splitting into different versions of yourself to survive?"

Win tutted. "Surviving makes it sound dramatic."

"I didn't—"

"I know, Freya. All I'm saying is that this is just me, and how I deal with things, and I'm OK with that." She looked at the girl on the far end of the sofa, tried to soften what she was saying. "I don't need you feeling sorry for me because I'm not sharing every little piece of myself with everyone."

"I wasn't feeling sorry for you," Freya said.

A second later her phone flashed up and the two of them retreated to the things that made them feel safe: Freya to her friends and Win to her revision.

SOPHIE

Something about Lucas was nudging at the back of Sophie's mind. A memory without substance. Not like the ones that crowded in as the car edged over the bridge and into the genteel hybrid of Georgian architecture and high street chains, where every square millimetre brought back a snapshot of Freya. The yellow-painted bricks and bright hanging baskets of The Teeswater Sheep reminded Sophie of queuing up, determined to pass for eighteen, only for the bouncer to swat away Freya's attempt to flirt by saying, "I've got a granddaughter older than you, pet." Or the hours spent lurking in the aisles of Sainsbury's, waiting for the rain to let up; or sunny days sitting on the bench outside the bakery, challenging each other to eat a jam doughnut without licking their lips. That was the cashpoint where Freya had squealed in delight after getting her first pay cheque before insisting they go to the chippy, her treat...

"I didn't even know this many Year 11s *existed*," Sunny said from the back.

There must have been hundreds of them, too many to fit on the pavement, students spilling out to trickle through the gaps between the parked cars. Buckthorn was the biggest contingent, a river of green skirts and grey trousers and scribbled white shirts flowing onto the high street from the bridge to join the Campion crowd. United in taking over the town.

"It's because of what happened last year. Both schools

banned muck-up, so someone started a campaign for us to get together down here," Sophie said, scanning the blue shirts of the Campion boys, looking for Kellan Spencer out of habit.

Do you think he'll turn into a frog?

Who?

The Campion Prince – like the frog prince in reverse. Kiss him and he might go all amphibian on your ass.

I don't care. I just want to kiss him.

And she had. A hazy August evening, Freya and Kellan had vanished from where the rest of them were hanging out down by the wharf, later emerging from behind the wall of Sainsbury's car park, Kellan's fingers twisted with Freya's, the two of them competing for who could look the most smug. The hottest of the Campion lads and the most popular girl at Buckthorn. A couple that made sense on paper and looked perfect on Instagram.

Something dislodged at the back of her brain…

"You OK?"

"Mm?" Sophie glanced across at Win in surprise. The only people who ever asked that question were the ones who knew to check in on her lupus.

"It's just…" Win's attention was on the road as she shrugged. "You looked like you'd thought of something."

Because she had. Lucas's name hadn't come up in a conversation about Freya's job, but about her boyfriend. And it had only been once. Back in September.

"I was thinking that I hope Lucas still works at Rabscuttle," Sophie said. September was a *long* time ago.

"And if he doesn't?" Win asked. But Sophie didn't have an answer.

"Do you think he's Campion?" Sunny blared from the back.

"There *are* other schools, Sunny," Win added.

"Ooh. *Or colleges*. Maybe he's a sixth former?"

But Sophie shook her head, the memory finally taking a recognisable form.

"I'm pretty sure he's our age…"

"Fifteen!" piped Sunny.

"Turned seventeen back in October."

"I meant mine and Freya's," Sophie murmured.

She *always* meant her and Freya.

September – 118 days before Freya left

The amount of school work that Freya had dumped on the bed made it look like Sophie'd missed the first two months, not the first two days.

"Yeah. It's been pretty intense." Freya looked at the books and worksheets, realised there wasn't any room for her, and moved the whole lot onto the floor. Kicking her shoes off, she settled onto the end of the bed and reached for a slice of the toast that Sophie's mum had brought up along with her guest.

"So what's wrong with you and is it infectious?"

Sophie shrugged. What was wrong was that she felt tired and achy, her body too heavy for her to walk any further than the bathroom. She'd spent the last week of the summer holidays napping all day and lying awake all night.

"Mum thinks it's glandular fever, but we'll know tomorrow when my blood test comes back." Her third that year. "If it's that, then you're only at risk if I spit on you."

Freya looked at the toast, then at Sophie. "You didn't, like, lick the butter when I wasn't looking?"

"No."

Freya took a bite and gave Sophie's foot a squeeze through the duvet. "Here's hoping it's a false alarm. My stepbrother got that partway through uni and had to retake his first year."

"Mm." Sophie wasn't exactly a keener, but the thought of missing so much school she couldn't sit her GCSEs was scary enough that she didn't want to think about it. "I'm feeling better now anyway. Today I sat in the garden and stroked Woof for ten minutes. Might actually get as far as school on Friday."

Freya finished her slice of toast, then burst out with, "*God*."

She did this sometimes, started a conversation in her head and only said anything out loud once she was halfway through.

"You'd think just because I mentioned another guy's name I'm cheating on Kellan."

Given the triangulation of information she received from the selfies on Freya's Instagram, her live-feed messages to the group chat and the quiet, private messages she sent Sophie afterwards, there was no possible way Freya could cheat on Kellan without Sophie knowing about it.

But then, she'd not heard her talk about any other boys…

"Whose name?"

Finished with the toast, Freya had moved on to the box of nail varnishes on the bedside table. "Oh. Just Lucas. Is this quick drying?"

"It says 60 seconds on the bottle but I'd leave it five minutes. And also: who?"

"The guy who started in the kitchen a few weeks ago." Freya tested the varnish on her little finger. "The one I get on with."

The way Freya said it made it sound like Sophie should know who they were talking about, so she muttered a vague, "Of course", but if Lucas's name had come up, it hadn't been when Sophie was listening.

"So … what've you been saying about him?"

"Ugh! *Nothing*." Freya screwed the lid back on the bottle and gave it a violent shake.

Freya's moods had always been as fickle as her focus, but today Sophie felt like she was missing something bigger. Like only realising there'd been a storm by looking out the window and seeing puddles.

"Freya, I wasn't—"

But Freya interrupted her. "Sorry." She put the nail varnish back and gave Sophie's foot another squeeze through the duvet. A double this time. "It's not you I'm cross with. It's just … people. Am I not allowed to talk to a boy without it being suspicious?"

"Apparently not."

"Ha."

Sophie wasn't sure how to make this better. Freya was a flirt and that was fuel for people who preferred to speculate about other people's drama rather than admit to their own. Until she'd started seeing Kellan, it hadn't been an issue.

"Presumably you haven't been doodling Lucas's name in your notebooks and drawing hearts around them when I'm not there to stop you?"

Freya grinned then. "Actually I've been practising my signature for when we're married." She left it a beat. "Because whoever I marry I'll be keeping the name I have now, thanks very much."

But she went serious again, frowning down at the pattern on the bedding, tracing a spiral with the newly varnished finger, the light from the window bringing out the pearly sheen of the polish.

"I feel like I'm being watched all the time, everyone waiting for me to make a mistake."

"Maybe don't post so many photos of your boyfriend on your Insta and all the girls at school will stop checking in to see if you've broken up?"

This got a proper, wolfish grin and Freya grabbed her phone, holding it out to show Sophie the most recent upload, even though she'd been the first to comment with a good-natured *#goals* like someone who actually had the energy to think about dating.

"But he so pretty…" Freya crooned.

"And this Lucas chap isn't." It wasn't exactly a question. Except it was.

"I never said Lucas wasn't pretty," Freya said, attention back on her phone as she scrolled through more of the comments. "But it's not like that. I'm just excited about having a new work buddy. Someone the same age who doesn't make dirty jokes or patronise me. Someone I can be me with. You know?"

"The way you are with me?"

"Don't be daft." Freya was still looking at her phone. "Nothing like I am with you."

WIN

When they passed the turning for their estate, Sunny made a very loud case for being allowed to go and get changed out of her uniform before Win silenced her with the threat of dropping her home and leaving her there. Sophie remained quiet until they passed the petrol station by the roundabout.

"Freya and I used to walk from hers to go and get ice cream here."

Win nodded like this was new information and not something she'd seen more than once, when she'd been sitting in the passenger seat herself, Mama at the wheel, driving Win over to one of her babysitting jobs.

"Win's lactose intolerant," Sunny said from the back, entirely unprompted. "Ice cream makes her fart."

Exactly the sort of personal information Win liked to share with attractive, popular girls from the year below. But Sophie just smiled across at Win before turning to look out of the window at the fields zipping past faster and faster as the speed limit approached sixty. Eventually, just past the next village, an elegant sign with gold lettering on a green background directed them through a sweep of parkland to Rabscuttle Hall – Hotel & Brasserie.

"What? Do they sell *bras*?" Sunny snickered away at her own joke.

The hall was as imposing as its name: a stately home-turned-hotel with ivy-clad stonework and three floors of long, elegant windows leading up to a skyline of well-proportioned chimneys and crenellated gutters. At ground level, a row of sleek and shiny cars tucked themselves into its shadow, their hub caps worth more than Mama's little silver Dacia.

Taking extra care, Win edged into a space, as Sunny announced, "There's a dish here costs eighty quid!" thrusting the menu she'd been Googling on her phone through the gap between the seats.

"I'm trying to park, Sunny."

But Sophie glanced at the screen and shrugged. "I've been here a couple of times – the food's not all that."

Win killed the engine and exchanged a loaded glance with her sister in the rear-view mirror. Rabscuttle Hall was a far cry from Sunday dim sum or birthday dinners with a sparkler cake at Remy's.

As befitted someone who saw themselves as a customer, not staff, Sophie made straight for the main doors, carrying herself like someone who feasted on foie gras and kumquat foam every other Friday.

"Hello?" Sunny's voice cut through Win's thoughts. "Are we going inside or are we just going to lurk out here like car thieves?"

"You can't drive. How exactly are you going to get away?" Win picked up the pace. "Break in and wait for the police to give you a lift?"

Inside was as classy as the façade. The floral arrangement spilling out of the fireplace could have rivalled Chelsea Flower Show and the air thrummed with the gentle walla-walla-chuckle-backslap of people in suits fresh from a successful meeting. As Sunny's head threatened to swivel off her spine, Win threaded her study of their surroundings with surreptitious glances at Sophie, arms folded comfortably on the slab of marble, leaning in as she talked to the person behind the reception desk.

Once they found Lucas and handed over the parcel, that would be it. Win would offer to drive Sophie home and she'd become nothing more than a once-used number on Win's phone.

"Oh yeah?"

"Mm?" When Win turned, Sunny was wearing a wily smile that brought out her dimple.

"Sophie Charbonneau…?"

"Shut up."

"You *like* her," Sunny hissed, too busy trying to laser the information out of the side of Win's face to realise that Sophie was coming back.

"I said" – Win lifted her foot and leaned all her weight onto her sister's toes – "Shut. Up."

"Come on," Sophie said, nodding back out of the entrance, oblivious to the way Sunny's face contorted in pain. "There's a door round to the kitchens we can use."

SOPHIE

While the front of Rabscuttle Hall had been lavished with greenery for its guests, the area for staff was stark and practical. No vibrant flowerbeds and sweeping lawns, just tarmac and outbuildings and a pervading sense of purpose. Not a world Sophie found as easy to fit into as she had the ostentation in reception, but she had always been good at faking it – and the last few months had turned her into an expert.

"They said to turn right and follow the signs for deliveries to get to the kitchen," Sophie said, setting off in that direction and concentrating on keeping her pace even, masking the discomfort blooming in her left leg. That one was always the first to go. A dull ache spreading through her muscles like when she'd had her 3-in-1 jab. Bearable, though.

"Are we just going to march into the kitchen?" Sunny asked, bouncing along next to her. "All, 'hello, chef, we want to speak to the pot washer'?"

"Might have better luck if we use his name," Win murmured from behind.

That was the plan: find the kitchen, ask to speak to Lucas and hope that the chef didn't shower her with swears and throw a pan in her face like an episode of *Kitchen Nightmares*. Although if a less risky alternative presented itself, she'd take it. Maybe there would be an office, or staff taking a cigarette break or … someone conveniently rattling boxes around in that shed opposite the door marked KITCHEN ONLY.

She had little chance to exchange a triumphant smile with the others when whoever it was emerged from the shadows and Sunny emitted a squeak that would have pained a bat. "He's *hot*."

He had his back to them as he wrestled with the bolts, so all Sophie could see was an inch too much of his boxers and a heather-grey T-shirt that sat snug on a body that looked as soft as it was strong. When he stepped back, his hand rose to brush an impractical flop of soft dark curls from his face and Sophie gave a start.

"That's Big T."

"You know him?" Sunny's voice radiated hope.

"Just house parties and stuff. He's Campion, one of Kellan's mates." Sunny's lust at first sight could wait until after they'd dealt with Freya's parcel.

Before Big T disappeared back into the building, Sophie approached with a cool and confident, "Hey there."

When he turned, Sophie looked for what it was that Sunny had seen, noticing lips that met in a pleasing curve and kind eyes framed by longer-than-average lashes. And that blink, like it was something he did on purpose rather than a reflex. If "swoon" was a sound, that was the one Sunny just made.

"Er, hi." Then, "Sophie?"

"Hey, Big T. Good to see you." Next to her, Sunny rasped a none-too-subtle, *"Introduce us."*

Rolling her eyes, Sophie held out an arm like a ringmaster introducing a new act. "This is Win and this is her sister Sunny…"

"Hi." Sunny lunged forward, holding out her hand like she expected him to shake it. After a second's hesitation, Big T dusted his hands on the front of his apron and reached out to take it.

"Hi." Blink. "I'm Lucas."

LUCAS

This kind of quiet meant there was something wrong.

Lucas's default was to assume it was him. Clammy hands? The stench of the spring onions he'd been shredding? Sweat stains spreading from under his arms?

He glanced down to check.

Nothing.

It had been a while since he'd seen Sophie, but she looked no less formidable in her signed school shirt than she did dressed for a night by the river or round at Kellan's. Her face was rounder than he remembered, her hair longer, gleaming like copper wire in the afternoon sun – but Sophie was someone you saw once and never forgot.

And she was looking at him like he was a stranger.

"But … everyone calls you Big T," she said.

"I mean, yeah, they do." At least everyone Sophie knew. "But it's not my name. Sorry." He didn't know why he felt guilty about this, but Sophie was frowning like he'd done something wrong.

Only then her friend, Sunny, swooped in.

"So is there, like, a silent 'T' in Lucas or something?" Her expression was free from any of Sophie's irritation. Nothing but bright, bird-like curiosity.

"My surname's Antoniou – Antony – Tony – T. And, well. Y'know." He shrugged. The "Big" wasn't ironic.

"None of my names are Sunny really and I've got, like, a million."

"You've got two," her sister said mildly from where she'd

been standing like a shadow behind the others.

"And neither one is Sunny." Sunny shot her sister a look like she'd rather those names weren't mentioned, before turning back to Lucas. "But the names we choose are the ones that are most real, right?"

Lucas smiled. "Right."

He'd known this girl less than a minute and Lucas couldn't think of a name that would suit her better – although he'd quite like to know the others. Or anything else she felt like telling him about herself.

"I don't get it." Sophie interrupted whatever he'd been thinking of saying to Sunny. "How come you're here?"

Lucas shrugged. He wasn't supposed to be – as of last week he'd had to say he couldn't work any shifts while he had his exams. This afternoon was a one off. "Ed asked me to cover the start of his shift because he had to pick his mum up from the station and, well, money's nice."

"No. That's not—" Sophie waved away his explanation. "I didn't know you worked here. You should be down by the river for muck-up."

"Well ... shouldn't you?"

He wasn't sure why Sophie was the one who got to ask all the questions. Whether she knew it or not, this *was* where he worked – Sophie was the one who didn't belong. Guests weren't supposed to come back here.

The three girls exchanged the same look before Sunny's sister stepped forward. Lucas was used to confidence that liked to announce itself in the loudest voice possible, but this girl wore hers quietly – in the short, sharp line of her fringe, the set of her shoulders and the way she looked him in the eye as she spoke. Even if her clothes hadn't indicated she was in sixth form, he'd have figured it out.

"Actually, we're here to find you."

"You are?"

"You used to work with Freya Newmarch, right? Well, she sent Sophie a parcel this morning. Inside was one addressed to me – Win" – a gentle acknowledgement that he might not have caught her name – "and when I unwrapped mine…"

She flipped round the parcel she'd been holding and Lucas saw his name scrawled across the front.

Lucas Antoniou

He took it, casting a glance at Sophie that didn't quite land. Her confusion made sense now. Freya had never called him Lucas anywhere other than here. Around Kellan and the lads – which meant around Sophie as well – he'd only ever been Big T.

"You going to open it?"

"Sunny!"

"What, I—"

But Lucas had already torn the paper a little too hard, right through the middle of his name, sending a cascade of shiny little triangles spinning to the ground like the seeds of a dandelion clock.

Freya had been a name on the roster before she became a face. Blonde hair swept up into a big clip that couldn't contain all of it – and a face too beautiful for Lucas to take seriously. (Or – more truthfully – too beautiful to take *him* seriously.)

They got on well, though.

While the kitchen staff treated him as one of their own, the front of house crew could be a bit distant, all their best manners used up on the customers and all their best jokes on whichever chef was running the pass. The kid washing the dishes got the conversational equivalent of whatever they scraped into the slop bucket.

Freya was the only one who made an effort.

First shift together, she'd asked for the ketchup that Ed kept under the sink and tried to tempt Lucas into eating the chips the customers hadn't. It didn't work. Lucas had no problem squeezing the literal crap out of prawns or helping wipe down a blood-drenched prep area, but he drew the line at eating someone else's leftovers.

She'd grin if she caught his eye, call out a guess as to what tune he'd been singing, and leave him plates that were scraped clean and stacked neatly.

For someone still finding his feet, it felt good to have a friend, even if it was only for the length of the Saturday lunch shift and every other Sunday afternoon.

The first time they clocked out together – weeks after he'd started – Lucas emerged from changing his T-shirt, ready to collapse onto a bed made up with ancient brushed-cotton sheets until he got called down for his dinner. All he had to do was get there.

"Hello." Freya was waiting by the back door, hair freed from its clip, spilling onto the shoulders of her denim jacket, ends curling up like the frilled edges of a fresh lettuce.

"Hi."

"I wondered if you'd like a lift home?" she asked. "My mum's picking me up."

"I've got my bike." Technically, it was his cousin's bike – like the house he'd be cycling to along the path that cut between Rabscuttle and the edge of the estate where his aunt and uncle lived. A home that had only been his since the 25th of July.

"But you'll keep me company while I wait?"

Exhaustion rested across his shoulders, weighing down his every move. And yet…

"Sure."

They sat on the break barrels, and Lucas cracked open the bag of crisps he'd found in his rucksack. Auntie Helena had been slipping snacks into the side pocket every shift as if she didn't trust the restaurant he worked at to have any food in it. His favourites were the homemade Greek stuff that his mum had never bothered with – sweet pastries, like *bougatsa*, or maybe a spinach slice. But he was perfectly happy with bananas on the cusp of becoming too ripe, or Aldi biscuits wrapped in a bit of cling film. The crisps he'd found were fake Wotsits, also from Aldi.

Lucas held the pack out for Freya, who took one between thumb and forefinger and told him they were her favourite.

("Well, the branded ones, but I'm not that fussy.") They finished the crisps in silence, still recovering from their shift, then Lucas pressed the pack flat, scored the sides and folded it lengthways into three.

"Are you going to make it into a triangle?"

"I am."

"I've always wanted to do that."

"I can show you, if you want?" he said, turning to look her in the eye.

"I'd like that," she said, only then she added, "I have a boyfriend."

"That's good."

"I just." She frowned, a genuine frustration that Lucas wasn't sure he deserved. "Sometimes people get confused."

Lucas nodded; he could see why. Flirtatious was her default state – and she was gorgeous – but Lucas was perfectly clear where he stood, and happy with his location. "Well. How about me and you stay mates and I show you how to make a triangle out of a crisp packet in a non-romantic way?"

When she smiled properly, Freya's face lost the cool beauty he'd seen when he first saw her. She became adorable.

"I'd really like that."

SOPHIE

As the others hurried to chase the triangles caught on the breeze, Sophie crouched down to collect the ones by her feet.

All that "I've no idea who Lucas is" in the car and it turned out to be Big T all along.

She felt sick and ashamed, pranked by someone she trusted. Why hadn't Freya said anything once Big T became part of Kellan's posse? All that time Sophie'd spent hanging out with the lads, her and Big T having the last few puffs on a balloon down by the river before it got too cold to stay out, and that time they'd teamed up during The Great Jaffa Cake Debate … Freya could at least have *mentioned* that she worked with him.

She might have grown a little cagey about sharing every detail of her life with the rest of the world, but Freya never had reason to hide anything from Sophie. Or, at least, that's what Sophie had believed.

"Sophie?" The question came from above, Sophie's face level with the faded knee of Win's jeans. She'd not realised that she was still crouching. Standing up, Sophie gritted her teeth as her left leg protested. Too much crouching today.

"You OK?"

"Yup." The word was tight, clipped short by discomfort and residual embarrassment over Lucas's identity. "Are these crisp packets?"

"Seems so." Win held out the heap in her palm. Wotsits and Quavers and Skips … the less it resembled a potato, the more Freya liked it.

Before they could speculate on the *why*, someone dressed in kitchen whites emerged from the building. A folded bandana kept the woman's hair back from her forehead, exposing a glare that could have blistered the skin from a chicken at fifty paces.

"Looks like Lucas is in for a bollocking," Win muttered.

WIN

As Lucas bargained with his boss for a five-minute break, Win reached across and returned Sunny's jaw to the correct elevation.

"Stop drooling."

"I was *breathing*."

"Of course you were."

"You can talk," Sunny said, darting a glance at Sophie.

Win would happily have killed her sister if she'd thought Sophie was paying even a pixel's worth of attention, but now the parcel had passed to Lucas, he was the one she was watching.

None of this made sense. Lucas was someone Sophie knew; and someone she didn't. He was Freya's friend at work; her boyfriend's mate at school. Sophie and Freya's best friendship was coloured by overlapping layers of living in the same place, doing the same things and seeing the same people.

If Freya hadn't seen fit to let Sophie in on the secret of Big T's identity when she lived here, doing it like this seemed a little callous.

Once the angry chef returned to the kitchen, Lucas turned back to the others, an over-saturated shade of embarrassed.

"I could take her," Sunny said, scowling at the door. "If you want me to."

"Thanks, but I'd like to keep my job." There was a depth and warmth to the way he smiled at the side of Sunny's head that Win wished her sister could see.

He held open his pocket for the girls to drop fistfuls of shiny triangles into his apron. When Sunny asked why Freya had sent them, Lucas shrugged.

"I showed her how to make them." An effortless explanation that Win wouldn't have been able to offer if someone had seen her Pride flag. She darted a glance at Sophie, wondering if Lucas's gift had made her question whether Win had received one, but all Sophie's attention was on the parcel in Lucas's hand.

"So…" Sophie nodded to the half-opened parcel in Lucas's hand. "Who's next?"

They drew closer together to watch, Lucas making quick work of the rest of the paper, scrunching it into a ball that he shoved inside his apron pocket before turning the parcel over to reveal the lucky winner.

"*No.*" Sophie's voice turned harsh with horror. "Absolutely not."

"Huh?" Lucas was frowning at the parcel in his hands like the name was hard to read.

Next to her, Sunny muttered an excited, "Ooh, I know that one!" Like this was a test she'd been pleased to pass.

As per usual, Win remained without a clue.

"Can someone tell me who Ryan Krikler is?"

SOPHIE

Curiosity burned through every part of Sophie's body – hotter, more insistent that any of the aches that had her adjusting the way she sat.

If she'd been the one left with the parcel, she'd have opened it; to hell with the rules.

As it was, she'd have to wait until Lucas took it to give to Ryan at Kellan's party. A thought that soured the anticipation she'd been feeling all week.

As they pulled out of Rabscuttle's drive, she became aware of Sunny's jiggle. She counted two fields before Win's patience gave out.

"Bie dong."

The jiggling stopped.

"What language is that?" Sophie asked. Neutral territory that had nothing to do with Freya or Lucas or the name written on the next layer of paper.

"Mandarin," Win said, slowing as a pheasant made a bolt for it across the road. If Sophie's brother had been driving, she'd be clinging onto the door and praying for a swift death along these country lanes. With Win at the wheel, the car remained on the correct side of the road without threatening to lurch into a ditch at every corner.

"Are you bilingual?"

"I'm fluent enough to get by."

"She's being modest," Sunny bellowed from the backseat. "She got a 9 in her GCSE and last summer, when we stayed with our grandparents, they kept saying how amazing she was and looking at me like I was a changeling who brought nothing but shame and disappointment."

Win rolled her eyes, leaning forward to check both ways before they pulled out onto the main road. "It wasn't that bad."

"I spent a whole meal singing all the songs from *The Greatest Showman* under my breath and no one noticed. That's how little they want to hear my terrible English accent."

"Your *English* accent's just fine."

Something vaguely related to a smile tugged at Sophie's lips. Win's humour suited her.

"So." Sunny plunged forward and Sophie tried not to roll her eyes. The combination of her bad mood and the pain made it harder to humour Sunny's constant need for attention. "That was a bit of an Iron Man moment back there."

"What does that mean?" Sophie said, since Win clearly wasn't going to.

"With the Big T/Lucas thing. Like at the end of *Iron Man*. When Tony Stark's all, *I'm Iron Man*."

"If you say so."

Sunny ploughed on. "God. Lucas better *not* be like Tony Stark."

"I thought everyone loved him after the last movie?"

Win muttered a warning, "Don't get her started…" as Sunny shouted, "A CHARACTER REDEMPTION ARC DOESN'T EXCUSE A LONG HISTORY OF BEING AN ASS-HOLE."

"Your favourite character is Loki," Win said mildly.

"Lies! You *know* it's Hulk!"

Sophie stopped listening, her thoughts boomeranging back to the moment pass the parcel stopped being fun. Maybe her mood could have recovered from the Big T/ Lucas reveal if she'd been given time to retro-fit a theory for why Freya never thought it was important enough to mention, but *Ryan*?

"This party tonight." Sunny again. "Is it strictly Year 11s only?"

"You'd have to ask Kellan."

"Yes. About him. Who is he?"

"Freya's ex."

"And?"

"Lucas's pal."

"And?"

Sophie closed her eyes. How did Win not have a permanent migraine? Or a criminal record for sororicide?

"Ryan's cousin," she said.

"And we don't like Ryan."

"Sunny. Could you maybe shut up?" Win was glaring in the rear-view mirror, but venting about Ryan was something Sophie could get behind.

"We *hate* Ryan."

"When you say 'we'…"

"Freya. Me. Anyone who talks to him for more than thirty seconds."

"He can't be *that* bad…"

"He can. He *is*." Rage hotter than lava solidified into loud, sharp words. "He was. To Freya."

September – 113 days before Freya left

On his first day, the new Year 11 English teacher walked in, said nothing and wrote *MR COCKBURN* right across the middle of the whiteboard.

Then he turned to the class and said, "Hi."

As soon as the noise died down, Cockburn invited them to make all the jokes they could about his name to "get it out of their system" – offering a prize to anyone who could come up with something he'd not heard before. So they did. For five minutes they shouted abuse at their teacher, everyone cracking up and trying to out-do themselves. Once the jokes dried up, Cockburn moved on from his name to the concept of euphemisms. Getting them into pairs, he assigned each a theme – death, sex, pregnancy, drugs and so on – and asked them to write a script between someone who was trying to communicate that concept to the other, without ever actually saying the word.

Writing about masturbation was A Lot for Sophie's first day back at school, but Freya was happy to take over, cackling away at her own wit.

"You know he's going to make us read this out?" Sophie said in horror as Freya wrote the immortal line *Don't tell me you've never flicked your bean?*

"No way. This is a hand-in piece for sure." She didn't even look up from the paper. "Help me think of a really innocent bean-based joke."

"Please take the flicking the bean bit out…" Sophie tried

to reach across and put a line through it. "Stick to all the guy stuff, there's loads for them."

"Coward." Freya elbowed her away, grinning.

Once the time was up, everyone looked very pleased with themselves and Sophie followed Freya's glance back to where Ryan was rocking his chair against the back wall, hands crossed behind his head. Next to him Joe T was grinning away, and the two of them looked unbelievably smug.

When Ryan caught them looking, he gave Freya a vicious scowl and mouthed, "*What?*"

He'd been a staple of their summer, part of the crowd playing (or watching) Smash Bros round Kellan's and messing around on the wharf, the link that forged Freya's connection to Kellan. At times, it had almost been nice to have Ryan there to take the piss out of all the giggling and fight-flirting that was going on.

The second his cousin and Freya had become something more than casual, though, Ryan had turned intolerable. Morgan had diagnosed a classic case of jealousy, but Freya had been weird with her about that. Since then Sophie had focussed firmly on the practical and steered clear of the hypothetical.

Ignore him Sophie scrawled in the margin of Freya's notes.

He makes it hard ☹ Freya replied – then scribbled over their words.

"Right then," the teacher was saying. "I've seen some really strong work as I've been going round, but I'd like to hear some of these conversations read aloud." Before he'd finished the sentence everyone was roaring in protest, and Sophie slid Freya a jubilant look.

"Anyone?" Cockburn looked hopeful, but writing something down and reading it out were wildly different asks and everyone kept their hands tucked safely away, avoiding eye contact with the teacher.

Until Ryan spoke up. "Ask Freya, sir."

Freya whipped round with a hiss of, "Shut up, Ryan."

"What?" The grin on his face was pure malice. "I have it on good authority you'll do anything for cock."

And he pointed at the name still on the board.

Amid sniggers and people telling him not to be gross, Mr Cockburn called him up to the front, saying that Ryan knew full well this kind of language wouldn't be tolerated out of the exercise.

As Ryan slouched past, because he couldn't help acting like a gold-star douchebag, he brought a fist towards his mouth and punched his cheek out with his tongue, eyes on Freya the whole time.

"Another euphemism for you, sir," he said, without a hint of shame. "Means blow job."

WIN

When Sophie asked if they could listen to the radio, Win turned it on just that little too loud. A trick she'd learned from Dad, who knew all the gentlest ways of easing Sunny from her default state of constant chatter into something like silence. Once they passed back through the high street and over the bridge, the sat nav directed Win onto a road lined with larger, older houses, whose roofs flitted by above privet hedges and weathered brick walls.

After they dropped her off, Sunny switched to the front and turned the volume down on a man and his synths doing an impression of Ed Sheeran that Win had hated the last six times she'd heard it. If the alternative hadn't been talking to her sister, she might have been grateful.

"So."

Win rolled her eyes beneath her eyelids, before remembering she was driving and snapping them open so fast she pulled a muscle.

"That was all very interesting," Sunny said.

"If you say so."

"Er. You get a mystery parcel from our old neighbour, spend the last hour steaming up the windows with Sophie Charbonneau, introduce me to the man of my dreams, and all you've got is *if you say so*?"

"Exactly how have I been steaming up windows with Sophie? You make it sound like we're in *Titanic*. I gave her a ride—"

"I'll say you did."

"Are you auditioning for *Love Island*? That wasn't an innuendo."

"I would be *excellent* on *Love Island*—"

"You're fifteen. You would be illegal."

"Whatever. What I'm saying is, you need to text Sophie and tell her we're going to Kellan's party."

"Oh really?" Win hit the brake a little hard as they came to a red light and both of them bounced against their seatbelts, Win turning to give Sunny an incredulous look. "I need to tell her that me – and for some reason *you* – are going to a house party we've not been invited to?"

"And offer to pick her up on the way. Obvs."

A car behind let out a little "peep" and Win turned round to glare. She was not in the mood for impatient drivers or ridiculous sisters or Year 11 house parties.

"Listen to me very carefully." The car stalled. Win squashed the bubble of frustration swelling in her chest, killed the engine and started it back up, pulling away less smoothly than usual. "I am not going to text Sophie. About anything. I do not want to go to a house party. And if I did, I *definitely* wouldn't take you with me."

"But—"

"Oh my God, Sunny, just *stop*."

"Stop what? I was just—"

"Stop. Talking."

"Why are you always telling me to shut up?"

"Because you're *always* talking!" Win swerved to the kerb, slammed on the hazards and pressed her head against the top of the steering wheel. "I can't drive with you like this."

"Like what?"

"Being all" – she waved a hand in Sunny's direction – "you."

"What's wrong with being me?"

Win pressed her lips together to prevent her giving in to the temptation of listing all her sister's flaws. (Too talkative, excessively horny, can't take a hint, never replaces the loo roll...) Sunny wasn't the problem. She was just *there*. Or she was until she started clambering out the door.

"What are you doing?" Win said, watching her.

"Making sure you don't have to listen to me any more."

"Sunny, don't be like that—"

But Sunny ducked down, all her heat and light concentrated into a single furious beam. "Don't be like what? Me?"

The force with which she slammed the door sent a shiver through the charms hanging from the rear-view mirror and Win collapsed forward onto her steering wheel once more.

She preferred her Fridays with a lot more chill and a lot less intrigue.

She hadn't asked for any of this. Didn't have enough of a claim over Freya to care one way or another what happened next. Whatever treasure was in the middle of that parcel, Sophie, Lucas and Ryan were welcome to it.

Someone knocked on the window and Win looked up to see a grumpy-looking man point at the ground and shout, "It's a double yellow!" through the glass. Win gave him a resigned sort of thumbs up and turned back into the traffic.

Her sister had made it halfway down the hill and, when Win drove past, Sunny flicked her a double V-sign.

Win parked up in a bay a little further along. Tempted as she was, it was too far to make Sunny walk all the way home. When her sister was nearly level, Win called her name out of the window. Sunny made no indication that she'd heard – unless walking faster counted.

Win sighed, tried a different tactic.

"How am I supposed to take you to a Year 11 house party that we're not invited to if you're ignoring me?"

Sunny's angry march turned to a dawdle, then she pivoted round and edged towards the car until she could see the message Win was holding up on her phone.

Hi Sophie. Sunny thinks we should go to the party with you. She definitely has ulterior Lucas-shaped motives, but the offer of company (and a lift) is there if you want it?

"Shall I press send?"

LUCAS

Too many people and too few bathrooms was one drawback of living in this house. Sharing a bedroom was another.

"What?" Lucas said. His cousin was looking at him in the mirror instead of paying attention to the ancient laptop that was open on his knee.

"Do you have a date or something?" Alex asked.

"No." Lucas turned to face him. They weren't much alike, but there was a family *something* there. Lucas spent a lot of time looking for it in all of them – Alex and Kat and little Xen.

"Then why all the…" Alex copied the way Lucas had been faffing with his hair, then waved a hand at what he was wearing. On Lucas, the whitest of his T-shirts and dark jeans was the equivalent of a tux.

"Party. End of school as we know it and all that."

Saying those words flicked the switch for a moment, fear so glaring it stunned him. Not only fear of spending every exam in a cold sweat of confusion, but fear that he'd disappoint all the people who wanted more for him. No one from home would have gone through old Maths papers at the kitchen table, like Uncle Vas, or downloaded the audiobooks of his English texts like his aunt. Here there was Alex and Kat, who'd done their GCSEs recently enough for their revision notes to be helpful, and Xen was the kind of ten-year-old who enjoyed testing him on his German over breakfast just so she could correct him.

That was the one good thing about no one being bothered: no risk of letting them down.

"How do I look?" Lucas asked.

"Why do you care?"

"I don't."

"Then why are you asking my opinion?"

"Forget it."

But Alex was already grinning as he summoned his sisters with a yell, the two of them appearing in the doorway a split second later, Alex lying back on the bed and basking in his cousin's obvious unease.

Lucas wished he knew how to be comfortable with this much attention. How not to take Xen's dismissive "Bit basic" as a bad thing, or how to let Kat tweak his hair and pick fluff from his T-shirt without tensing as if for a fight. His cousins had grown up in each other's pockets, with two parents who were around enough to know all their business. The three of them fussed as intensely as they fought and after nearly a year of pretending to be one of them, he still struggled with knowing how to ask for space.

Xen got bored first, drifting back to whatever YouTube crafting video she'd paused, then Kat left to finish the other half of her make-up in preparation for a night out with her work friends, until only Alex remained.

"Sleep with one eye open, mate," Lucas said, hooking his track top off the end of his bed, "because you're for it when I get back."

"Planning on a late night, are you?" Alex grinned and made embarrassingly loud kissy noises that followed Lucas out of the bedroom and down into the hall.

By the front door, Lucas checked the contents of his

work rucksack – the bottle of Jack Daniels that absolutely hadn't been acquired via the commis chef and the package for Ryan Krikler resting on a shimmering bed of crisp packet triangles.

He'd have to be careful. Kellan wouldn't be too pleased about his ex sending a present to his cousin, and the last thing Lucas wanted was to get shot as the messenger.

But then, if Freya hadn't chosen him for the job, he'd not have met Sunny.

Lucas had no reason to think she'd be at the party. If she'd been in his year, her shirt would have been signed the same as Sophie's – and he'd definitely have noticed her if she'd ever been down the river. Lucas didn't think he'd ever fancied girls specifically enough to have developed a type, but there wasn't any aspect of Sunny that he didn't find appealing: the shape of her body and the length of her legs; her long straight hair and *very* pretty face; smiling eyes and braces and dimples…

Yeah. He'd definitely remember her.

September – 102 days before Freya left

Moving from a mixed north London academy with 1,500 students to a Catholic boys' school half the size, with twice the real estate, came as a bit of a culture shock, but fancy uniforms and semi-regular church attendance didn't change how people behaved in the classroom. Everyone at Campion could be measured on the same scales as at Lucas's old school, from keener to couldn't-care-less, D&D in the library to footie in the yard via I'm-with-the-band in the hall. And the most revealing measure of all: the people who wanted to be someone else and the someone else they wanted to be.

Kellan Spencer was that someone else. When he was in the room, conversations skewed his way – people calling for him to settle an argument, talking a little louder if the topic might interest him. Everyone wanted his attention, and Kellan gave it as readily to the nervy lads with the bad haircuts as he did to his own mates.

A likable quality in someone Lucas expected to be an arsehole.

Not that he aimed for any of Kellan's attention. All Lucas wanted was a group to sit with at lunch and ask questions of when he'd not paid enough attention in class. Lads he could talk to like the kitchen staff up at Rabscuttle.

Only problem was that none of the groups wanted him. The most conversation he had during the first week was when his classmates tried to get him to say "Newcastle" so they could take the piss, or were told to partner with him on a science practical. Three days into the second week and Lucas figured the rugby try-outs were the best chance he had of proving he was worth knowing.

A plan that worked better on paper than on the pitch. Back home he'd been a decent second row, but coach divided everyone into groups so that Lucas ended up with a bunch of Year 10s who only passed to each other and one other Year 11 who was clearly competing for the same position as Lucas. By the end of the session, Lucas was cold and bored and sick of trying to impress a bunch of people who didn't care if he was here.

As special dispensation, the coach sent everyone straight for lunch, where they flooded the dining hall with Campion's blue-and-white stripes, dusting the floor with clumps of mud and wisps of cut grass. Lucas was standing, scanning the crush for a seat, when someone said his name. One table over, Kellan Spencer was twisted round to look at him. Like Lucas, he'd been at the try-outs, cold autumn air still pinking his cheeks, sweat spiking his hair, and he pushed out the chair next to him.

"There's a seat right here, if you want?"

After ten days of asking for permission to exist, Lucas was grateful for the invitation. When Kellan talked to him like he actually wanted him there, he could have wept. It felt good to have someone talk to him, even if it only lasted for the length of a hot dinner and a custard slice.

Only it lasted longer. Down to the changing rooms, then back up to their form room, Kellan kept the conversation going whenever Lucas slowed things down to give him a chance to escape. When they got to the classroom, Kellan went over to where his mates were sitting, nodded to Matthew Fry and told him to budge up to make room for the new boy.

Glancing back to Lucas, he pointed to the nearest chair. "Seat's free, if you want it?"

And when a small, welcome grin warmed Lucas's lips, Kellan returned it.

Just like that, Lucas became part of a crowd, so that even when Kellan wasn't around, he had someone to sit with in lessons or lunch, to walk with down the corridors, or out the school gate to the newsagent.

Like (Matthew) Fry and Jonathan "Jonno" Gibson, Lucas's name quickly morphed into one that sounded better bellowed out during a rugby match or across the classroom, until he was Big T to everyone except the teachers.

The first offer of something more solid came during History, as Lucas frowned at the board, copying a timeline of events preceding the Bay of Pigs. Next to him, Kellan doodled a load of pigs storming a beach, cigars in their mouths and machine guns in their trotters. The kind of student who could waste every lesson and still get top marks for his essays.

"I'm meeting the lads down by the river after tomorrow's match." Kellan missed the sharp look Lucas gave him, too busy adding red biro spurting out of the severed neck of one of the pigs. "Don't know if you've got any plans, but you can come with, if you fancy it?"

Kellan's signature delivery was to offer his company like it was optional – as Lucas accepted with a forcibly casual "That'd be cool", he wondered if anyone ever took the alternative.

The match was tough. They were playing a team from across the county who'd had an hour's drive to work up a bit of steam that they weren't shy of letting off. But Campion were at home and, when they remembered how to play, they were pretty good.

The win was all that mattered for the start of the season and the mood in the changing room was buzzing.

"Good to go?" Kellan said, coming to stand next to where Lucas was finishing stuffing his kit away.

"Sure." Shouldering his bag, Lucas felt suddenly self-conscious walking next to someone whose jeans-and-trainer combo cost more than Lucas could make if he worked double his usual hours from now until Christmas.

Campion sat at the bottom of the high street and the two of them stepped through the gates into a valley of shadows and fading light. This was the hour between the shops shutting and the pubs swelling, and Lucas enjoyed walking in a different world from the one he knew from helping Auntie Helena with the shopping, or heading to the barber who gave Uncle Vas and Alex and Lucas a "family" discount.

"Is it just the lads?" Lucas asked, aware that Kellan hadn't brought their plans up around any of their teammates.

"Just us, some people from Buckthorn. My girlfriend and her friends."

Kellan had mentioned his girlfriend before. Never by name, just by title, and Lucas was curious to see what she was like. Also nervous. Not so much about who'd be there – unlike some of the lads at school, Lucas actually knew how to talk to girls (like they were people, it wasn't hard) – but about what it meant to be asked. He should be starving from the match, but his insides had knotted themselves with nerves and the adrenaline of hope buzzed all the way from his heart to the tips of his fingers, fisted tight in his pockets to stop them trembling.

He wanted *friends*.

"Here we go." Kellan nodded to the wharf where the

river cruiser stopped during the day, bulbs strung up like bunting along the water's edge.

Something in Kellan changed as he approached the top of the steps. A straightening of the shoulders, and the confident stride of someone who belonged everywhere he went. He glanced back, tilting his head towards the people round the benches. "You coming?"

Lucas hurried down, eyes on the steps, scared of stacking it and crashing through the crowd on the wharf with all the grace of a bowling ball.

At the bottom he came face-to-face with the girl who'd come to give Kellan a slightly more special greeting than everyone else.

"Big T," Kellan said, arm resting casually on his girlfriend's shoulder, "this is my girlfriend, Freya – Freya, this is Big T. He's new around here, but we like him."

"We do?" She looked at Lucas, her eyes sharp, smile fixed and fake, and before Lucas could say anything, she said, "Hello Big T. Nice to meet you."

WIN

Their parents had been suspicious of having a party sprung on them, but Sunny had a way of getting permission that no one wanted to give – permission that would be withdrawn if they saw what she planned on wearing.

"Ann Summers called – they want their mannequin back," Win said.

Sunny stuck her tongue out at the mirror where she was fixing a couple of false lashes at the corner of her eye. "Ha. Ha."

"I'm serious." Win was having trouble choosing between disapproval or disbelief. "I'm not going to a party with you dressed in your underwear."

"Just because it's *lace* doesn't mean it's *underwear!*" In an attempt to instil a little modesty, Sunny gave the hem of her dress a savage tug – and exposed the top of her bra.

Win tugged it back up. "Put them away."

"What's wrong with them?" Sunny folded her neck over like an ostrich to check.

"The fact that you've tried to stuff them into a bra that's a cup size too small."

"My friend Olivia said that's how to make your boobs look bigger. Everyone does it…"

Whereas Sunny had messaged her mates to brag, Win had messaged hers to stress. Gatherings of more than four people were as far from her cup of tea as a tequila slammer. She could do without Sunny rocking up dressed as jailbait in a nightclub.

"At least wear something that covers your boobs and your bum at the same time."

Win rooted through the clothes on the bed, looking for an alternative. As she navigated a landscape of inside-out tops twined with leggings and a rainbow array of bras hummocked across the sheets like sand dunes, Sunny wriggled out of her dress and picked up a skirt with a neon pink lightning bolt down the thigh that was so tight Win had to help her tug it on.

"At least I'm not dressed like a generic lesbian," Sunny added, frowning at Win's outfit.

"Straight girls wear checked shirts too."

"Fitted ones."

"Fake news *and* homophobic assumptions. Chuck in a little racism and you can run for office."

Sunny thwapped her with the vest she'd just picked up.

"I'm just saying…" She paused long enough to get the vest over her head. Despite plunging lower than Win would consider, it was an improvement on the original neckline. "Why would you wear *that* to a party?"

Underneath her favourite charity-shop shirt, Win wore a gun-metal grey tube top and a pair of tracksuit bottoms that sat exactly as she wanted on her hips. Between the two was a slightly daring expanse of stomach. She was making more of an effort than Sunny thought.

"I'm going to be hideously uncomfortable in a house full of people from the year below, so I'm wearing clothes that make me feel better." And nothing made Win feel better than this over-washed, cotton-soft charity shop bargain.

Sunny rolled her eyes. "Would it kill you to show a little cleavage?"

Win thrust a flimsy hoodie into Sunny's chest.

"Would it kill you to show a little less?"

"Fine." Sunny shrugged it on and yanked the zip all the way to the top. "Happy now? Lucas won't notice me and I shall spend the entire night crying off my perfectly applied lashes in Kellan's toilet."

"Was your plan for your breasts to obscure your personality?"

Like that was possible. On either front.

"Because that's what you like about Sophie. Her *personality*." They were halfway down the stairs, Sunny raising her voice so she could be heard over the thump of her own footsteps.

"*Sunny*." Win directed a meaningful look towards the light coming from the kitchen doorway.

Her parents knew. When Win made a plan, she carried it out. Like she'd said to Freya, she'd waited until after Liu and Dom's wedding that summer, then she'd sat her parents down at the dining room table and told them she was a lesbian.

There'd been some shock, some concern, some tears. There had also been love and effort. But acceptance was a slow process – Win's mythical future husband no longer crept into every other conversation, but her mythical future wife had yet to make an appearance – and Sunny announcing "WIN HAS A CRUSH ON A GIRL CALLED SOPHIE" wasn't something Win felt ready for five minutes before leaving the house.

In the lounge, Dad dozed, socks and sliders up on the recliner, *Sky News* scrolling on mute in the background, although he stirred long enough to tell Win that there was no shame in leaving a party early if she wasn't enjoying herself. Mama was still in the kitchen, tidying up from dinner.

"Stay close to meimei," Mama said, giving Win a distracted pat on the arm while frowning at her youngest. "This is her first party. No trouble."

It was Win's first party too but she thought better of mentioning it, in the same way that she made no impossible promises about keeping Sunny out of trouble. At the door, Win went for the same faded Converse she'd worn all day, Sunny putting her feet into something that more closely resembled a collage put together by an enthusiastic toddler than trainers designed by someone so exclusive they'd cost every last penny of the money she got at New Year.

"Like I can cause trouble dressed like a nun..." Sunny started as they walked down the drive, and Win tipped her head back and silently begged the sky for a reprieve. "... boobs shrouded beneath my habit. Lucas won't even look at me, let alone think about kissing me."

"Look. Either someone wants to kiss you or they don't." Win double-checked the pockets of her tracksuit bottoms – phone, money, house keys, car keys. "A tiny dress and a push-up bra isn't going to change that."

"Hard disagree."

"That's because you want boys to kiss you. They're shallow. Girls are different."

"Yes but *you're* the one who wants a girl to kiss her, not me."

Win felt like banging her forehead repeatedly on the roof of the car before she got in it.

"Stop talking. You're annoying me."

"I can annoy you without talking…"

Win gave her sister a plaintive look. "That wasn't supposed to be a challenge."

SOPHIE

Sophie's room was the best in the house – Mum had sacrificed size for an ensuite and Christopher had claimed the loft extension for his lair. Next to her bed was a huge bay window looking over the drive, and there was enough wall space that, even with a double wardrobe and a chest of drawers, there was still room for posters and photos in a haphazard jigsaw of charity-shop frames.

Sophie lay on her bed and tried to talk herself out of The Fear.

That parcel, finding out about Lucas, then seeing Ryan's name … it was a lot to process. The hurt and confusion that came with it took energy Sophie couldn't afford to spare and anxiety gnawed away at what was left. She feared the slide from how she felt now to how she might feel later tonight – or tomorrow. More than anything, she feared that once it started it wouldn't stop – that she'd find herself hurtling towards the bottom once more.

She'd been there before. Two months ago, when she'd have expected her medication to make things better, she'd been worse than ever before. The drugs she was on brought on an almost insurmountable fatigue and left her so nauseous that she'd sobbed through every meal. On her worst days Mum had to hold a straw to her lips because her arms were too heavy to lift them herself; even breathing became an effort. On her best – on the days she dragged herself to school with all the verve of a week-old corpse – Sophie would struggle through lessons and spend break crying in the toilet or trying to get comfortable in the sick bay.

Back then she'd been frightened beyond all reason that this was her life now. She'd been betrayed. Told this would help. At her lowest, she'd prayed to come off her meds and go back to the rotation of pain she'd been so desperate to be rid of.

Then her rheumatologist had given her something different. Changed her meds and changed her life. Nowadays the pain was OK – not great, but survivable, the fatigue less persistently pervasive.

That something could happen, that she might relapse back into living like that, was a threat that terrified her.

When the alarm went off on her phone, Sophie hit snooze.

She probably could have showered, made a real effort with her clothes and her hair. But there was always the risk of more to come from Freya's parcel. More names, more uncertainty, more strain on an already half-broken heart.

Better to save herself with a little dry shampoo and a spritz of Marc Jacobs.

Next time the alarm sounded, Sophie turned it off and put some music on for motivation.

"Get up."

She stayed where she was, staring at the ceiling.

"Come on."

There were clothes heaped on the window seat, outfits she'd shortlisted the day before that didn't feel right today: a couple of dresses Mum had helped order – smaller sizes than she'd ever needed before that would invite comment on how "good" she looked from people who didn't realise it wasn't a compliment if it wasn't a choice.

Opening her wardrobe, Sophie grabbed a shirt new enough that she'd not worn it a thousand times already. It was bold and bright, tropical birds so loud they'd obliterate any chance someone had of noticing the shape of the girl who wore them.

Put it with shorts and high-tops and she wouldn't hate seeing herself in other people's pictures.

Make-up next. Steroids had given her a mild case of moon-face that made contouring compulsory and didn't leave much time for her eyes. When Sophie reached for a fast-to-apply liner, her hand wavered and her heart failed her.

It was three for two so I got you one.

But I never wear black...

Which is why this one is green.

Freya had dropped it into the bag Sophie was carrying and kissed her on the forehead.

You're welcome.

Crying wasn't an option. Not ten minutes before Win would be here to collect her. Instead of falling down the rabbit hole of thinking about Freya, Sophie thought of Win. How lucky Sunny was to have a sister that enabled her crushes – Sophie had once said something nice about one of her brother's friends and Christopher had done nothing but torture her until she could no longer risk being in the house if his friends were over.

And maybe there was a part of her that felt grateful on a smaller, more selfish level. She'd liked having Win around this afternoon, someone to share a secret with so that it didn't weigh as heavily as all the others Sophie carried.

Truthfully, she couldn't have done this alone.

September – 102 days before Freya left

Freya's moods had grown more unpredictable. Either that or Sophie was finding it harder to predict them – but she didn't like the thought of that.

Today should have been a good day. It was one of those late September days where the sun still carried warmth that would last long enough to make a Friday by the river worth their while. A night ahead that caught the interest of more than the usual suspects, although it seemed that the weight of everyone else's excitement was bringing Freya down.

"You still want to come back to mine first?" Sophie asked during Geography.

"Yeah. Why wouldn't I?"

"I was just checking. You don't seem in the mood for socialising, that's all."

Freya answered with a shrug. "Socialising with you I can tolerate."

Which was hardly the most flattering way of putting it.

After last bell, they made it through the melee of people calling out that they'd see them later, asking what time they were planning on getting there, did Freya know if the Campion lot would be there…

"Oh my god," she hissed, finally making it as far as the gates. "Why am I the one they're asking?"

Sophie bit down on the inside of her lips to stop herself from answering, and they walked on in silence for a few paces before Freya looked across the road at the crowd by the bus stops and announced that she'd rather walk.

When she heard Sophie's sigh, she frowned.

"What's up?"

"Just tired, that's all." Last night she'd fallen asleep over her Chemistry book, then stayed awake until 3 a.m. waiting to do it again.

But Freya had zero sympathy.

"You're always tired. The fresh air'll wake you up. Come on."

And Sophie did as she was told because disagreeing with Freya when she was like this meant losing more than an argument. Five minutes down the road, Freya sighed and sort of collapsed into Sophie like she was the one who needed the support.

"Sorry," she said.

"For what?"

"For being impossible today."

Sophie slipped her arm through Freya's. The pavement here wasn't wide enough for anyone to pass, but Freya showed no signs of letting go and as a woman with a couple of shopping bags approached, the two of them bundled into the wall that ran along the pavement in a fit of "oofs" and laughter.

The woman and her shopping did not approve.

Once they recovered, Freya let go to adjust the bag on her shoulder. She'd all her stuff with her and Sophie thought about offering to carry it for a bit, but as the offer made a slow shift from thoughts to words, Freya stopped her with a, "It's Kellan."

"What about him?" The Kellan Spencer spam-a-thon that had once flooded Sophie's phone had thinned to a dribble and she felt some retrospective guilt at how relieved she'd been. She was still interested, but demonstrating that interest was hard to maintain.

"He'll be out tonight." Not exactly news. Freya only went down to the river when Kellan did. "He keeps dropping hints about the fact that his parents have gone away for the night and won't be back till after lunch tomorrow."

"Hints?"

When Freya glanced across, her gaze didn't quite land. "You know, sex hints."

"Oh." Sophie walked on a couple more paces. "Is that a bad thing? I thought—"

"You thought what?"

"I'd thought you'd want to."

"I never said I didn't." Freya was walking a little faster now, like she was trying to outpace a conversation that she'd started.

"OK, it's just—"

But Freya tutted like whatever Sophie was about to say had already pissed her off.

"Never mind. You wouldn't understand."

"I'm trying to." Sophie felt more than a little helpless. "Please, Freya, just talk to me about what's bugging you."

She tugged on the strap of Freya's bag, slowing them both to a stop.

The two of them stood, looking at each other a moment, as if each thought the other should go first. Sophie had said so many wrong things, she didn't want to risk another, but Freya was the kind of stubborn that didn't bend. Ever. And Sophie didn't want to see her break.

"I'm sorry," Sophie said. "I'm not trying to annoy you. I don't know what the right thing is to say."

But even that had been wrong – she could tell by the ripple of disapproval in the way Freya looked at her.

"Maybe don't say anything," she said. "Maybe just let me talk."

"OK." Hadn't that been what she was doing? Sophie tried to backtrack through their conversation, but the words had turned to mist, too hard to hold on to.

"OK," Freya said, nodding, and threading her arm through Sophie's once more. "Maybe later."

But it seemed that was all she'd needed to say. On the walk to Sophie's, over tea, while they messed around trying on nearly every item of clothing in Sophie's wardrobe, Freya's mood lifted so far that by the time they got to the wharf, she was higher than ever before.

And at the end of the night, when Sophie looked for her, Freya had left with Kellan.

LUCAS

Kellan's offer of friendship wasn't entirely without conditions. The flip side of people always wanting his attention was that when no one else was around to ask for it, he expected his mates to do the honour. Texts had to be answered and invitations accepted – a small price to pay for entering the inner circle, but a price nonetheless when Kellan's moods swung from sunny skies to stormy waters.

Tonight, Lucas figured Freya's parcel might tip the barometer in a less favourable direction.

Best to find Ryan nice and early, hand it over and get on with celebrating the illusion of freedom that would last until he actually did some revision.

Kellan's road was lined with tall trees and posh cars and houses with columns framing the front doors like a row of red-brick Greek temples. Passing through the fog of burnt fruit and fist bumps from the vapers on the steps, Lucas walked in through the open front door into the hall. Left was the massive lounge, already bouncing, and behind the stairs was the door to the dining room, but if you followed the hall round to the right, you got a choice between the kitchen and the nook.

Even after months of calling Kellan his mate, Lucas still felt like it was an honour to be allowed in the nook, with its Banksy print and shelves of games around the 65" TV. The room could fit ten people, absolute max, and there were eight already in there – some girls Lucas didn't know plus the usual suspects. Kellan didn't even look up from the screen when he gave dap – too busy working his way through an 8-player Smash – and Lucas propped a bum cheek on the arm of the sofa next to him.

"Where you been?" Fry asked, tipping right back on his beanbag to look up. He wasn't holding a controller, keeping himself busy by sorting a bag of party balloons into different colours across his lap, ready for later.

"Work," Lucas said. Pulling out the Jack Daniels, he twisted the lid and gave Fry a nudge in the shoulder.

But it was Kellan who paused the game and held his glass out for a refill.

"This real?" he asked, giving it a sniff.

"Can't believe you'd doubt me."

Kellan downed it and held his glass out for more. "You not having one?"

"Maybe later."

"Maybe now." Kellan was all smiles and jokes and accepting was inevitable. Taking the nearest empty glass, Lucas tipped a slug into the bottom and knocked it back with a grimace. He loathed drinking anything neat.

"Better with Coke."

"Cuck."

"No, *Coke*."

Kellan's mood was magnetic and when he laughed, good humour rippled round the room. It wasn't often Lucas was fast enough to get a laugh like that and it boosted his confidence.

"I thought Ryan would be here tonight?"

"He will be," Kellan said, un-pausing the game without

warning anyone else. "There's noz, there's drinks and a ton of food that trash panda can shove into his pockets. My cousin will definitely be here. Why?"

Lucas considered his answer, eyes on the screen as Mewtwo annihilated the opposition.

"Oi." Kellan nudged Lucas's ankle with the toe of what looked like brand-new trainers. "I asked you a question – what do you want with Ry?"

Lucas hated lying. He always had, but sometimes the truth wouldn't work.

"Think some girl out there was looking for him."

"Send her my way, Big T," Kellan said, mouth wide in the grin of someone who knew he had his friends on-side. "We all know I'm the pretty one in the family."

September – 101 days before Freya left

Lucas and Freya were working the same shift the day after they'd seen each other by the river. She was still tying the strings on her apron as she walked into the dropzone.

"Why did you pretend not to know me last night?" Lucas said.

Freya tutted.

"I was doing us both a favour."

"Being ignored by someone I thought was a mate didn't feel like a favour."

Freya finished knotting her apron with vicious little jerks before looking up, her expression set in serious lines, lips pressed tight, eyes pulled wide with accusation, brows and cheeks all angles and no give.

"Are you really that dense?" Her voice matched her face. "Kellan would be weird about us already knowing each other."

"Why?"

"Because Kellan is a lighthouse. We only exist when the beam hits us. I'm his girlfriend and you're his new favourite. We're not allowed to be like this."

Before he could say anything more, she was gone, preferring the demands of the customers and the company of the wait staff to a second longer with Lucas.

He didn't know what she meant by "like this". They were only friends – or at least they had been. He had no idea what they were now. As the shift progressed, conversation was no more than the scrape of steel on china and the clatter of cutlery thrown into the bucket to soak. No chat, no teasing, no eye contact.

Lucas hated it – and he hated the problem Freya had created.

The best thing to do would be to go back to the night before, correct Freya's "Nice to meet you" with a puzzled frown and make a joke about her not recognising him without an apron. But Lucas wasn't quick enough to have thought of it at the time.

Now he'd lied, he was trapped.

Lucas read people better than Freya gave him credit for. Kellan liked to be the one with the magic touch, humouring lesser beings in return for universal respect, elevating a select few to tend the altar. By befriending Freya before the appointed time, Lucas had accidentally given himself a promotion. Owning up to it immediately might have been a bit awkward, but now the two of them had lied…

That was worse.

He clocked off at the same time as Freya and there was no way for her to avoid him as they went to get their coats.

"What am I supposed to say to Kellan about work?" Lucas said as he chucked his apron in the laundry bin and took his rucksack and helmet from where he'd left them hanging on the pegs.

Freya didn't even turn round as she pulled her jacket on and lifted her hair from the collar.

"How about nothing?"

"I don't like lying—"

She turned then.

"And you won't have to. It's not like Kellan's going to ask, is it?" When she looked at him, Lucas felt like she was seeing another person entirely, not the boy she'd smiled at across the dropzone and teased for singing a Jonas Brothers song. "He's already decided who you're going to be. He doesn't need to care about who you already are."

"What do you mean?"

"I mean Kellan likes how big you are." Her eyes flicked up and down all six feet of him. "It's good to keep someone around who can take care of themselves – and him. Especially someone so agreeable."

That hit home. Lucas hadn't always been so eager to please – but if Freya thought keeping the peace was something to look down on, it was because she'd never made the wrong people angry.

"So I'll just pretend not to know you?"

"Shouldn't be so hard." Freya turned away as she heard a car pull into the back yard. "It's not like anyone does."

WIN

Sophie had been subdued when they picked her up, but by the time they walked through the front door and into Kellan Spencer's very posh house, she had transformed into something more. Everything about her levelled up: her smile, her manner, her confidence. When she saw the group of girls lurking by the bottom of the stairs, she welcomed them with an exuberance to rival Sunny – a social chameleon, slipping into a different skin to suit her surroundings.

"Guys, this is my friend Win." Sophie reeled Win in towards her.

"Hello," Win said, enjoying their polite surprise. These Year 11s might only be half-familiar to her out of uniform and in full make-up, but she was practically invisible to them. When Sophie introduced Sunny, she leapt forward, elbowing Win out of the way to bombard Sophie's friends with compliments. About someone's skirt, how did they get their eye-liner so symmetrical and where was that nail varnish from and—

Then she stopped mid-sentence and snatched the carrier bag of supplies that Win was holding.

"We'll just put these in the kitchen and get a drink..." As Sunny towed her across the hall, Win cast a slightly despairing glance back towards Sophie, who stood with her friends managing to look completely cool, if a little bit baffled, before a couple of boys tapped her on the shoulder and snared her attention.

Almost the second they rounded the corner, Sunny melted against the wall dramatically.

"Oh my God that was Ewan Moore. Don't look!"

Too late, Win had stepped back to check the boys they'd just run away from. "And?"

Sunny yanked her back out of sight.

"And I sent him a not-so-anonymous Valentine's card that he totally ignored and now I think I might die."

"Which one is he?"

"The one with the hair."

Win wrinkled her nose. Ewan Moore was more hair product than human. "Come on. Here's hoping there's no more of your failed conquests waiting in the kitchen."

The two of them followed the corridor round to where they'd (correctly) presumed the kitchen would be. As ostentatious as the hall, the kitchen/diner was bigger than their lounge, with a huge breakfast table pushed up against a cool blue wall, a neon DINER sign illuminating the people sitting below as they argued about whether it would be better to have a cat's tail or a cat's ears.

"Ears," Sunny whispered once they'd passed, lifting her hands up to swivel them round, then flattening them against her skull and hissing, "Cats' tails are useless. You can't even use them to grip stuff."

Ignoring her, Win offloaded the Haribo and Cherry Coke they'd brought as offerings to the party gods. Between carrier bags and boxes of crackers and biscuits stood bottles of every soft drink going, stacks of plastic cups and a huddle of mugs. Alcoholic options consisted of a half a supermarket's worth of WKD, Jägermeister and dry Martini, all of which Win would have no problem avoiding. Selecting a small bottle of lemonade and a couple of cups to take back to the lounge, plus the can of Monster Sophie had stopped to get, Win startled as a whir and a series of clunks tore through the murmur of the ears/tail debate.

Sunny had found a pint glass (from where?) and was holding it under the ice dispenser on the fridge, oblivious to the fact that everyone in the room had turned to stare. Doubling down on the embarrassment factor, she ignored Win's subtle nod towards the hall, and veered towards the door into the dining room with an over-excited, "Oh my God…" before disappearing entirely.

Which meant Win had to follow.

As soon as she walked in, she understood Sunny's reaction.

"Wow."

In a starkly dressed room, devoid of party guests, two enormous gilt-framed communion photos exerted a gravitational pull towards a gleaming sideboard, where Sunny stood as if in supplication. She glanced back at Win and pointed to where a boy beamed with all the poise of a child actor sitting for a head shot: wide eyes, neat little doll's teeth and a chestnut quiff combed back with enough gel to reflect the photographer's flash.

"Do you reckon that's Kellan?"

"I mean, I really hope so." Win came to stand next to her. The girl in the other picture – presumably Kellan's sister – wore the dead-eyed stare of someone hating every second.

"If he's not on that wall and this is his house, I foresee a lot of therapy."

Sunny leaned in to look at the cluster of normal-sized photos framed in hallmarked silver on the sideboard.

"I found Ryan!" Displaying the facial recognition of an AI that had spent one thousand hours studying the boys of Buckthorn Academy, Sunny picked up a photo taken at someone's birthday (in Remy's – Win recognised the sparkler cake) and pointed to a boy with a severe haircut that made his ears extra-obvious and a smile that looked more like a scowl. He looked like trouble – and Sunny was emitting the "I think he's cute" hum.

"Really?"

"I like his ears," Sunny muttered with alarming intensity, but then she put the photo down and shrugged. "But not as much as I like all of Lucas."

"Lucas I can get behind," Win conceded – he had good hair and a kind smile and looked like someone to be held by. "Maybe if I squinted I could understand the Ewan Moore thing, but you've really lowered the bar with this one."

"Like Freya did?" But when Win didn't follow, Sunny looked at her like she was a fool. "Well what's your theory on the parcel that's addressed to Ryan and not Kellan?"

"I don't have one…"

Sunny popped an ice cube in her mouth and bit down, giving Ryan's picture a look loaded with implication.

"Don't stir."

"I'm not! I'm hypothesising." A hard word for someone with a mouthful of ice to enunciate.

"Don't do that, either." But the mention of the parcel had reminded Win of why they were there. She glanced down at the can she'd been intending to take to Sophie. "We should get back to—"

"BORING."

"OK, well, I'll get back to Sophie and you do a tour to see if there's someone more interesting."

"Lucas."

Win rolled her eyes. Like that needed saying. "Just … don't cause any trouble."

Sunny swiped a halo above her head, turned on her heel and bounced back towards the kitchen, leaving Win to go looking for the lounge. Not that it was hard to find from the squash by the door and the volume of the music. Win weaved her way through the room, navigating the valleys between other people's backs and hoping for a sighting of Sophie…

She was with her crowd. As she should be. But the skin she wore was the one Win knew from the lunch hall, or on the bus when Sophie had come home with Freya. The Sophie she'd admired from afar, not the one she'd liked more up close.

Win always liked people best when they weren't performing. This afternoon, driving round, Sophie had sometimes seemed as if she were easing into a more truthful version of herself. As crushes dictated, Win had liked Sophie as much when her temper seemed a little short as she had when she'd smiled at something Win had said. And earlier, when Sophie had walked down her drive to get in the car, Win had felt like maybe Sophie hadn't only wanted her there to hitch a ride, she'd wanted her around for the night.

Seeing her with her friends, it looked like Sophie had all the support she needed.

Turning, Win caught sight of the conservatory at the far end of the room. Somewhere quiet and out of the way, where she could mess around on her phone – maybe chat to Felix, who could close the distance between them with nothing more than a well-chosen GIF and a couple of sympathetic messages. Sophie's friends were here, but so were Win's, if she wanted them to be.

SOPHIE

When Sophie followed the others into the lounge, Morgan greeted her with what felt like a rib-crusher of a hug, then she and Georgia showered her with compliments – her top was wild, her hair awesome. If this had been the old days, the four of them – Morgan and Georgia and Sophie and Freya – would have got ready together for a party this big. Usually at Morgan's house, where there was a mirror for everyone and parents too trusting to check for alcohol. Seeing them so polished – Morgan's hair straight and glossy and Georgia's face YouTube-tutorial perfect – was one more way for Sophie to feel like a square peg hammered relentlessly into a round hole.

So much of Sophie's most recent socialising was the quiet kind that involved a laze around after school or a late night in pyjamas with a film she and her friends could talk over. But a lot of her crowd still went down to the river, or met up with the Campion lot on weekends to kill time in the park or go mooching round town – places that had always appealed more to Freya than Sophie.

Now, here she was, in the place that appealed to her best mate most of all.

And it felt wrong.

Kellan's house shouldn't exist without Freya, but exist it did, the monstrous lounge filled with familiar faces from school and a wider circle of Campion lads that Sophie only knew from the half-dark of Friday nights out in town, or the background of other people's Insta. People whose world kept turning while Sophie's had ground to a halt without its axis.

She needed to get it going again. Forcing herself into party mode, Sophie plastered on a knowing smile.

"So I see that Ewan Moore's looking particularly fine tonight, presumably to impress…"

But Morgan had widened her eyes and was staring over Sophie's left shoulder.

Dismayed, Sophie whipped round to check Ewan wasn't standing right behind her, only for Morgan to cackle with glee at the wind up, Georgia thumping her in the arm and saying that she was mean. But Sophie was laughing too, maybe louder than the joke deserved because bursting with fake laughter was better than bursting into very real tears.

She didn't want to be here. She wished that instead of talking to her old friends, she'd stuck close to Win and Sunny, where she felt safe. A team of three on the hunt for answers. Twisting round, she scanned the room, wondering if they'd made it back from the kitchen yet…

But the crowd by the door were parting for someone more important.

Kellan Spencer.

And, edging in after him, Lucas.

Seeing him now, dressed up for a party and looking a little less stressed and sweaty, she saw more of what Sunny had.

"Why are you looking at Big T like that?" Morgan sounded suspicious.

Sophie shrugged, a lie slipping out under the cover of the truth. "Haven't seen any of these guys in a while. I'd forgotten how cute he was."

She knew the look she was getting for that, and ignored it as Lucas scouted the room, missed seeing her through the crowd and made to move in deeper.

"I'll just go…" But as Sophie rose from where she'd perched on the arm of the sofa, it wasn't Lucas who saw her.

"Hey Carbonara!"

Kellan walked right past a group of girls who cast a disgruntled look in Sophie's direction, not realising she was a zero-risk threat. Firstly, whether she was here or not, Kellan was Freya's. Secondly, as Freya's best friend and relationship confidante, Sophie knew of the less-pretty personality traits lurking beyond that killer combination of good looks and charm.

Still, good looks, charm – and history – were enough for Sophie to accept the hug Kellan was offering. The emerging flu-like ache of muscle pain in her shoulder made his grip a little uncomfortable and when Sophie let go, she was disappointed to see that Lucas had vanished.

"It's been a while," Kellan said. "Don't think I've seen you since Christmas?"

Time that had only added to Kellan's appeal. Something in the slant of his smile and the lazy cast of his eyelids suggested he knew this.

He reached out and gave her shoulder what passed for a gentle squeeze. "I was starting to think you were avoiding me."

"As if." But Sophie found it hard to meet his eye when she said it.

When Kellan had got to know her, Sophie had been shining

in the spotlight next to Freya. The Sophie he knew enjoyed a drink and could beat him three times in a row on *Rainbow Road*. Now the lupus threatened her kidneys and she couldn't hold a controller without paying for it the next day.

And Kellan was someone who *saw*. The pretty face and easy smile reeled everyone in, but it was his attention that kept them hooked.

Attention that Sophie didn't want.

"I hear you're the only one Freya's still talking to. How is she?"

And there was the other reason Sophie had been reluctant to socialise with this crowd.

"Oh, you know. Unbearably smug about how amazing Manchester is." She aimed for a smile, but Kellan looked almost as sad as she felt.

"I still miss her, you know."

"Same."

Kellan frowned and the look he gave Sophie froze every cell in her body. "But you're still in touch?"

"I could FaceTime her every hour and it wouldn't be the same as having her around." Sophie took the drink he was holding and pretended to take a sip – casual and comfortable. "Not like we can hang out and get ready together like old times."

"Shame. Maybe she could have steered you away from that shirt?"

"Ouch." She grinned and gave him a playful shove.

"I'm joking." Kellan slid an arm around her shoulder to give her a kiss on the side of her head. Each point of contact felt sensitive and tender and Sophie marvelled at how she'd never noticed how vigorous Kellan's affection was. "Gorgeous as always, Carbs."

"Whatever." The name had reminded her. "Is your cousin here?"

A question that tightened the line of his shoulders and the press of his mouth. "Popular man, our Ry."

Lucas had already asked, then. Sophie raised her eyebrows. "Well? Is he here or not?"

"Didn't think you two were pals." The way Kellan was looking at her had changed. A plate shifting beneath the surface, threatening a disaster that Sophie would rather avoid. She'd skirted the subject of Freya safely just now, but unless Kellan's name was on the next layer, she'd prefer to avoid any mention of the parcel.

"We're not." She got her phone out as a diversion and scrolled her feed for the photo Joe T had posted. "I was just wondering if Ryan was still modelling this work of art…"

Getting the dick off his forehead had taken a while. He'd scrubbed at it with soap, washing-up liquid – even a bit of laundry powder. If it hadn't been for Jules, he'd have been tempted to take his chances with toilet bleach.

"Is that permanent marker?"

"No, I went and got a massive cock tattooed on my forehead." Mood as raw as the skin on his face. "Course it's marker and I can't get the fucker off."

His sibling had scampered off downstairs, slammed every cupboard door in the kitchen, then returned with a bottle of sunflower oil and a wad of kitchen towel.

"Try this."

The oil worked.

"Where'd you learn that?"

"Chemistry."

"Nerd."

"Dickhead."

Thirteen years old and smart as shit. If Jules hadn't been the only person in the world Ryan loved, he'd have hated them.

Jules followed him the two steps it took to get from bathroom to bedroom, where Ryan dug about in the heap of laundry Mam had upended at the bottom of his bed.

"Where you off to?"

Ryan didn't say immediately. The top he'd picked up had a hole in the armpit, but if he couldn't find anything better it would do.

"Ry?"

"Kellan's having a party." After pulling on a less-weathered T-shirt, he glanced at the door to find Jules had gone. Jules never liked it when Ryan and Kellan hung out, but tonight it wasn't about choosing one over the other, it was about the last night of school. Ryan had to do something and Kellan's party was the only something to do. The muck-up down by the river had been a bust after some old fart called the community cops. If anything was going to happen, it would be at his cousin's house. Ryan wasn't prepared to have his face missing from all the shitty photos that got posted, or to spend the twenty minutes before every exam lurking in school reception listening to everyone else speaking in a post-party code he couldn't crack.

Not even for Jules.

A twenty-minute walk to the far side of the park, butter-coloured sun smeared on the grass between the shadows of the trees, then Ryan was there, ducking in through the side gate in order to skip the crowd out front. There was a half-arsed ice bin by the tap – not that there was any ice in it, just the end of the hose, a six pack and a couple of bottles with their labels soaked off. Lifting one out, Ryan cracked the lid on the tap and sucked up the foam.

The key to arriving late was to saunter in like he'd been there from the beginning.

The kitchen was buzzier than the garden – some lads cluttering up the sink and a group of Buckthorn familiars getting rowdy at the table. Ryan swiped a bag of Haribo from the pile and stuffed it in his back pocket for later.

Ignoring the people at the table, he made his way towards the door, aiming for family privileges in the nook.

He made it all of two steps before a girl lunged off the doorframe and landed right in front of his face.

"Ryan, right?"

"Uh huh."

He leaned back and tried to take her all in – which was hard because there seemed to be a lot of her. Not physically so much as just ... energetically. Her clothes were three times brighter than anything else in the room and the spotlights glinted off a smile that was as much metal as teeth.

"Do we know each other?" he asked. Girls didn't usually look this pleased to see him.

"We do now. I'm Sunny. Same school, different year. Anyway, I know someone looking for you." To Ryan's delight, she grabbed his arm and in full view of everyone in the kitchen, dragged him across the floor and into the dining room.

"Umm... OK, hold up." Ryan dug his heels into the thick pile of the carpet, wary there was some kind of humiliation waiting for him on the other side of the door that led into the hall. "Look, you're cute and all—" His companion punched him in the bicep. "Ow! What the fuck?"

"There are a million flattering words out there. Choose *any* except that one."

"I wasn't paying you a compliment." A lie. "I was trying to ask what you're playing at."

Whatever joy he'd felt at having Sunny drag him in here

soured to resentment as Ryan rubbed his arm where she'd struck. That had hurt.

"I'm not *playing* at anything," Sunny said.

"Then why'd you say you were looking for me, Sunny from a different year?"

Her eyes and lips narrowed like she suspected he was taking the piss. Which he might have been – taking the piss was his default setting.

"Look, it's a long story, but basically, there's a package for you."

"Expand on that." Ryan set his beer down on the sideboard and took the Haribo out of his pocket. A moment after opening it he held the bag out to Sunny as a peace offering. No hesitation – Sunny dived in, muttering, "These are the same ones we brought!"

"Who's we?"

"Me and Win."

"Again with the who?"

"My sister."

"Let me know when you plan on making sense."

"Let me know when you plan on shutting up long enough for me to explain."

Ryan smiled, a barely-there tug in his lips. He liked her.

One second's pause and she was off.

"This morning Sophie got a parcel. Inside was one addressed to my sister and inside *that* was one addressed to Lucas…"

So many names, so little information. Although if her sappy little sigh was anything to go by, then Sunny from a different year was well into whoever this Lucas was.

"Inside his parcel was one with your name on. Ryan Krikler."

"I know my name."

She gave him a second-long stare. "Yay. Sarcasm."

Ryan popped another Haribo to hide his smile, then, "You mentioned a Sophie. Which one?"

He knew at least three.

"Charbonneau."

Ryan froze.

"Who sent this parcel?"

"Freya Newmarch." Sunny cocked her head to the side, a calculated innocence to the way she said, "Aren't the two of you friends?"

Ryan took another long swig of his beer before he set it back down.

"Absolutely not."

October – 86 days before Freya left

Between the two of them, Ryan and Jules had been very good at dodging Auntie Lou's Sunday dinner for the last four weeks – but they couldn't avoid it for ever. Mam gave them both a once over, making Ryan change into jeans rather than joggers and grunting her approval of Jules' neutral, muted outfit of skinny jeans and white shirt. No make-up, no jewellery, hair tied back into an unremarkable ponytail, the dye through the ends left to fade for this week.

"It's been ages since we've been over…" Mam started as she locked up, handing Ryan a carrier bag containing a bottle of wine that still had the sticker on it from the newsagent. Ryan reached in to peel it off. "What with Jules' band practice and you getting sick"— her offspring exchanged a flicker of a glance – "Lou'll start thinking we're avoiding her."

"Auntie Lou's not the problem," Ryan muttered.

"Not this again!" Mam's voice was sharp enough that the old couple they walked past gave her a startled look. "I don't know what happened between you and Kellan over the summer – you practically lived there for half of it and now all you do is snark about him."

Summer had been an odd one. Years he'd known Freya – just another girl he went to school with. Although maybe there had been something more there, recently. The two had got into a way of talking that felt more playful than hostile … then she saw Kellan. And Kellan saw her. Both of them had been as bad as the other, thinking they were being subtle about the way they were using him – the bridge between Freya's Buckthorn lot and Kellan's Campion crowd. Maybe it hadn't been so hard spending lazy days in the park and nights on the noz, a summer of half-started barbecues and never-ending game play feeling like people actually wanted him around.

Only as a charity case, though. As soon as his cousin and Freya got together, the charity stopped – and Ryan resented both of them for it. He and Kellan could barely be civil without supervision and Freya wound him up just by existing.

Now he'd be sitting across the table from both the fuckers.

At least with Freya there, Kellan would be on his best behaviour when it came to Jules.

When Mam wasn't at work, the only time she didn't spend on the phone to her sister was when she was in her house, but Auntie Lou greeted the three of them like she'd not seen them since last Christmas, with squeals and kisses and more love than Ryan knew what to do with. Steering them into the conservatory, she introduced Mam and Jules to "Kellan's lovely girlfriend, Freya", who looked like she'd come dressed for work experience as a teacher.

"Ryan not getting a mention?" rumbled Uncle Tim, from the corner chair. "Or are we finally excommunicating him?"

"Him and Freya go to the same school."

From Freya's face it was clear she wished they didn't, but Kellan squeezed her knee, giving Ryan the smile of a satisfied shark.

"Got Ry to thank for introducing us."

Ryan jammed his hands in his pockets and asked how long till dinner.

They ate in the dining room, the photos of Kellan and Heather beaming down from the family shrine, eyeing up his mound of roast potatoes and looking virtuous.

Modelling his behaviour on Jules – who always became a quieter, more watchful version of themselves in Kellan's company – Ryan gave short, straight answers when questioned and shoved another forkful into his face to avoid saying anything more. It wasn't so hard. Despite the fact that neither Heather nor her fiancé were there, all Auntie Lou talked about was the wedding, Tim nodding along like spaffing half his salary on a covers band didn't bother him.

Ryan enjoyed Freya's surprise when she found out they were having it at Rabscuttle.

"Oh. That's where I work." She darted a glance at Kellan that no one other than Ryan noticed.

"Well hopefully you won't be working on New Year, poppet," Auntie Lou said, patting her hand, her face creasing up in a smile. "You'll be there as a guest. You're family now."

Given that Freya had been going out with Kellan approximately 20 seconds and had yet to meet Heather – the actual bride – this seemed like a bit of a leap, but Auntie Lou's heart was as big as Tim's budget.

Inevitably, clearing the table fell to him and Kellan – Jules the baby, Freya (despite being family now) the guest. The two of them made short work of it, Ryan gathering up all the plates, scraping what little was left into the composting bin, already overflowing with peelings and prep, so that when Auntie Lou breezed into the kitchen to collect the crumble, warm from the oven, she invoked the "be a love" clause of nephewhood and had him take the lot outside.

When he came back, Freya had joined her boyfriend by the sink – the pair of them completely ignoring the jug of custard they needed to bring next door.

"Break it up." Ryan elbowed them aside so he could wash his hands.

"While you're there, mate" – Kellan held out most of

a bottle of wine – "chuck that lot down the sink. Dad says it's corked. Not fit for drinking."

But Freya intercepted the bottle, frowning. "Not wishing to show your dad up with my waitress credentials, but screw tops can't be corked." She gave it a sniff. "This is fine."

"It's not fine," Kellan said, gently removing it from her grasp and holding it out to Ryan. "It's a corner-shop bottle of piss that no one is going to drink."

Dismay dawned as Freya looked from her boyfriend, to Ryan, via the wine Mam had brought round. Ryan took the bottle and started pouring its contents into the sink, but Freya was in the way, tipping the neck back so that some of it splashed out across the striped sleeve of her top.

"What? No. This is a waste. Where's the lid?"

Kellan held it up a second before he clenched his fist round the cap, crumpling the metal. "No idea."

"Kellan!" she hissed, giving him a shove. "You're being an absolute wanker. Did your dad even say anything, or are you just trying to wind him up?"

But Kellan gave her a scowl that Ryan knew all too well. "Maybe you should stay out of family matters, yeah?"

Whatever her reply, it got drowned with a twist of the tap as Ryan rinsed away the wine staining the sink. Freya was still there when he'd finished – although Kellan had vanished along with the custard.

"There's nothing wrong with that wine," she said, voice drenched in pity. "You could have taken it home and used it in a sauce or something."

"Do I look like Jamie fucking Oliver?" Ryan hated her

for seeing what just happened, hated the pity in her voice.

"Drink it then—"

"You really don't know how to take a hint, do you?" Ryan snapped as he dried his hands. "This has nowt to do with you."

"I was just trying to stick up for you—"

"*Why?*" Ryan hissed, anger turning him mean. "Kellan's the one you're banging. Not me."

LUCAS

For all Lucas had done a lot of telling himself not to expect to see Sunny tonight, that hadn't stopped him from *hoping*. The sight of her sister sitting on her own in the conservatory, hip propped on the window sill, was a shot of adrenaline into the heart of that hope. If Win was here, surely Sunny was too.

"Hi? Win?"

Win glanced up. Her make-up and her clothes were just that little bit edgier than earlier. "Lucas. Hi. Just a sec." As cool and collected sitting on her own at someone else's party as she'd seemed up at Rabscuttle. Lucas watched her finish whatever she was typing and wished he could feel that comfortable asking someone to wait ten seconds for his attention.

"Want some?" Win held up the bottle next to her.

"What is it?"

As she studied the label, Lucas thought how she looked so much and so little like her sister, same as the similarities between his cousins. "According to this it's a *zesty lemon-infused beverage with maximum flavour and minimum sugar* but I would have gone with 'lemonade'."

"In which case, hit me up." He accepted the cup she handed him, glad to have something to take away the taste of JD that lingered at the back of his tongue. "So … um … are you all here then? Sophie" – the safest name to say first, before he looked down at the contents of his cup to finish with – "and Sunny?"

"Yes." When he looked up, Win was smiling like she knew something he didn't, a curve of the lips and no sign of any dimples – nothing of Sunny in her smile. "We are. Sunny's exploring and Sophie's out there." She tipped her head in the direction of the lounge. "We're all here to help."

She raised her cup and tapped it to his.

"*Gan bei*." She tucked away a smile. "Cheers in Mandarin."

"*Ya mas*." He grinned. The only Greek he'd picked up from his family was to do with eating and drinking and cursing. All the best forms of love.

Win looked over his shoulder and nodded. "Looks like we're about to have company."

Lucas turned to stand next to her – if that company was Kellan it might be best for Lucas to do the introductions. Friends of friends got warmer welcomes than cold-callers.

He needn't have worried. Sophie was with him and when she saw Win, she immediately came to sit with her and slip a casual arm across her shoulders. He felt Win tense, but then Sophie was saying something about being worried she'd lost her and Win twisted round to pick up a can of drink and pass it to her, so that he was the one who felt out of place.

"Check this out." Kellan held out his phone to show him a picture of Ryan, still in his school shirt – a massive spunking penis scrawled across his forehead. Ryan's face was pure fury and the ear in shot looked hot enough to melt off the side of his head.

"Don't think the lass who's looking for him will be so interested if Ry's still got this on his head." The way he was looking at Win framed his question and Lucas gave a slight shake of the head.

"This is Win, she's—"

"With me," Sophie finished decisively.

"Oh yeah?" Kellan stared down at Sophie like he was hoping to get more out of her, but Sophie sweetened her silence with a smile. Giving the two girls a final speculative look, Kellan twitched his head towards the door and said to Lucas, "Going out for a smoke. You coming?"

"Actually," Sophie leaned across and looked at Lucas, her arm sliding from around Win. "I was hoping to borrow him for a bit."

"Need a bodyguard do you?"

When Sophie smiled, it was with the same brand of confidence as Freya – that sleepy, slightly flirty vibe that came when she knew she was about to get her own way.

"I know someone who'd like to get to know Big T a little better." She gave the slightest nod in the direction of the lounge.

"First Ryan, now you…" Kellan shook his head like he wasn't sure what the world was coming to, grinning all the while. "Buckthorn girls used to have *taste*." He saluted the girls and gave Lucas a jock-like slap on the back. "Let me know how it goes."

The three of them watched as he went out the door, arms spreading wide as the group littering the patio furniture turned to welcome him. Then, before Lucas could ask Sophie what she'd meant about someone wanting to talk to him, Win's phone flashed up.

She held it up to display a picture of someone pulling a cat-eared beanie all the way down over their face with the contact name *Most Annoying Avenger*.

"I'm guessing Sunny's found Ryan."

SOPHIE

Going back through the house was like walking through a microcosm of memories. The back garden had reminded her of summer evenings sitting with her feet in a paddling pool; the conservatory of whispered misery the night Freya and Kellan had fallen out over how hot she thought Shawn Mendes was because even famous men were a threat to the ego of the Commissioner of the Thought Police.

Then there was the nook, with its standby-button glow and perma-scent of Diesel and leather, where Lucas had left his bag next to a sofa weighed down with boys more interested in gaming than girls.

It wasn't until the three of them stepped back into the hall that Sophie remembered she'd kissed one of them at Kellan's last big party – or rather, the last she'd been to. They'd kissed here, on the stairs, when whoever-he-was misread friendly for flirty and Sophie figured she had nothing better to do since all her friends except Freya had already gone home.

He'd tasted like the e-cigarette he'd been smoking on the front steps.

The next day Freya had laughed herself half-silly about it, turning a disappointing snog into something Sophie could laugh at too.

I thought you were off boys?

I am, but this one was right there. Boys are so much easier than girls.

Too easy, clearly.

"Sophie?" Win was waiting for her by the arch that led into the creepy dining room.

They found the others by the wall of worship. Sunny was a firework close to exploding the second Lucas noticed her, while Ryan modelled the hunched shoulders and shifty expression of a dealer about to get picked up by the police.

On seeing Sophie, his eyes narrowed to nothing.

"Big T," Ryan said, flicking the briefest of glances at the others. "Girl I don't know—"

"That's my sister, Win!" From an indignant Sunny.

"Carbs. This is a horrific surprise."

"Anything to do with you is horrific," Sophie said, putting her can down on the side and scanning his forehead for any trace of her drawing. "How's the head?"

All she got was a scowl.

"So." Ryan slid his hands into his back pockets, one of them crackling with the pack of sweets Sophie could see stuffed in there. "What's all this about a present?"

Hearing him call it that annoyed her.

"It's a parcel. Not a present." To spite him, she added, "There's probably one for someone else inside."

"Yeah, well, hand it over."

Sophie looked to Lucas. This was it, then. She was glad they'd found Ryan so soon – no, *relieved*. An hour was enough to convince Sophie she didn't have it in her to last much longer. Another hour, tops. Constantly standing, walking, paying attention when her brain kept buffering would have been hard enough, but being in his house and seeing Kellan was *definitely* too much.

Pretending she was fine took more energy when *all* the things were sub-optimal.

Lucas was rummaging in his bag for the parcel, finally handing it over with a, "Here you go. From Frey—"

"Shut the fuck up!" Ryan snatched the package. "Anyone ever tell you what subtle means?"

Apparently no one had told Ryan, either. The way he stuffed the package into the waistband of his trousers and swept a glance round the empty room was anything but. Sophie had expected scorn, something dismissive and mean, but *that* was fear.

"You worried about Kellan?" Lucas asked, and Sophie thought of the way Kellan had reacted when she'd asked to see Ryan.

"Don't want him in my business, that's all."

"Do you two not like each other or something?" Sunny piped up.

"He's family," Ryan said, lips sealing the sentence shut as he shot a warning look at the rest of them.

But Sophie had exhausted what little patience she possessed: the only thing that mattered was the next layer of the parcel.

"Are you going to open it? We can go somewhere—"

"I'm not going anywhere with you." Ryan was watching her too closely. Had *seen* how much she cared. With a spiteful twitch to his lips, he edged round them and out into the hall. "Think I'll go somewhere a little more private. Enjoy the party."

RYAN

The safest place to open Freya's parcel was at home, far away from prying eyes. But that required patience and Ryan was running on empty. Five months was too long.

In the year following his parents' divorce, when Mam and Ryan and Jules had lived here, the downstairs toilet had been a dingy little panic room he ducked into whenever he wanted to escape. Time hadn't changed his instincts, but it sure as hell changed the décor.

While Mam spent all her free time trying to make money, her sister spent all hers wasting it. Like everything else in this house, the toilet had been done up in the last year: a fresh coat of paint; new sink that looked like a shallow glass bowl; a posh new loo. Still the same Auntie Lou flourishes – towel folded in perfect pleats over the rail under the sink, hand cream and soap lined up with the labels on show, and on the far wall a row of wooden letters spelled out the word *fresh!*

Lowering the seat, Ryan sat down and tore into the parcel, shredding the paper in his haste to reveal the treasure inside.

When he got there, all he could do was stare.

Dad's T-shirt. The one he'd hidden and hung on to because he'd wanted something of his dad, Mam binning everything else – forever determined to erase every trace of the man she'd married, regardless of what her kids wanted.

If he'd known Freya had taken it, he'd have told her to keep it. It had been something of his dad; maybe Freya had wanted something of him… But now she'd returned it.

A sheaf of envelopes splashed to the floor as the material unfurled. Ignoring them, he bunched the shirt in his hands and held it to his face for a sniff. Flowers. A scent that smelled ... his eyes shifted to the word on the wall ... *fresh!* Like Freya.

October – 76 days before Freya left

The sky was trying to flush itself clean. Thirty seconds outside and your clothes would be soaked, skin pimpling with the cold of it, hair and lashes dripping.

Rain to drown in.

The doorbell went again.

Ryan was the only one home – Wednesdays Mam worked till the gym closed at ten and Jules went straight round their mate's house for band practice that lasted till long after tea.

The front door always got sticky when it was wet and he had to yank it out of its frame before he saw who'd called. "What are you doing here?"

Freya shrugged. The rain had plastered her hair to her scalp, drops forming at the end of every sodden tendril, and she shivered inside the rain-stiffened shell of her denim jacket. "Thought I'd drop by."

Her lashes bunched together, framing the challenge in her gaze as she waited for him to say something. To ask why she was there or make a joke, force her to beg for shelter.

Ryan pushed the door wide and, after a second more of

that gaze, she stepped inside. He had to brush past her to shut the door, feeling the heat of her body beneath the chill of the rain.

"Well," he said, standing back. "You've dropped. Now what?"

"Now I need to get dry. I'm soaked."

"I can see…" Her jacket was open enough that he could see her school shirt sticking to her bra.

But that was all he saw before she tugged the jacket tight around with one hand, freeing the other to wallop him on the arm. "Don't be a perv."

"Ow."

"You deserved it."

"When do I not?" he threw back over his shoulder as he started up the stairs, then turned, waiting for her to follow. "Bathroom's up here. So are all the dry clothes."

After a moment, she came up after him, following Ryan into his bedroom where the walls were patchily papered with pages ripped from magazines – half-naked women laid over sweaty footballers in the world's tamest orgy. Every surface was crammed with glasses or cans, plates and pens and paper, tatty school books and little models of old obsessions – footballers, Pokémon, Minecraft. A torch that needed a battery. A fake Fitbit with a broken strap. A pair of headphones, copper wire peeping out of the rubber.

Freya took it all in with a single glance.

"Newcastle?"

"Runs in the family – Dad's side," he added, before she

pointed out that Kellan bled Boro red. "Why are you here, Freya?"

"You said something about dry clothes...?"

"Here at my house, not here in my room." But he went over to the pile of clean clothes heaped on top of his chest of drawers and dug about for something she could change into before she left a puddle on the carpet.

"Me and Kellan fell out."

"Oh yeah?"

"Don't sound so hopeful." She'd picked up an interlocking puzzle Jules had left on the window sill. "Kellan's fine. You can't hurt someone's feelings if they don't have any."

"So you fell out with Kellan. What's that got to do with you being here?" He balled the clothes he'd picked up in his hands. "Why not call your mam?"

"Don't want the hassle."

"Go round Sophie's then—"

"I don't want a *friend*, Ryan, or I wouldn't be here." She put the puzzle down a little too hard, the plastic slapping on the sill with a crack, either the cold making her clumsy, or anger making her careless. "I just want to be somewhere that doesn't belong to the rest of my shitty life."

Ryan looked at her, wondering how the hell someone who had everything she wanted could possibly call her life shitty when she was standing in his shoe-box bedroom on a carpet that hadn't been changed since the last century and stank like stale socks.

"You mean you want somewhere to hide," he said.

"And someone who won't tell anyone about it."

He didn't know if she meant at all, or just Kellan. Either way, Ryan wasn't going to spill.

"I can manage that."

"I know you can." Something that might have been a smile lurked in the shadows of her lips. "But stop pretending you want rid of me. You had your chance to tell me to jog on when you opened the door."

Every word of that last sentence quivered as she fought to stop her teeth from chattering and Ryan thought better of forcing more out.

"Dry clothes. As promised." He handed her a pair of tracksuit bottoms and a long-faded T-shirt with SECURITY: KRIKLER in cracked print across the back. A T-shirt that had lasted a hell of a lot longer than the job – Dad had never liked being told what to do.

"Thanks." Freya was already undoing her shirt, as she nodded back out the door. "Bathroom's the one opposite, right?"

Ryan nodded to hide the way his gaze had dipped down to where her fingers fumbled the button. "Right."

A knock on the door.

"Someone in here!" Ryan called out. "Go upstairs."

There were three bloody bathrooms to choose from – they couldn't *all* be occupied.

Leaning forward, he gathered up the envelopes that had tumbled out of the material. One for each of them – Sophie and Lucas and that girl Win. One for him. His gaze traced the "y" of his name, one long swoop that curled back on itself.

Ryan spent a long time trying to remember all the different ways his name could sound coming out of Freya's mouth. The one everyone heard, of patience thinned too far.

And the other times, other ways Freya said his name, when there had only been Ryan to hear.

Tucking a finger under the flap, he tore the envelope open and went to lift out the letter.

THUMP. THUMP. THUMP.

"Someone in here!" Ryan yelled back savagely.

"Oh *is* there?" His cousin's voice. "Hi Ryan. Having fun are you?"

And then THUMP. THUMP. THUMP. The envelope trembled, Ryan's hands less steady than a second ago.

"I'm having a shit! Leave me alone!"

"Last time you took a shit this long you flooded the en suite."

Kellan would only spin a tale like that if there were people other than Ryan to hear it. More banging on the door, some name calling and an overloud "Shitler!" that no doubt came from Jonno, who'd used the same insult many times in the past – usually when Ryan was caning him at Smash Bros. Giving up on his privacy, Ryan flushed the empty toilet and pulled his dad's T-shirt on over the one he already wore. Better than trying to stuff it down his trouser leg, or explain why he was carrying it. The envelopes went in his back pocket to join the Haribo. He could deal with them later.

Now for Kellan.

Ryan squirted some air freshener into the air for authenticity and snatched the door open, with a, "Fuck off, will you?"

There weren't many of them, just Kellan and his entourage: Jonno as per the "Shitler" dig and Kellan's Fry-shaped shadow, plus a couple of other Campion hangers-on. Nothing to get worked up about.

"All right, coz." Kellan made a playful swipe for his head that Ryan was too slow to duck. "What is it with you and that loo?"

"What? I was having a shit…"

"He was having a wank!" Jonno shouted, the others cackling in glee.

"I was not!"

But this was Kellan's house and Kellan's friends and the only words that mattered were the ones that came from Kellan's mouth.

"You were, though, weren't you?" Kellan slung an arm round Ryan's shoulder, fingers digging into the socket to give him a shake. "Overcome by all the girls next door, you couldn't wait to crack one off."

"I'm not the one who goes to an all-boys school." This quip exceeded his humour allowance and Kellan shoved him away a little too hard, so Ryan had to catch hold of Fry to steady himself. Face saved, Ryan straightened and made as if to go.

"Thanks, mate." One of the Campion anons was holding up the Haribo he'd pulled from Ryan's back pocket, grinning as he grabbed a handful of whatever was left. A charade wasted on Kellan, who was looking at an envelope that had fallen to the floor. One whose top edge had already been torn open.

Time rippled a moment before there was movement, Ryan reaching out with a strained, "Forgot I still had that on me…" as Kellan leant over. Kellan was faster. The envelope was in his hand, lifted high enough that Ryan had to lunge for it.

That was a mistake.

Kellan twitched the envelope further away, dodging from Ryan's reach, laughing, asking him if he wanted it back, tossing it to Fry, who passed it to Jonno…

"Give me that!" Ryan snarled, furious at them all, with himself, and very *very* frightened.

"Ask nicely."

"Just fucking give it."

Kellan rolled his eyes and plucked the envelope from Jonno. "All right, you whiny little diva. Here you go…"

One moment Ryan was reaching out for his letter, the next

he found himself sprawling through the toilet door and onto the floor, limbs taking a bruising as the door swung closed, cracking shins and ankles before the latch clicked shut.

"NO!" Ryan hurled himself at the door, forcing all his weight down on the handle.

Whoever was on the other side was stronger.

"LET ME OUT!" Ryan smashed his fists against the wood, hard enough for the force to jar every bone in his body. Again and again he flung himself at the door, the panels flexing with each blow. Through all the noise he could hear Kellan starting to read the letter out in a loud, camp drawl.

"This is the hardest letter to write. Maybe that's why it's taken so long for me to…"

"Kellan I am going to *kill* you. Do *not* read that letter!" Ryan gulped back air, trying to smother the terror ballooning in his chest. "Do you hear me?"

But there was no answer. The handle remained immovable, but beyond the door Kellan had fallen silent.

LUCAS

Lucas suspected he had Win to thank for the fact that he and Sunny were alone together. After Ryan disappeared with the parcel, she and Sophie had gone outside and her parting shot to Sunny had been a warning about not getting into any trouble, eyes darting to him as she tucked away another of those knowing smiles.

The trouble they weren't getting into so far had been to drop his bag back in the nook, obtain a pint of ice from the dispenser on the fridge and "explore" upstairs at Sunny's request. Now they stood, side by side, in one of the passageways that led off the landing, staring at yet another Spencer family portrait, lit up by a spotlight that had come on when Lucas hit the light switch at the top of the stairs.

"Kellan's family really like looking at pictures of themselves, huh?" Sunny said, before popping a shard of ice into her mouth and crunching it like candy.

She wasn't wrong. When Lucas first came here, he'd been surprised by all the photos. Not that there weren't plenty of family pictures up in his aunt and uncle's house, but they were all normal size, not blown up like gallery art and made the centrepiece of the stairwell or the dining room. This one had been taken at Heather's wedding – she'd got married at New Year and had the reception up at Rabscuttle on a day Ed had been rostered to work and that Lucas had been pleased to avoid. In it, the bride and groom stood at the bottom of the sweeping central staircase, Heather's parents a few steps up, Kellan with his elbow propped on the bannister looking like he'd been born to model menswear.

"Don't you think it's weird how there are so few of Ryan?" Sunny said, tipping her head to the side. "I mean, those two are close, aren't they?"

Lucas wasn't sure what close really meant when it came to Kellan and his cousin. Kellan seemed to loathe Ryan as much as he loved him – the two of them could hang out every night for a week, but the second anyone brought up Ryan's name, Kellan'd be the first to talk him down. Not in the good-natured, piss-taking way that Lucas was used to with Alex, but with sharper words that cut too close to the truth for Lucas to feel comfortable with what he was hearing.

"Maybe Ryan just hates posing for photos?" he suggested.

"Unlike Kellan."

"You sound like you don't approve."

Sunny grunted. "I don't like people who think they're good-looking."

"I'm safe then."

"More than safe." She gave him a sidelong look through her lashes, cheek dimpling a second before her expression dissolved into dismay and she gripped his wrist in alarm. "No! Wait! Does that make it sound like I agree that you're not good-looking? Because I don't. I think the opposite. Like, Kellan's here" – she crouched down, hand a little above the ground, then she stood – "but you're here." Sunny stood on tiptoes, stretching out so tall that the tips of her fingers brushed the crystals dangling from the light above.

Lucas laughed, hand coming up to rub at the back of

his head as he blinked, aware of the difference in the way the world saw Kellan and the way it saw him. Perhaps not Sunny, though, who made a sound like a mouse trying to squeeze through a too-small hole as she looked at him with eyes as wide and brilliant as her smile.

"How about we agree to disagree?" he said.

"Deal." She sparkled up at him, her expression sucking all the oxygen from his lungs.

There was nothing he wanted more than for Sunny to like him.

She crept further along the corridor, craning her neck to peer into the rooms at the end, saying something about seeing if there were any more pictures, but he touched a hand to her elbow, skin thrilled at the contact, his face warmed by the glow of her smile as she turned to look at him.

"We should head back." He nodded towards the landing. "This bit of the house is supposed to be off limits."

Not really knowing how to interpret her disappointed little "Aw", Lucas approached the top of the stairs with a frown. The people they'd passed on the way up, the girls who'd been sitting on the floor of the landing, even the couple who'd been blocking the other passage as they kissed up against the wall, were all leaning over the bannister, watching whatever was going on in the hall below.

Just as Lucas was about to ask what was up, the crowd flinched and one of the girls turned away, scrunching her eyes with a horrified, "Oh my God, that's blood..." as a less squeamish friend took her place, eyes wide as she gasped, "Is that *Kellan*?"

RYAN

Ryan's attempt to make a bolt for it when the door opened didn't exactly work. All that happened was that he cannoned into Fry.

"You don't want to get involved..." Ryan murmured, more plea than warning, but Fry was Kellan's friend, not Ryan's. Not when it mattered.

A split second and Kellan yanked him round, fist smashing into his face.

"The fuck you think you are?" The material of Freya's T-shirt was bunched into Kellan's hand as he pulled Ryan so close that the blood dripping from his nose bloomed crimson on the crisp white collar of Kellan's polo shirt. "You back-stabbing piece of shit; she was my *girlfriend*."

Ryan's eyes darted down to the paper scrunched in Kellan's other hand, a fist ready to land another hit.

What the hell was in that letter?

Like he could ask. Kellan was already lunging in again, the two of them squirming around in the kind of fight they'd had many times as kids, fingers scraping against bare skin as they grappled, Kellan thumping any part of Ryan's torso he could. "Get off!" Ryan tried to throw him, tried to kick and elbow, then punched down, aiming for a nut-cracker that bounced harmlessly off his cousin's thigh.

Squirming free, Ryan managed to land a hit, Kellan staggering into the little table by the stairs, knocking over a bowl of crystals that skittered across the floor in applause.

As he lunged forward, aiming for Ryan's throat, Kellan slipped, bringing both of them down. Ryan was first up, quick to get a knee over Kellan's chest, giving him a chance to actually do something to slow this fight down, give him a chance to actually *say*—

"Don't think so, mate."

As Ryan made to bring his arm down, someone caught his elbow from behind, twisting his arm back so that Ryan squawked in agony, forced to take his weight off Kellan as he staggered up and back.

Even through a veil of pain so intense his vision had blurred, Ryan saw the sadistic intent with which Kellan hauled himself up.

Freya's letter sat on the hall floor between them, the paper curved and crinkled as a sea-shell.

"You want this?" Kellan crouched down and picked it up, smoothing it flat against his thigh. He took a couple of slow, deliberate steps towards Ryan.

If it hadn't been for whoever was shoving his elbow up between his shoulder blades, Ryan would have made a run for it.

Instead, he spat a glob of blood and spit that landed on Kellan's shoe. It did nothing to slow him down – he just held the letter up to Ryan's face.

"Can you read it?" He drew closer. "No? Here?"

The paper swooped close enough that it filled Ryan's vision, but when he lifted his free hand to take it, Kellan twisted his fingers back.

"How about *here*."

Kellan smacked the paper into Ryan's nose, the heel of the hand holding it forced so hard into his face that spots of pain fired white across the inside of his eyes. A thumb forced its way into the corner of his mouth, forcing his jaw down as Kellan jabbed the paper inside, knuckles knocking against his teeth.

He couldn't draw breath, everything hurt and Kellan was leaning in, his next question a venomous hiss intended for Ryan alone.

"You think you can do that behind my back and get away with it?"

Not that Ryan could answer.

One second he was choking on the words that had got him into this mess, the next he staggered back as whoever was holding him let go. Someone fierce and fluorescent was shoving their way through the crowd and into the space between Ryan and Kellan, forcing the two apart.

Ryan swiped the paper out of his mouth to haul in some air, staring at the furious figure of Sunny.

"Get off him!"

"Stay out of this—" Kellan made to push past her – a tornado barrelling towards a bird – but Sunny braced her shoulders.

"No. I won't."

Kellan's face, flushed from the fight, deepened from anger to rage. "This is my fucking house!"

"So. He's my fucking" – she glanced back at Ryan with a frown – "acquaintance."

No one said anything and for one awful moment, Ryan

wondered if Kellan was so far gone that he'd shove Sunny out of the way to get to him.

Then he came to his senses, realised how many people were in the hall, lining the stairs, all of them watching. People who were murmuring among themselves, asking what the fight was about…

Kellan's eyes flickered down to the letter in Ryan's hand, then back up to his face. The menace in his gaze was chilling and Ryan wished he knew exactly what was in there, how much Freya had told him. How scared he should be.

"Get the fuck out of my house, Ry. And take your girlfriend with you."

"She not my—"

"Sunny's with me," someone said from over Ryan's shoulder.

Turning, Ryan came face-to-face with the person who'd been holding him. Lucas stood there, looking miserable, a bloody streak smeared across the broad white expanse of his T-shirt.

But Sunny looked him up and down, just once.

"I'm not with anyone, actually." Ignoring the crushed look on Lucas's face, Sunny jerked her chin in the direction of the door. "Come on, Ryan. Your cousin's an absolute wanker."

WIN

Going outside had been an excuse to give Sunny a little time with Lucas – and perhaps to give herself a little time with Sophie. Win's shoulders remembered the weight of her arm and, when she sat next to her on the wall at the bottom of the drive, she caught a faint waft of whatever perfume she wore. A smell that made Win think of white flowers and warm summers.

But if Sophie were a flower, it was one that had wilted.

"Are you OK?" Win asked. She clearly wasn't, but what else do you say?

"Just tired." The words were more sigh than sound. "I need to sit quietly for a bit."

"Oh." Win stood and hitched her thumb back towards the house. "If you want I can—"

"No. Stay."

"I don't have to."

"You're peaceful to be around." Sophie smiled at her, eyelids low and lazy, and Win's heart swept itself up for a beat. "I miss having someone I can be quiet with."

Presumably that was a Freya reference. One that Win wouldn't have made – whenever a conversation threatened to get too relaxed, Freya would prod it back into action with a question that demanded an answer – but if that parcel had shown Win anything, it was that Freya might not have been the same person around Win as she had been around Sophie, or Lucas, or (presumably) Ryan.

Win shrugged her shirt closer around her body. The

sun had dipped beyond the line of the trees, the sky above a wash of the most virulent oranges and pinks, glowing with the last of the light. Everyone in the world loved a good sunset, but they weren't the only beautiful thing to look at.

Win allowed herself a glance at the girl next to her, as fast and subtle as a breath.

Behind them came the click of the front door and the two of them turned, Win to her left, Sophie to her right, the two of them drawing close enough that it was easy to hear Sophie's muttered, "Ugh. Ryan."

"Would it cheer you up to see that he's bleeding?"

"Yes. It absolutely would."

But Win only had a fraction of a second in which to share Sophie's slightly wicked smile, because Ryan wasn't alone. Sunny was with him. Win was so fast up the drive that Sunny hadn't made it three steps from the front door before Win was there, hands on her sister's shoulders, holding her still enough that she could inspect her for damage.

Suspicious of Ryan, Win switched to Mandarin. "*Zen me le? Ni mei shi ba?*"

"Calm down. I'm fine." But there was a tremor in Sunny's voice and something unhinged about her smile.

Ryan ignored both of them, just carried on down the drive, lifting his top up to dab at his nose, exposing a pale, skinny torso, the skin splotchy like he'd been grabbed and pulled and punched by sharp, vicious hands. There was a flash of a glance as he passed Sophie, still sitting on the wall, and then he'd turned down the road and away. Sophie looked up the drive to Win, then she too was gone, following Ryan because he was the person who had the parcel and, when all was said and done, that was what she cared about.

Before Win could form anything more coherent than a "What—" she was interrupted by the sound of someone at the door.

Lucas.

Sunny turned away so fast that she practically propelled herself down the drive with a single step, trainers slapping angrily on the brickwork.

Win didn't know what was happening, didn't really know where to start. But since both Sunny and Ryan had run off, the only place she could start was with Lucas.

"What happened in there?"

"I made a mistake."

"What kind of mistake? Did you hurt Sunny?"

"*No.*" His reaction was horrified and honest. "I was with her upstairs—"

"*Upstairs?*" She took a step forward and for all Lucas had the physical advantage of someone twice her size who hefted barrels and crates on a semi-regular basis, he took a hasty step back.

"On the landing, looking at Kellan's sister's wedding picture." Lucas relaxed a tiny bit when he realised Win wasn't about to reach down his throat and pull his testicles up through his digestive tract. "Someone was knocking the shit out of Kellan – or – I *thought* so – and I didn't know it was Ryan … he had a different T-shirt on…" An excuse so flimsy he looked ashamed at having made it. He brought a hand up to his head, fingers combing a savage path through his fringe. "I didn't know Kellan was going to smack him about like that. I'm so sorry…"

RYAN

Ryan hadn't wanted company, but he had Sophie at his back, ready to interrogate him about that bloody parcel and Sunny bouncing around in front of him, nagging at him for bleeding. Short of climbing over someone's front hedge and sprinting through their house, he was trapped.

"You can't walk all the way home!" Sunny grabbed him by the arm, then quickly let go as he snatched himself free with a scowl.

"You don't even know where I live—"

"Enough!" Sunny's sister had caught up with them. Win – that was her name. She was nothing like Sunny. She looked tough, spoke with authority and wore an expression that squashed Ryan's instinctive urge to argue. Instead he slouched back against the sign for Kellan's road and had another go at his nose. Less blood came away than last time.

The whole group seemed to take a breath. Win's presence slowed Sunny to a less vigorous jitter and Sophie leaned against the lamp post, a far cry from the girl so angry she'd savaged his forehead with a Sharpie. Beyond all of them, hulking in the shadow cast by one of the trees, stood Lucas.

"Ryan," Win said. "Are you OK? Do you need to see a doctor or something?"

"Ha! *No.*" Clearly none of them had seen a fight before. His attention darted to Lucas, who looked guiltily away. Correction: none of the *girls* had seen a fight.

"Ryan…" The second Lucas spoke, everyone else went extra silent, Sophie's gaze dancing round all of them as she tried to piece together what was going on.

Ryan decided to give her a little help. Just for once.

"You come to say sorry?" The words dislodged something and Ryan spat out a dark, shiny globule before carrying on. "Or did Kellan send you to finish what you helped start?"

"That's not what happened. I was trying to break things up." For all he was looking at Ryan as he said it, they all knew he was talking to Sunny.

"My face says thanks."

"I really didn't mean to hurt you—"

"Says the guy who got chucked out of his last school for breaking someone's arm."

"What?" Sunny hissed, all of them turning to look at Lucas so that they missed Ryan's satisfied little smirk. Revenge sweet enough to cut through the taste of blood.

"I didn't – that's…" Lucas sighed. "I didn't get chucked out."

To be fair, Ryan couldn't recall the ins and outs of Lucas and his reputation for being tough. Knew he'd broken someone's arm – the one thing he wasn't denying. Too honest, that one. Ryan would have denied it in a heartbeat in his position – and if he'd been Lucas, they'd have believed him.

Felt kind of weird to be the one people listened to.

"Whatever." Ryan sniffed and dabbed a thumb to his nostril. "I'm out of here…"

"Wait." Win pulled a set of keys from her pocket and nodded at a car parked across the road. "My car's just here. I'll give you a lift." Then, "Sophie, I can come back to get you if—"

But Sophie was shaking her head, pushing herself up off the lamp post.

"No. I've had enough partying for one night."

For one awkward moment, no one said anything more, but then Win looked at Lucas. "What about you?"

"If you're sure…"

But Win had already turned away, pointing her key at her car, pulling the driver's seat forward for Ryan to get in the back. He hadn't meant to accept, but Win commanded a level of authority that Ryan found hard to rail against. Besides, he was tired, he hurt and a lift wasn't such a terrible idea.

Sunny was in next, then Lucas, his bulk squashing the three of them into an awkward tangle of elbows and knees as they battled to put their belts on, Sunny squealing indignantly when Ryan accidentally elbowed her chest.

"So is this it?" Sophie twisted round from the passenger seat, fixing Ryan with a steely look and a sigh that was either exasperation or exhaustion. Maybe both. "Wasn't there anything else inside that parcel?"

"Well there was this." Ryan pointed at his T-shirt and there was a murmur of "I told you!" from Lucas. "And some letters."

"*What?*" Sophie tried to twist round further, the seatbelt jerking against her neck, an angry dog restrained by a leash. "For us?"

But Sunny was talking over her.

"Was that what was on that piece of paper Kellan was so angry about?"

Ryan gave her a sidelong glower that she interpreted perfectly – and ignored.

"*Oh my God, what did it say?*"

"Like I know. He got to it first."

"And the others?" This time the panic came from Lucas. Serve him right.

"I've got them here…" But as he reached for his back pocket, Sunny, squashed as she was between him and Lucas, objected with a squeak and a "You have *really* pointy elbows!" while Sophie held her hand out, demanding he hand hers over—

A short sharp *parp* of the horn silenced the chaos.

"Stop this," Win spoke into the silence that followed. "Why don't we go somewhere quiet, all of us together, and sort all this out."

"What's there to sort?" Ryan muttered, feeling a little disappointed when Win sighed, like she'd known he'd be the one to object.

"When Sophie found me this morning there was a note from Freya." Win looked over at Sophie, like she expected her to say something. When she didn't, Win carried on. "She said there was treasure at the end of the trail – I presume she means the letters, but…"

"But what?" From Sunny.

"I don't know." Win might give the impression of having an answer for everything, but she sounded no more sure than any of the rest when she said, "What if the letters all interconnect or something? One last puzzle we need to solve together?"

SOPHIE

"Up here." Sophie pointed to a narrow road just before they hit the bridge into town. The road led up a long slope, past houses built with money as old as the bricks, sash windows framed in white-painted wood and ivy.

One of them was her gran's house. Something Sophie would have pointed out if it had just been her and Win. She'd meant what she'd said in the garden. Some people were a drain to be around, but Win's company was the closest thing to replenishing that Sophie ever got. Except they weren't alone, and with a row of people on the back seat, Sophie stayed quiet, thinking back to the week when she'd had to walk up here after school to feed the cats and water plants while her gran had been in hospital.

Freya came with her every time.

"Sophie?"

"Mm?"

The car was at a turning and Win was looking at her for directions.

"Oh. Follow the road round the…" Whatever word she was looking for had gone missing.

"The green?"

Sophie nodded, ignoring the concern in Win's frown. She could do this. She was sure. All they were doing was reading the letters, giving Freya an opportunity to have her final reveal, then she could go home.

The car bobbled along the road, wonky little cottages on one side, the green on the other, shadowed in twilight. No one said anything until Win pulled into a small car park at the end of a row of houses. Beyond that, beneath an indigo sky, stood a sandstone church, glowing in floodlight.

"We're here," Sophie said.

After they'd finished at Gran's, she and Freya would grab a bag of strawberry sherbets from the tiny little shop on the green and come up here. On the far side of the church, beyond the graveyard, a row of memorial benches looked down over the valley.

Do you think the ghosts come and sit here to take in the view?

Can ghosts sit? Wouldn't they go straight through the bench?

They can stand, can't they?

So you're saying they stand on the bench?

Shut up.

Freya hadn't understood why Sophie had been miffed to find Freya had brought Kellan here because it was "romantic". She didn't get that some things were meant to be special.

LUCAS

Last time Lucas came here the light felt cold and the trees were stripped down to their bones.

Tonight it was Lucas who felt naked, the best parts of him snatched away from the surface, revealing all the things he'd rather no one saw. Having lived so long with someone who knew how to expose his flaws, Lucas was aware of his limits. But he'd thought – believed – that he'd grown since coming here, so that if things got rough, he'd step back and *think*.

And if he had, maybe he'd have remembered that for all he was a mate, Kellan had a vicious streak.

November – 32 days before Freya left

"What is this place?"

"It's a church, you prat." Kellan strode on through the graveyard, aiming a lazy kick at a pot of plastic flowers someone had set by one of the headstones. As Lucas passed, he nudged the pot upright with his toe, sending a silent apology to David Travers, who lived on in the hearts of those who knew him.

Kellan hadn't been the easiest company that week. In lessons he'd been silent and sullen and if his classmates caught his attention, it held more chill than warmth. When he had announced an alternative activity for tonight, none of the lads had voiced objections, but that didn't mean

Lucas didn't have any. The location wasn't the issue; the bundle of golf clubs propped over Kellan's shoulder very much was.

Lucas tugged the edges of his track top as tight around his body as it would go and followed his mates beyond the shadow of the church, until all four of them were looking down the hill to where the town nestled in the crook of the river's elbow.

"You can be caddy." Kellan shoved the clubs at Jonno and watched him struggle not to drop them. Then he jumped up, quick as a cat, onto the low stone wall and settled a golf ball at his feet, holding a hand out for a club. "Hand me the fairway wood."

Jonno looked at the clubs the same way Lucas had eyed all the different kitchen utensils the first day of his training at Rabscuttle. "I – er…"

"Fucksake." Kellan wrenched the one he wanted from Jonno's grasp, the shaft catching him squarely on the mouth. No one said anything, aware of the bite that Kellan's mood brought to the crisp winter air, and Jonno waited until Kellan's back was turned before running his tongue over his lip.

"Fore!" Kellan called, as he sent the ball arcing into the sky to plummet into the middle of the river. If he'd wanted to, Lucas knew Kellan could have sent it across the water and through someone's window. Town looked a lot closer from up here than the church did from below.

"Fancy a go?" Kellan jumped down from the wall and prodded Fry in the stomach with the end of his club.

"Kellan, pal…" There was none of his usual bravado as Fry eyed his best mate, then the golf clubs. "Last time I played golf it was on top of the cliff at Whitby and it took me ten swipes to get my ball past a bloody windmill."

"And?" Kellan said, eyes as cold as the sky.

"Don't expect me to actually hit it," Fry mumbled, giving in and grabbing the first club he laid hands on.

True to his promise, Fry's technique was less Tiger Woods and more tiger chasing its tail as he whirled round with every swing, the iron whistling over the top of his ball several times before he scuffed it straight into the grass.

"Warned you." Fry accompanied his complete lack of concern with a wry smile that Kellan didn't return.

"Big T." Kellan had already selected a club and was holding it out for Lucas to take.

"Look." Lucas raised his hands and stepped back. "I'm not up for this. We could hurt someone."

"Says the guy who broke a dude's arm!" Jonno's voice had the over-loud edge of someone relieved to be out of the spotlight, but Kellan ignored him.

"Tell me," he said, turning his attention back to Lucas. "How's Freya?"

Lucas shook his head, not sure what he was supposed to say.

"You work at the same posh hotel as she does, right?" Behind him, Fry stuffed his hands in his pockets and kicked at the ground with his heel, avoiding Lucas's eye. "So. You must see her."

Here it was. The moment that Lucas had hoped never to face, the one he'd avoided by asking questions about everyone else's weekends and never talking about his own, his guard up around his job, pretending it was because he was ashamed he needed to have one.

"The roster changes week to week…" he began, hating that he was about to cover one lie with another.

"You don't know then." Kellan nodded – a pantomime of trust before his gaze narrowed. "She and I are on a break."

This was news – to all of them, judging by the looks fired behind Kellan's back.

"Oh, mate, that's rough." Lucas edged closer, aimed a hand at Kellan's shoulder for a firm sympathy shake.

"Just a bit." Kellan hefted the golf club and lowered the grip until it was level with Lucas's free hand. "So if I want to blow off a little steam, the least my mates can do is help me out. Right?"

Lucas took the club.

"Right. Of course. If I'd known…"

But Kellan wasn't letting go of the golf club.

"Just remember where your loyalties lie, Big T."

WIN

The sky was the same vibrant blue of Van Gogh's "Starry Night" and Win slowed, tipping her head back to admire it. She wished she had a real-world eyedropper tool that she could use – select the colour of the sky and fill the wall behind her bed so it glowed in the hour between dusk and darkness. For a night that she'd entered with optimism, buoyed by the hope of hanging out with Sophie, perhaps seeing Sunny get a little closer to Lucas, Win now felt as if all Freya's parcel had done was drive everyone further into themselves and away from each other. Her attempt at unifying everyone for a grand letter opening seemed pointless – the second they had the opportunity the group had fragmented faster than if Thanos had dusted them with the Snap.

Sunny hung back the furthest, rolling a fir cone under the toe of her right trainer, all her fizz turned flat.

"Ni hai hao ma?" Win nudged her forward. Given neither knew where they were going it was best not to lose sight of the others entirely.

"Bu tai hao." Sunny darted a look at Lucas's back, then switched to English. "He held Ryan while Kellan … I mean, he didn't hit him exactly…"

This was all sounding very *Hollyoaks* – the sort of trouble Win was supposed to be keeping Sunny out of.

"… he had Freya's letter and Kellan sort of shoved the paper in Ryan's face, tried to make him eat it."

Sunny's shoulders drooped with the same melancholy as

the boy ten paces in front of them. But when she looked at Win it was with a hopeful, "We've all done something we regret. Right?"

Win considered how to answer, wanting to find a way to offer Sunny hope without letting Lucas off the hook.

They passed a row of huge arched headstones whose words were nothing more than shadows, then a couple of granite cubes, gold letters slicing out the names of the dead. Up ahead, Lucas paused by the corner of the building before he followed the other two round.

Maybe it was that they were near a church, but the word "penitent" sprung to mind.

"I think you'd have to talk to him. If Kellan's that kind of person, and Lucas is hanging around with him..."

"But Freya went out with Kellan!"

"We're talking about Lucas," Win said gently, tugging her shirt closer and tucking her thumbs through the buttonholes. "I don't know if I could fancy someone who got on the wrong side of a fight."

"Not even as a Marvel villain?"

"*Only* as a Marvel villain." Since there was no one to see, Win reached round her sister and gave a soft, affectionate squeeze. "IRL we deserve heroes."

As they rounded the corner, the town below opened up into a jumble of buildings accessorised in sequins of light. Win let her arm slip from around her sister as they joined the others: Sophie on one bench, Lucas on another, with Ryan leaning up against the wall opposite, back to the beauty of the view. His hair was roughed up, lip swollen on one side and the blood he'd been dabbing at earlier had crusted round his nose. Win would have offered him a tissue, if he'd not despise her for it.

Without having to discuss it, Sunny went to sit with Sophie, leaving Win to sit with Lucas: all five of them in a small, broken circle.

SOPHIE

It was Lucas who spoke first.

"Ryan, mate, I really am sorry." He was leaning forward, forearms resting across his thighs so that he was looking up through his fringe at Ryan, somehow still soft, even as he was apologising for a fight. "About earlier."

"Doesn't matter."

"I was trying to break it up."

"Yeah." It was more scoff than acknowledgement. "Whatever."

Sophie had run out of patience for this. There was no apology that Ryan would accept; no rejection that would stop Lucas from offering.

"All that over Freya's letter?" she asked. She couldn't be the only one wondering what had been in it, but Ryan shrugged, kicking at the grass with his heel.

"Are you lot really that vacant?" Sunny's voice was loud enough to bounce off the building behind. Undeterred, she held out a hand and reeled off an explanation, point by point, on her fingers. "Freya addresses a parcel to Ryan and not the person she'd actually been dating; Ryan acts shiftier than a cartoon cat with a mouthful of mice; inside is a letter that makes Kellan rage so hard he literally tries to shove it down Ryan's throat."

Sunny's expression as she looked from the bench next to her, then back to Sophie was the definition of incredulous.

"Those two were totally doing it."

One moment for it to make sense, then laughter bubbled

up from a murky pit of horror and hilarity to burst out of Sophie's mouth in a bark. Because no. Freya might be a *flirt*, but no way, not in a thousand trillion years, would she ever be that combination of desperate and stupid enough to go there. Not with Ryan.

But none of the others found this even half as funny as she did – and Ryan might have been looking at the hole he'd made in the grass, but even with his head lowered, eyes down, there was no mistaking the glimmer of a smile.

"No need to look so surprised," he muttered.

No. Absolutely not.

What started as laughter shifted into something else.

"You're lying."

"Am I?"

He *had* to be.

"She'd never…" This time she might know the words, but there was no getting them out. "Not with you."

Ryan finally looked up, smile snatched away in a storm of anger. "Listen to yourself. You're such a fucking snob."

"She hated you—"

"No – *you* hate me, Carbs," Ryan spat back. "Maybe think about that while you're so busy asking yourself why she never told you."

Her hands rose reflexively to her face to stop it melting off in horror because … he was telling the truth, wasn't he? The two of them. Together. And Freya never said. Never *once* let on…

"I think I'm going to be sick."

"Fucksake," from Ryan, as Sunny shifted a little away

from her on the bench with a "Please be exaggerating…"

But this wasn't just about Ryan. It was a swell of misery that threatened to purge all the secrets from her system. She swallowed it back, she could do this. Front it out for that little bit longer. If there was one part of her that had grown stronger recently, it was her will.

"Just give us the letters," she said. She knew she was crying now, but consigned that fact to the same part of her brain that was dealing with the pains in her hands and the aches that stiffened the muscles in her leg and shoulder: just because it was happening didn't mean she had to admit to it.

Ryan pushed himself off the wall and yanked a sheaf of crumpled envelopes from his back pocket.

"Lucas… Win…" Ryan handed the others theirs. Because of course he did. Sophie refused to stand and Ryan refused to step closer until Sunny lunged forward and snatched the letter from him and handed it to Sophie without sitting back down.

"You guys. I swear…"

But Sophie wasn't listening. Didn't care. Today was twice too long as it was and she was done. *This* was done. Here was the treasure at the end of the trail. The promise of a piece of Freya that Sophie got to keep to herself.

Without waiting, Sophie tucked a nail under the flap of her envelope and tore along the top.

WIN

"Thought the plan was to open them on the count of three?" Ryan was saying as Win looked down at her name on the envelope. Freya had written the one name this time: *Win*.

Win wondered about that – about all of this. How Freya had chosen to write everyone's name in full on each layer because she'd wanted them to be able to find each other without needing Freya's help…

So much work for everyone except Freya.

"Is this a wind up?" Sophie rose from the bench and took a step towards Ryan, glaring at the paper she was holding, then at him, face mottled from the tears the rest of them were pretending not to notice. "Where's my letter?"

"In your hand," Ryan snapped back.

"This" – the paper made a snap as she whipped it in the air, making herself wince – "can't be all she sent me. There must have been something else in there."

Ryan edged back a touch, bringing him closer to Sunny, like he might welcome her protection once more.

"Er … there wasn't," he said.

"Like I believe you." Sophie held her hand out, palm up as if expecting him to spit out whatever he was withholding the way a toddler might relinquish a half-chewed Lego brick. "Hand it over!"

"I gave you it already." But there was amusement in the way he said it. "Just because you don't like what she—"

An angry hiss slipped through Sophie's teeth before she

went for him, shouting that it wasn't funny, that she knew he had it…

And Ryan was laughing, trying to push her away – and Sophie looked so angry, so pained, that Win couldn't stand by any longer.

"Stop!" She stood, pushed Ryan beyond Sophie's reach and got between them. "The pair of you … just … stop yelling at him and *you*" – Win turned to channel as much disapproval as she could at Ryan – "could you maybe take one minute off being a complete and utter tool and perhaps not wind her up?"

"She started it."

Whatever expression accompanied the warning finger Win aimed at his chest, it was enough to shut him up. But when she turned back to Sophie, she was holding herself like a puppet who'd lost her strings yet still felt compelled to perform.

"You want to know what's in my letter?" Her voice wobbled with every word and Win wanted to tell her *no*. She didn't want to hear whatever it was that Freya had said to do this to her best friend. She hadn't wanted to be a part of any of this – her connection to Freya had become weaponised against someone to whom she meant so much more.

"It says, *Hey Soph*." Her segue into Freya's voice was uncanny. "*Thanks for trusting me. Miss you tons. Speak soon. Love F.*"

The others waited as a she wavered on a breath. Only nothing further followed.

"Huh?" From Sunny. Blunt and to the point. "Trusting you with what?"

"How about *absolutely nothing*?" Sophie choked back at her.

"Hey, don't yell at Sunny for asking—" Lucas stood up and reached out to touch a hand to Sunny's arm.

"Why not?"

"I'm sure Freya didn't want—"

"You're sure, are you? How? Because *I'm* not sure what she wanted," Sophie shouted back at him with more rage than she had for Ryan; her whole body was trembling, voice shaking with it. "Why the *fuck* would I presume to know *anything* about my so-called best friend's life?"

Sunny and Lucas backed away, drawing closer to Win and Ryan, like that could protect them from whatever bomb was about to detonate. Swear words didn't sound right in Sophie's perfect Queen's English. Her cut-glass accent smashed into shards and flung in their faces.

A side of her that Win hadn't known was there.

"Until today I hardly knew any of you existed! You know what I thought when I opened that thing this morning? Who the hell is Winnie Su? I had to ask at the school office! And *you*" – she scowled at Lucas like he was the one who'd lied – "all this time you've been two different people. Some guy from work that she stopped talking about once the novelty wore off and Kellan Spencer's pal that she never even talked to."

Her gaze slid to Ryan and the disgust on her face said it all.

"Whatever," Ryan muttered. "So she didn't tell you about a couple of mates? Big fucking deal. At least you still get to talk to her."

"*Do I?*"

"All the…" Ryan thumbed the screen of an invisible phone. "You know where she is, how she's doing. She didn't ghost you like she did everyone else."

"Didn't she?" Sophie trembled with the force of whatever she was holding back, her voice hoarse.

There was a moment in which the answer to that question changed from what Win believed – to what she *knew*. The way Sophie had dialled Freya in the car knowing she'd not answer, the look on her face whenever she talked about her leaving … how had Win not even *guessed*?

"But…" Ryan started. Win wished she could reach over and slam his mute button. "You said. Every time someone asked – I heard the answers. About how she's doing with her dad, why she's not posting anything online…" His frustration snowballed into rage, so that he was practically shouting. "You *said*!"

"I LIED!"

The truth tore out of Sophie with a force so strong it blasted through Win's body so that Sophie's pain felt as real and terrible as if it were her own.

"She just *left* and I didn't know where she'd gone and I didn't know why and I thought" – a sob broke free – "I thought I must be wrong. I thought she'd call. I thought … she was my best friend." Tears broke over the shores of her cheeks, a tide running down her face. "And now I find I was worth less to her than a bunch of *strangers*."

The paper in her hand screwed into a ball as she clenched a fist around it.

"I'm not even worth a letter."

She threw the balled-up paper towards them, but for all her rage it got no further than if a light breeze had puffed it from her fist. Then Sophie was gone. Not back to the car, but hauling herself over the stile set into the wall. As Win called her back, she twisted round to look at them.

"Fuck this." The words came out low, trembling with the strength of her feelings. "I'm done with all of you."

RYAN

Ryan had spent all his life convinced no one wanted anything to do with him. He didn't have to look far for the proof: his dad leaving; Mam blaming him for trouble he didn't even start; all his mates so desperate for an invite to Kellan's place they forgot who'd introduced them.

Just for a bit, Freya had him fooled.

Then she left too.

Not a word for him, for every Wednesday they spent together from that first time she showed up, soaked to the skin, or the spare moments caught when no one else was looking. But she'd had them for Sophie, hadn't she? That was the only person whose calls got answered, messages returned. He'd sat quietly in the classroom and listened, greedy for any echo of a word from Freya, even if none of those words were for him.

A month after she left, Ryan gave in. Swallowed his pride and asked Sophie how Freya was doing. Expected it to be hard, because it wasn't like he and Sophie were pals, but the way she looked at him like he was dirt…

And I'm supposed to believe you care when you made her life hell right up to the moment she left?

Sophie made it sound like she *knew* – like Ryan had done something so terrible on December 31st that Freya couldn't forgive him. But he'd thought – he'd believed – that night had made things right between them. That weeks of keeping his distance, punishing him as much as her for what they'd done, could be put behind them.

But the next day Freya had left. And she'd told Sophie why.

...*you made her life hell*...

All this time, Sophie'd been spinning her bullshit and Ryan had swallowed the lot. He had to work very hard not to laugh as the girl he'd envied for so long, for so little reason, staggered down towards the river through the long grass, as if finally finding out the truth had knocked it out of her.

Good. Because of Sophie, he'd spent months thinking the girl he'd risked everything for hated him so much she'd shat all over her own life to get away.

"Shouldn't we go after her?" Lucas said, but Win shook her head.

"When someone runs off it's because they want space."

"There's a lot of that going around," Sunny muttered, shrugging when her sister gave her a stern look. "What? Like running off isn't exactly what Freya did?"

"We're not talking about Freya—"

"Why not? She's the person behind all this."

She was. And each one of them had a letter from her that no one other than Sophie had read. Ryan glanced at the time on his phone. "Anyone want to start a book on how long it'll take Carbs to climb down from that shit fit?"

"Don't you *dare* joke about this." Win's words lashed across the quiet of the churchyard.

"Newflash. When I make a joke, you'll fucking laugh."

"I fucking *won't.*"

Ryan was almost impressed. *Almost.* "Why are you having a go at me?"

"Because this is all your fault—"

"It's really *not*," Ryan snapped back. "I know Sophie's doing a very good job of acting like the victim, but if we're playing who's got the tiniest violin, then how about the guy whose evening started by trying to wash off the penis she inked on my forehead and ended with his cousin trying to knock his teeth in?"

There wasn't any sympathy in the way Win was looking at him; she just crossed her arms like she thought he'd deserved it.

"I'm not the one who wrote her best mate a one-line letter," Ryan said, bringing his voice back to something less than full volume. "And it sure as hell wasn't *my* idea for all of us to come here and open them in case there was some puzzle to figure out."

Win drew back, the shutters coming down on her expression after that little nugget hit home.

"Since Freya left, Sophie's been on my case like this was all *my* fault." And he'd believed it – how could he not, when he was the last person she'd talked to?

He *really* needed to know what was in his letter.

"So, if I want to take the piss out of Sophie, then you'd better believe I'm owed it."

His next breath dislodged something bloody in the back of his throat and forced him to hock it out onto the grass. Wiping his mouth with the back of his hand, Ryan gave the others the full force of his glare – Win, her mouth pinched in a rigid line and Lucas, who stood back, brows raised like he might actually have been listening. He didn't look at

Sunny. Didn't want her to think he cared what she thought.

"I'm going home," he muttered. "You lot do what you want."

He was long out of the graveyard and halfway down the road before Ryan decided that no one was coming after him.

Like he wanted them to.

SOPHIE

Sitting on a fishing jetty, her back to the church and the fields leading up to it, Sophie stared across the river to the jumble of mews houses opposite. Round to the left – past the wharf and the car park – hulked the riverside apartments, whose balcony windows blazed a little bigger, a little brighter. To the right, the path led past the beer garden of The Sheep, the murmur of conversations and clink of glasses mingling with the *whish* of cars crossing the bridge.

She hurt. Nothing new, but a shattered heart made everything else that much harder. Sitting was all she felt up to, waves of revelation washing over her, each bigger than the last. First Win – just a name on a parcel – then Lucas and his alter-ego, then *Ryan*. She wished she could unknow all of them, go back to believing that Freya was the person she knew best in the world.

As it turned out she'd not known Freya at all.

For months, Sophie had been turning over every memory, an archaeologist studying her own history, looking for clues as to why Freya had left. She'd blamed Freya's mum for being so cold and closed off, Kellan for failing to live up to his promise as a boyfriend, Ryan for making Freya's life so miserable at school…

But quietly, Sophie held a belief so secret that she barely acknowledged it herself: her best friend had left because Sophie had failed her.

Tonight, Freya was the one who'd failed.

A creak of a board.

Turning, Sophie saw that Win had come to fetch her, dark as a shadow, thumbs tucked through the cuffs of her shirt.

Glancing away, Sophie pressed the heels of her hands to her eyes, wiping away tears she didn't want anyone else to see. All of them – Win and Sunny and Lucas and Ryan – had already seen too much.

"I don't want to talk about it," Sophie said. She made no move to stand, and Win made no move to sit.

"OK." Then, "I came to offer you a lift home."

"You don't have to."

"I know. But that's what I'm doing: would you like a lift home?"

"Depends if I have to share with Ryan." Not exactly a joke, but Sophie expected something other than a sigh.

"I'm not taking sides in a grudge match I don't know anything about – and don't want to." Win's hands rose to ward off whatever Sophie had taken breath to say. "Winning the league of who hurts the most isn't that great a prize, Sophie."

"Like Ryan feels anything."

"Just because someone doesn't advertise their feelings, doesn't mean those feelings don't exist." Her words whipped out louder, a calm sea stirred by a storm. "People are complicated – and you don't get to shit on them just because you're sad."

"Sorry if I'm not dealing with this perfectly, OK?" Sophie didn't know where she found the energy to sass, but reducing the way she felt to a three-letter word with all the depth of a single-tear emoji had stung. "Today was supposed to be about having fun with the friends I actually have left. Instead, the best mate who ghosted me rose from the ashes to give me a delivery job, and at the end my thanks comes in the form of a note written with as much care as an ASOS returns label."

And a bracelet she'd thought about flinging into the river – only her fingers had fumbled the catch and she'd given up.

"Doesn't mean you can take it out on the customers. Or the person who drove the delivery route." It felt like a telling off and Sophie drew back. Talking to Win was the one nice thing about tonight – the whole day – and Sophie liked her enough to care about being liked back.

"My apologies to the driver. Promise I'll give you a good rating on Yelp," Sophie said, voice a little husky from the strain of holding back a fresh swell of tears.

Win's lips twitched in what could have been a smile. When she spoke, her voice had settled into the calm Sophie was used to.

"Do you want a lift, or not? Ryan's already gone."

LUCAS

"Should we have gone after Ryan?" Sunny said as they walked back through the churchyard, two shadows beneath the brilliance of the floodlights.

"Bit late now." Ryan hadn't exactly been dawdling.

"We could run?"

"I don't think Ryan wants me chasing him. In the dark. In a graveyard."

But Sunny resisted his attempt to lighten the mood.

"Because he's worried you might break his arm?"

"Ouch."

"Yes, that's what people say when you hurt them."

Lucas knew he'd hurt her too, but not in a way he knew how to fix.

"Sunny—"

"I'm cross with you."

She didn't need to say it. All the happiness that had glowed out of every feature of her face, her voice, the way she moved, had been replaced by an equally intense anger.

When they got as far as the car, they realised they had no way of getting into it without the keys and Lucas hoisted himself up to sit on the wall, offering a hand to Sunny. She ignored him, scrambling up with no elegance whatsoever, holding the hem of her skirt below her bum.

Once she was there, she kept her eyes on the floor as she bounced the heels of her trainers against the stone wall.

"I thought you were one of the good ones," she said quietly.

"I'm sorry."

194

"What for, exactly? Hurting Ryan? Breaking someone's arm—"

"That was an accident."

The heels slowed and she looked up at him like she wanted to believe him too much to trust her own judgement.

"I never wanted to tell anyone," he said with a sigh. "It just came out one time…"

He and Fry had been round at Kellan's when Ryan turned up with half a bottle of vodka, and Kellan had been in a mood mellow enough to let him stay. Over a game of FIFA, Ryan and Kellan relived the story of Ryan's scar, how they'd been racing each other to the top of a tree in the park when the branch Ryan put his weight on cracked and he'd fallen out, nearly tearing his ear from his head and breaking his ankle. When Lucas spoke, he was squirly on alcohol he wasn't used to drinking and his, "Only bones I've broken belonged to someone else…" came out like a brag.

"I'm not proud of it," he said, trying to overwrite his memory.

"You don't have to tell me," Sunny said. "It's not like we're friends. Not properly."

Her words made him ache for that very thing: to be friends – and more. But if he wanted Sunny to stick around, he wanted her to do it because he'd been truthful. Anything else wasn't fair on either of them.

"It was my stepdad," Lucas said, not looking at her. "We'd been fighting. I caught him on the nose by accident and he fell – flung his arm out and cracked it on the edge of the work surface."

"You…" When she faded out, he looked up to see her frowning like the next sentence was a puzzle she didn't know how to put together. "What do you mean you were fighting?"

So he told her.

How it had always been him and Mum until Justin came along. How it had been good to begin with – although he didn't go into detail. Sunny, who glowed with health and wealth, wouldn't understand how growing up on scraping by gave you a deep appreciation of the moment heat and light and food stopped being things you had to choose between and became things you just *had*.

"The arguing started as I got older, until we only ever seemed to be yelling at each other, him and me. A lot of 'not in my house' or 'while you're under my roof' – I couldn't do anything right. He hated me asking for money for stuff, but flipped out when he found I'd been stuffing dog-walking flyers through every letterbox on our block. Thought it was embarrassing." That had been a pretty big one – though not as big as the next. "Week later he caught me looking through his toolbox and accused me of stealing them to sell, even though all I wanted was a screwdriver to fix my door handle. He wouldn't listen, tried to drag me out of the kitchen and I lost it. Fought back and, well…"

Lucas clicked his teeth, like that was the sound Justin's arm had made when it broke and not a sickening thud accompanied by an undignified yelp.

"Mum made me stay home while she ran him to the hospital."

"Your mum was there? When he – when you were fighting?"

Lucas shrugged. "Don't think she knew it had turned physical, just ran in when she heard a crash and saw all the blood from where I'd cracked him on the nose."

"You didn't mean it."

Lucas tipped his head to the side, not quite agreeing with her. There were better ways of not hurting someone than punching them in the face.

"We had a talk after that. Considered my options – Mum had already talked to her sister…" Family he'd hardly known because his mum had kept them hundreds of miles and a Christmas card's distance away. "Everyone agreed this was for the best."

"Will you go back?" Sunny asked. She'd moved her hand to rest on the wall next to his, her little finger grazing the side of his hand.

"Mum's pregnant. Reckon they'll need my old room for the baby." He shrugged. "And I don't want to. I'm happy here. Happier, I think."

But in the pause that followed, Lucas could tell both of them were thinking of what had happened at the party.

"You do have a knack for getting in trouble you don't mean to start," Sunny said, her voice wavering on the edge of forgiving. "But does trouble start a lot? Around Kellan I mean?"

Lucas recalled the last time he'd been here and the horror of striking his golf ball too sweetly, watching it clear the water and plummet to where a few brave souls sat out under the stars in the beer garden of The Teeswater Sheep. How Kellan had been disappointed when all it did was strike a heat lamp.

After the grudge match in February, when Kellan was the one who'd shouted the loudest insults until a fight became inevitable.

And the time Lucas had to separate a play-fight-turned-real between Kellan and Fry.

Lucas might have believed he was breaking up a fight back at the party, but he'd known Kellan long enough to be suspicious of how it started.

"He *had* just found out about Ryan and Freya," he began.

"So? Cool motive, still violent. And it's not like you knew that when you leapt in to help him – you just took Kellan's side because that's what friends do. But if I had a friend who threw punches rather than talking things through, maybe I'd stop taking their side." She sighed, frustrated. "Maybe I'd stop being their friend."

"I guess I could talk to him."

"You guess?"

"He's a hard person to disagree with." Lucas stopped what he'd been about to say, the conversation he'd had with Freya coming back to him. "Or maybe Freya's right and I just find it hard to disagree with people."

An "*UGH*" belched out of her. "Freya."

Which was confusing.

"I thought the two of you were friends?"

Sunny turned to stare at him, mouth an incredulous squiggle of a smile. "Why would you think that?"

Lucas waved back in the direction they'd come. "All this, the parcel, coming to Kellan's party."

"You mean the parcel that was addressed to my sister and has contained exactly *zero* references to me whatsoever?" A sentence that came out on a continuous breath. "You think *that's* the reason I invited myself to Kellan's house party?"

Lucas blinked in confusion and brushed the hair out of his eyes.

"Well … yeah."

"Well, no. It was because I wanted to see you." Her mouth was parted, just a little, and her eyes – dark and bright as apple pips – shifted between his mouth and his eyes. Then she sighed. "But seeing you hurt other people, I'm not so keen on that."

Lucas sighed, running his fingers through his fringe once more. "Kellan's a mate, though."

"Get new ones."

"Kellan was one of the new ones."

"Newer ones then. Mates are like iPhones. There's always new ones available, just costs a lot to get one."

It was impossible not to grin. "You're comparing friends to phones?"

"Only yours." The humour in her voice matched his. "Mine are diamonds. Priceless."

"Just like you?" He bumped her gently and grinned.

Only she made a frustrated kind of wail. "No! Stop it."

"Stop what?"

"Flirting with me."

"I wasn't." He was.

"I can't kiss people who get into fights. I have *principles*."

"Are you saying you want to kiss me?"

"*Obviously*." She sounded very angry about it and Lucas wasn't sure he'd ever seen someone master the combination of smile/glare quite like the girl next to him. "You're gorgeous."

"I am?"

"We've been through this. Stop fishing."

Her playful shove was hard enough to push him off the wall, the momentum taking Sunny with him, so that they stumbled onto the ground, grazing elbows against the stone and giggling as they struggled to keep upright. When she recovered her balance, Sunny left her hand where it was, splayed out across his chest.

He wanted to tell her that she was gorgeous too. That he'd been trying to store up every snatched image of her, from the moment Sophie had told him her name to the one they were in right now, her head tilted back to look at him, mouth in a braces-wide smile, hair wisping across her face, eyes brighter than the floodlights.

Between one blink and the next, she launched herself at him, lips bruising his in a kiss so forceful that she bounced off him.

"Dammit." She pressed her lips together and gave him a deliciously veiled look through her lashes. "That was not supposed to happen."

"Why not?" Lucas leaned his weight into the palm she'd not yet moved from his chest. "I liked it."

"Because I'm supposed to have some self-control. And those principles I mentioned."

Principles that Lucas didn't want her to compromise, because Sunny was someone who deserved to be taken as she was or not at all.

"How about you keep your principles..." He lifted a hand to her sleeve, watching as he twisted the material of her hoodie around his fingers, "And I keep out of fights..." His gaze flowed up to her face, trying to take everything in and failing because there was far too much of her – and not enough. "And we can keep kissing."

WIN

The two of them walked back up from the river in slow, measured steps and complete silence, each festering in their own thoughts. Win regretted being so hard on someone she liked so much – wished she could find a way to apologise that wouldn't sound too crawling and like she hadn't meant everything she said. Because she had. Ryan was by no means her favourite person, but what he'd said about the way Sophie treated him...

She might have told Sunny that she'd not be able to fancy someone on the wrong side of a fight, but Win had never felt more like she wanted to hug someone than she did right now. For all Sophie's anger, for the things she'd said about Ryan, Win wished she could take away some of the hurt Freya had inflicted on her best friend tonight.

She couldn't possibly have meant to. That last note had been written with the same breezy confidence as the one Sophie had shown Win in the common room, by someone so convinced in the unshakeable faith of her friend that she could ask the world and Sophie would deliver.

Freya was too far away, too far gone, to know that Sophie hadn't the strength to take it.

"Don't look now," Sophie said, nodding as they rounded the corner of the church, "but your sister and Lucas appear to have made up."

"Oh God..." Win groaned, then gave an apologetic look at the church next to her. "I leave her alone for *one* second."

"I thought you liked Lucas?"

"I liked him just fine before he helped beat someone up."

She felt like she'd been air-dropped as an extra into a final battle, each major character cresting their own arc while all she wanted to do was survive long enough to go home and have a cup of tea. If this was how Freya had lived, no wonder she'd done a runner. Other people's drama was *exhausting*.

"That's enough!" Win clapped loudly as they approached, making the *tsh tsh tsh* noise that Dad used for scaring squirrels from the bird feeder. "We're going home."

Ignoring the outraged Mandarin that Sunny was yapping in her direction, Win waved the rest of them into the car. Before she opened her own door, Win laid her cheek against the roof, just briefly, and closed her eyes.

How had Freya pictured the night ending? Did she really think that nearly five months of silence could be forgiven in a single day? That they'd all know the steps to this dance she'd led them on so that instead of everything falling apart, they'd somehow come together?

She felt awful for Sophie.

Awful for Ryan.

She'd feel bad for Lucas, if she'd not just interrupted him fondling her sister.

She had no idea how she felt about herself other than weary. Whatever was in the letter she'd tucked into her pocket, it had better be good.

LUCAS

There were no lights on downstairs when Win dropped Lucas outside his house. When Vas worked nights, Auntie Helena usually went to bed the same time as Xen, and Kat would still be out. Problem was, Lucas had left his keys in the side pocket of his rucksack – the one he could picture slumped up against the side of Kellan's sofa in the nook.

When he got his phone out to text Alex to come let him in, there were some messages on there from Fry that started off trying to find out where he was and ended with a photo of him kissing a near-empty bottle of JD. And just one from Kellan: *Where u go?*

Sighing, Lucas fudged an answer.

Felt like crap and left early. He added the appropriate emoji and sent it. Then another, saying that he'd left his bag at Kellan's and would come round to pick it up tomorrow. He didn't know how he was going to square things with Kellan, but maybe he'd have figured something out by then.

Alex answered the door in his shorts, hair fluffy from the shower he'd had before bed.

"The least you could do is come home late enough that I can finish having a wank," he said, pulling the door open and letting Lucas into the darkened hall.

"I did not need to know what I was interrupting," Lucas said.

"Gotta take what privacy I can get." Alex grinned, reaching out to ruffle Lucas's hair with a hand that (thankfully) smelled only of soap.

The two of them sloped through the lounge to the kitchen, Alex ordering a cocoa from Lucas as payment for letting him in, then interrogating him as Lucas filled the kettle and fetched the mugs.

Where was the party? What did they get up to? Who was there?

Lucas tried to hide the smile that tugged at his lips, but Alex had lived with his sisters too long to let it slide.

"Oh yeah?" He flicked the scrunched-up wrapper of his biscuit bar across the table right into Lucas's forehead as he set the drinks down. "Who is she?"

"No one you know." Lucas pushed his cousin's drink across and took a biscuit for himself from the tub.

"Don't be so tight. She must have a name."

"Sunny."

"And does she have a corporeal form that you could describe, or is she a ghost?"

"She's this tall and this kind of shape…" Lucas traced a vague "girl" shape in the air, conjuring about as much detail as the white tape marking the location of a dead body in a crime scene.

"Looks like…?"

"I dunno. Pretty." Lucas took a sip of his drink to try and slow up the questioning, but all that happened was that he scalded his tongue and nearly dribbled the whole lot down his front – to join the smear of blood that had darkened to a brown that could pass for chocolate in this light.

"Wow. Smooth." Alex sat back and shook his head. "You get with her, then?"

The grin that broke out was so wide it hurt Lucas's cheeks and it was all the answer Alex needed. Taking a second biscuit, Alex retired upstairs, leaving Lucas alone in the kitchen.

Reaching into his pocket, he took out Freya's letter.

She'd written his name with the same flourishing capital letters as on the parcel, the envelope posh enough to give the impression of containing something important. For a moment, he wondered whether he actually wanted to know, or whether Freya's words would hurt him the way they had both Ryan and Sophie.

But then … Freya hadn't the power over him that she had over them. She'd pushed him away months before she left. By the end they were contented co-workers, nothing more.

Sighing, Lucas tore open his letter.

Dear Lucas,

How's it going? Bet the tips have gone down now that the best waitress no longer works at Rabscuttle…

I miss it. Dad won't let me have a job. Thinks I need to spend every spare second on school work. (It's possible he has a point because OH MY GOD, GCSES!!!)

I have royally screwed up. In quite a lot of ways, but this letter is about you. The person I think about every time I have a packet of crisps. How we got to know each other as strangers and how I was so excited because you were the fresh start friend that I was looking for: you

206

didn't know anything about me, I didn't know anything about you and I got to be me. Do you know how rare that is? Finding someone to be yourself with when everyone already thinks they know everything about you?

Finding out you were friends with Kellan kind of took the shine off because how can you be my sparkly new friend when you're HANGING OUT WITH MY BOYFRIEND? I was gutted and I over-reacted and I'm so sorry. I said Kellan would have been weird about it, but really I meant me.

I wasn't in a great place at the time. Too many things weren't going the way I hoped and the way I dealt was to cut myself off from whatever was upsetting me.

Guess I kept going, huh?

Anyway. I'm sorry. Really and truly. I look back now and I think "Dick move, Freya".

Maybe if we'd been a bit closer I could have talked to you about Kellan. I know how much he likes having you around, but being around Kellan … it's not always so good once you get too close.

I know what it's like to be noticed by him. How you feel giddy at having something that everyone else wants, but it's the other way round. Kellan has you. He makes people into who he wants them to be. The name he gives you, the way he keeps you close when trouble's round the corner. He makes you feel special because he wants you to stick around. Stay loyal. Stay his.

And you're someone who lets people have their own way. (Believe me, if I'd really wanted to, I could have got you to eat leftover chips … you're a pushover.)

So the other people in this chain – Sophie and Win and Ryan – these are people who won't demand as much from you as Kellan, people who'll have your back if you feel like saying no. (Yes. I know. Ryan is a hard sell on this, but he's the only other person I know who won't put up with Kellan's bullshit. You need someone like that.)

And they all need someone like you. When I said I miss working at Rabscuttle, what I really meant was that I miss you.

Freya x

WIN

By the time Sunny went to her own room, it was well beyond midnight. At one point, Win thought that she might actually fall asleep curled up at the end of her bed like she had when they were little, on the nights Dad read them stories at least half an hour longer than Mama would usually allow. Back then, Win hadn't been in possession of a letter that she was increasingly curious to open.

In all the joy about Lucas (and the word-vomit that inevitably went with it) Sunny seemed to have forgotten why they'd gone up to the church in the first place.

Once she'd left, when the landing light was off and there was no hint of activity from the water pipes in the bathroom, Win went and got the letter from where she'd left it folded safely in the pocket of her trousers. Back under the covers, she angled the lamp next to her bed a little better and finally settled down to read whatever Freya had thought was so important it had to be buried inside the middle of a mystery parcel.

Dear Win,

I never fully appreciated how lucky I was to have you as a neighbour until I moved in with Dad. On one side it's Sky Sports WITH THE VOLUME TURNED UP where they cheer every time a United player so much as looks at the ball. On the other it's a toddler who spends every evening banging a wooden spoon on the shared wall while I try and revise.

If I'd known how noisy it was living here would I have moved???

Well. OK, yes.

I had to go. My life was full of a louder noise than any my new neighbours make. Escaping like this seemed the healthiest way to silence it. My counsellor seems to think I did the right thing, but lately I've been worrying that the right thing for me might be wrong for everyone else. The people that matter, anyway.

I know you probably don't think you are – but you're one of them. I admire you. Always have – my intimidatingly cool neighbour who I never thought would talk to me!

I admire you for how well you know your own mind. For being patient with your parents. For having the strength to divide yourself into different bits and each bit be as much you as the next.

When I tried to do that, all that happened was that I kept getting smaller. Thinner, like squash watered down too far to have any flavour.

But not you.

At least, that's what I think until I remember Pride. One of the best days of my life. I'd never done anything like that before – a day with someone I was still getting to know, meeting your friends (send Felix my love), all in a city so far from home... (Mum still thinks we went on a shopping trip to York.) Kind of weird how there's no record of it anywhere other than my camera reel. There's a photo on there that I love. Of you wearing that rainbow flag – like all the parts of you have come together. You look glorious, like you could conquer the world.

You once said that telling people took effort. That it wasn't easy. I understand some of that, a bit. Telling people what you're feeling is scary, but if I had, maybe I wouldn't have ended up as lonely as I got? Maybe I wouldn't have tried to only give out the bits of me that I thought would fit, forgetting that I need to be whole.

That Win I got to see, she looked pretty whole. I think she could take on the world and make it look easy.

I think not letting her out can make you feel trapped.

So in case you want somewhere to start, I thought maybe here would be good: Sophie and Lucas and Ryan. All the people I gave bits of my heart to when I should have given them the whole.

Freya xxx

Win read it again, jaw clenching harder with every word until her face ached by the end of it. If the parcel had irritated her, then this pile of patronising nonsense had pissed her off so much she felt like setting the whole thing on fire and hurling it out the window.

Instead, Win folded it over, again and again and again, until it was nothing but a fat little wodge of paper and stuffed it into the pocket of the jeans she'd left lying over the end of the bed.

Maybe tomorrow she *would* burn it.

RYAN

Ryan had read his letter on the way home. Re-read it sitting on the bottom of the stairs. And then again, sitting on his bed, soaking up every word Freya had written, beyond caring whether or not it was good for him. Not. Almost certainly not. But that was how it had been when she was here. He'd craved being with her and hated himself for it. Hated being needy, for wanting more of her than he was allowed to have. Hated that he could never tell her anything truly nice, in case she believed it and wondered why she was wasting even a second longer hanging out with him.

When she left, he'd tried to convince himself that she'd done him a favour.

In bed, the sheet wrinkling under him and the duvet knotted round his legs because he couldn't get comfy, Ryan gave in one more time. Rolling over, he flicked the switch on the shitty little lamp that had been beside his bed since he was a kid, a massive domed lampshade painted to look like half a football that he had to pile up on a stack of books and boxes.

Freya's letter sat scrumpled on top of the tissue box and Ryan reached across to get it.

Dear Ryan,

This is the hardest letter to write. Maybe that's why it's taken so long for me to write it? I'm a bit of a coward like that – easier to play the part that people want. The one where I'm supposed to be interesting and cool and perfect.

That's why I liked you. Both of us were pretending – but not to each other.

I could just ask for what I wanted and you gave it:

A place to hang out.

Someone to waste time with.

Someone to keep me safe, to keep me secret.

And then I started liking that secrecy thing a little too much, became swept up in the idea that I could ask for more and you'd give it...

I wish I could rewrite the last year as many times as I've rewritten this letter. Find a better order to put things in. Lose the bits that got too messy. But I can't. You mess things up, you just have to live with them, right? But living with them doesn't mean ignoring them. So this is me, not ignoring the fact that you were exactly the right friend when I really really needed one. And I am not ignoring the fact that I should have told you I was leaving.

For a few weeks, I thought you would be a good enough reason to stay.

Until I ruined things.

Some days, when I think about what happened, I wonder if I ruined things on purpose. If I had to burn all my bridges to force me into leaving because what I needed was to be away from everyone and everything and as long as there was anything I wanted to hold on to, letting go was harder.

So that month we didn't talk? That was actually what I needed. And I hated it.

But I'm glad we made up. In the end.

Of all the changes I'd make to our story, it would be that I shouldn't have been with Kellan when I wanted to be with you. But just to be clear, even though there's a ton of stuff I regret, I absolutely do not regret having sex with you. I really really *regret the timing, though.*

Ryan, I'm sorry. For all of this. But I'm also sorry that I left you to deal with things on your own. You needed a friend as much as I did and now I'm not there, who do you have? (Please don't say Kellan…) So. I thought maybe you could use some introductions. Just in case.

F x

"I absolutely do not regret having sex with you. I really *really* regret the timing, though…" Ryan closed his eyes and whispered a vehement "*Shit*" at his ceiling.

Half an hour after collapsing into bed, hair grips digging into her scalp and what little make-up remained still clogging her pores, Sophie lay awake, caught in the crossfire between a body desperate for rest and a brain incapable of sleep.

With sweet dreams off the table, she'd been composing arguments for the benefit of her bedroom ceiling.

How could you do this to me?

Is it because I kept skipping out on going down to the river?

Or was it something worse?

I thought you trusted me – I kept ALL your secrets.

And I know I got a bit sick of you and Kellan and never knowing if you wanted me to hate him or like him, but COME ON, that didn't mean you had to sneak around with Ryan.

I did everything I thought you wanted. I always messaged back. I said sorry every time I pissed you off. I tried, Freya.

I didn't know I could get it this wrong.

No Freya there to answer.

That's what Sophie had hoped for. Some explanation why Freya had never said she was going, why she simply disappeared, taking with her any chance Sophie had of a tearful goodbye and a promise to stay in touch.

130 days of uncertainty and she'd thought tonight that would end.

Maybe it could.

Sophie dredged up the last remnants of energy and reached for her phone. If Freya couldn't be honest, then Sophie could. She could stop pretending that she was fine, that sending Freya a cheerful message every single day – even the days when she'd had no cheer for anything or anyone – hadn't taken its toll the longer they went unanswered.

She could tell her the truth.

Typing was out of the question, but Sophie could leave a voice note. A literal cry into the void.

"Hey." Her voice was low, but Sophie could hear the steel in that single word. "What the *hell*, Freya? Five months you've been gone and I've been here all this time, waiting for you to remember that you left, to send me *something* to let me know you still think of me that you still care – that you *ever* cared."

A breath. This was too hard.

"Do you how excited I was to get that parcel?" Then almost immediately. "No. You don't. You can't even imagine. You know why? Because I've been sending you all these messages all this time trying to make sure you know I'm thinking about you, that I care – I've not even given you a chance to miss me.

"And you've not given me a chance to do anything else but miss you."

Sophie closed her eyes, letting the tears trickle down her cheeks so she could keep them from her voice.

"You are – you were – my best friend. My person. When that parcel arrived I think my heart actually burst because it was from you and it was for me … and then it wasn't. It was for Win. Then Lucas. Then *Ryan*." The disgust was enough. "And I kept on going, because that's what you asked, and

I trusted you because I always did and you knew it and …
I was wrong."

She squeezed her eyes shut, the next words coming out
on a whisper.

"You've broken that trust now. With everything you
asked of me today. And that letter. That nothing little note.
Friendship is supposed to work both ways. I guess I let you
down when you needed me – and you've been doing the
same every day since. Today you let me down for the last
time."

Sophie stopped. Watched the seconds of silence tick
over.

What had she got to lose? Freya was already gone.

Sophie released her words and collapsed.

SATURDAY

SOPHIE

Sophie's brain didn't get the memo about needing rest. Instead, she startled awake out of a dream that left all the physical traits of anxiety in its wake, piling in on top of the pain that was already there, more pervasive than yesterday's. Lying on her right side to ease the discomfort of her left, waiting for the beats of her heart to reach a calmer rhythm and her nausea to subside, Sophie stared in despair at the digits of her alarm clock.

9:02 was an ungodly hour to wake on a Saturday. But that was it. While Sophie had trained herself how to nap, going back to sleep seconds after waking was beyond her.

Getting to the bathroom was a chore. Yesterday's stress had triggered symptoms that had been dormant earlier in the week and the pain from last night had radiated from her shoulder down her back – tolerable for now, but not if she had to sit at her desk all day revising.

Mum was out on the landing, already dressed for the day.

"I'd have held off my morning yoga if I'd known you were going to be up this early. Could have joined me…"

God. Not the yoga thing again. Sophie wasn't yet operational enough for conversation and she let Mum lead her gently back to her room, going on about breakfast, something about brain food to set her up for a day of studying. Exactly like she had been with Christopher.

As Sophie shuffled back to her bed, Mum remained in the doorway, fists planted on her hips like a land girl about to win the war by digging some potatoes.

"First thing we'll have to do is tidy your room." She surveyed the jumble of clothes and make-up and books carpeting the floor, frowning when she saw the lid of Sophie's laptop, where she'd upended her box of earrings to look for something party-appropriate. "You can't study in a pig sty."

"Mum—"

"Don't worry. I'll do all the moving around, you can help with telling me where things go."

"I don't—"

"I'll call you when breakfast is ready."

As soon as she'd gone, Sophie closed her eyes and slumped sideways onto the bed.

Maybe she'd have been better off battling whatever it was she'd been fighting in her dream than waking to Maximum GCSE Mum.

"What's this?" Sophie stared at whatever it was Mum thought passed for breakfast.

"Smoked mackerel and poached egg on a bed of kale."

Sophie's cheeks puffed out as she retched. Mum gave her a Look.

"Don't you dare. Eat it. How was last night?"

"Fine." Why was Mum trying to make her talk?

"You came home later than we agreed."

"We didn't agree anything." And she'd been home *early*. The clock on Win's radio hadn't even made it beyond eleven.

"Sophie…" Mum's fingers tensed a moment as she held her cutlery over her plate. "You need your rest."

"I didn't know I was going to wake up this early, did I?" Sophie had made little progress – the egg remained untouched, the yolk wobbling ominously under a flimsy bit of white. "Do I really have to eat all this?"

"Right!" Without warning, Mum's cutlery clattered onto her plate a second before Sophie's was snatched from under her nose, Mum spinning away across the kitchen to the organic recycling caddy. "Don't eat your breakfast. Don't tell me why you're in such a bad mood. Why would you tell me anything? I'm just your mother."

"There's. Nothing. To. Tell." Sophie took advantage of Mum's back being turned and unlocked her phone on her lap.

"You were gone long enough for me to watch four episodes of *The Good Wife* and give myself a pedicure." Her voice rose over the sound of the hot tap on full blast before she dialled everything down a little. "And yet you went to a party and did 'nothing'?"

Sophie didn't have a comeback for that, too busy scrolling through the conversations she'd missed the night before, head too full of Freya to make room for anyone else.

Mum was still talking. "Look. I know all this is hard for you…"

Sophie made subtle little "yap-yap-yap" hand puppet motions under the table at Woof, who was sitting on the chair next to her, and paid Sophie about as much attention as she was paying Mum. There was something on here about Georgia and Ewan…

"Sophie Eleanor Charbonneau – I am *talking* to you."

"I'm listening!"

"You are not listening, you are looking at that *bloody* phone."

"With my *eyes*. I can still hear you."

"What did I say then?"

Sophie looked up, caught in a lie. "You said it was hard."

Mum narrowed her eyes. "What's hard?"

Crap. Something about lupus. Or revision. Possibly both.

"My ... life?"

Wrong answer. Mum threw her hands up, spraying the air with suds.

"See what I mean? You're never *here*. I was saying that I understand it must have been hard going to a party without Freya, but you've got to start focussing on the people who are here for you—" Sophie made the mistake of glancing down at her phone. "*Stop checking your phone.*"

"*God*. Make up your mind!" Sophie yelled back, the anger that simmered under her skin reaching boiling point faster than she was expecting. Her temper wasn't any better than her body at recovering overnight. "You literally just told me to focus on my friends."

Mum sighed so aggressively Sophie felt the force of it from across the room. She spoke with her eyes closed, voice low and dangerous.

"You know for a fact that is not what I meant." Mum's eyes snapped open and Sophie realised then that she was for it. "I am sick of trying to talk to someone who's too busy scrolling through Instagram to hear a word I say. I've tried to be patient with you about this, but you *insist* on testing me."

"How am *I* testing *you*?" She didn't know why she was doing this, why she wanted to push her mum this far, but she couldn't stop the words from coming. "You give me the most disgusting breakfast ever even though you *know* I find it hard to eat, badger me about staying out when I came home early and now you're angry that I'm trying to find gossip from the party that *you* asked me about!"

"That's *enough*." Mum crossed the kitchen, slippers slapping on the flagstones loud enough to stir Woof from his slumber. She held her hand out across the table. "You're not leaving the house this weekend. And I'm confiscating your phone."

WIN

Win woke early and angry. Reading Freya's letter before she went to bed had been a mistake, her words permeating Win's dreams and giving them that slightly-too-real vibe that made them feel more vivid, more threatening.

Dozing wasn't possible and when she picked up her phone, she found she didn't feel like messaging anyone.

So she did what she'd done after every exam last year, when her brain was too busy running over the paper she'd just done to think about revising for the next. Win dressed in shorts and a vest, spooned out a bowl of congee from the slow cooker – hiding it in the microwave in case Sunny rose early and ate it all like she had last Sunday – and called out to the garden to let her parents know she'd be back in an hour. Then, slipping her running trainers on by the door, Win stepped out into the morning, ready to chase away the stress of the day before.

SOPHIE

Whenever Sophie hadn't wanted to be in her own house, she'd gone to Freya's.

A bus across town and a short walk up streets lined with cookie-cutter houses and little snooker-table lawns. Freya's was at the end, everything about it the same as ever, from the hanging basket by the front door to the car parked on the drive.

But no Freya. Not that it mattered. Freya wasn't the person Sophie had come to see.

The bell chimed inside the house, followed a moment later by footfalls on the stairs. Sophie hoped it was Win. Sunny would be too much and this was a weird way to meet someone's parents.

When the door opened, Sophie's eyes settled on the feet of the person behind it. White trainer socks, slim calves and strong thighs leading to a pair of running shorts and a ribbed vest. Above the neckline, Win's chest was flushed and there was a sheen of sweat on her skin. She wiped her wrist across her face, leaving her fringe spiked up and uneven, and rested her hand on the doorframe, eyebrows sweeping up a moment before she spoke.

"Hi."

"Hi." Sophie didn't know what words came next. Win wasn't Freya.

"No deliveries today?" Win's eyes dipped down to where Sophie's bag hung at her hip. It looked like a Jammie Dodger and all it contained was her second dose of naproxen, some emergency paracetamol, a travel-sized sun cream and her purse. Also a tampon. Just in case.

"No," Sophie said.

"Good." Win pushed the door wider. "Do you want to come in?" Although before Sophie got any further than the mat, she added, "We're a no-shoes kind of house – although there's hotel slippers if you want?"

"No. It's fine." Sophie put a toe to the back of her slip-ons and tucked them next to Win's Converse. Red checks next to faded grey.

Stepping into the hall was like swigging a mouthful of coffee when Sophie had expected tea. The walls were papered a soft pink, the colour of a shell washed through a thousand million times by the sea, the carpet a dated shade of blush that felt as thick and luxurious as if it had been laid yesterday.

Nothing like the cold blue walls and wood floors of next— *no*.

No Freya. Not now.

"Shouldn't you be revising?" Win had stopped in the middle of the hall, like she didn't quite know where to go next. Sophie had clearly caught her in those few moments between working up a sweat and washing it off.

"I absolutely should be doing that. *Mais je vais faire les tenses francaise demain*."

"I did German."

"And Mandarin."

Win's eyes sparkled and her lips curved up at the corners. "And Mandarin."

Just then someone bustled in from the kitchen, flipping a tea towel over her shoulder. Same height as Win, slender like her sister.

"Who was at the door?" The woman's eyes alighted on Sophie as Win said, "Mama, this is Sophie."

"Hi Mrs Su."

Win's mum smiled like her youngest – wide and unselfconscious.

"Nice to meet one of Winnie's friends," she said to Sophie. "Let me get you something – a drink? Something to eat?"

Sophie's stomach made an angry snarl that meant she couldn't just politely say she was fine. The couple of crackers she'd forced down earlier so she could take her meds weren't enough to last.

"Umm…"

"Let me see what we have," Mrs Su said, already returning to the kitchen.

When Sophie turned back to Win, she looked the closest she'd seen to flustered, avoiding Sophie's gaze and bringing an arm across her body like a barrier, hand resting on a bicep that had more definition than Sophie's.

"How come you're here?" Win said, still not looking up. "Not that it's not nice to see you. I just… It's a long way to come. If you'd sent me a text I'd have made sure I beat Sunny to the shower."

"I couldn't text – Mum confiscated my phone. I'm grounded."

Win's gaze swept from Sophie's fringe to her feet and back to her eyes. "I can see."

Sophie pressed her lips together. Win didn't need to know that Sophie had got dressed, waited until her mum had gone out into the garden to inspect the strawberries, then moved as fast as her body would allow down the stairs and out the front door. She *especially* didn't need to know that Mum had an account with the local taxi company for days when she couldn't take Sophie to school, and that her daughter had shamelessly abused this account to get here.

"I came over to say that I'm sorry for how I behaved last night – all yesterday, really." Her whole world had crumbled apart and Win had been someone who'd helped her hold it together – coming to Kellan's party, sitting with her on the front wall, coming to get her after she'd gone down to the river... "I got so caught up in wanting to know what Freya was playing at that I forgot anyone else existed."

"She was your best friend, Sophie. I get it."

"I know you do. And" – she swallowed, hoping her throat might stop trying to squeeze itself shut – "it means a lot. All of it. Driving me round, coming to the party."

"Any time," Win said, with a wry smile.

"How about today?"

"Drive you back home? Sure, I just need to shower—"

But Sophie was shaking her head, conviction settling any doubt. "I came out because I don't want to stay home. I can't revise today, going over old work – I'm tired of looking at the past. Yesterday was all about Freya. I want to do something fun that's about us. *Now*." All of a sudden Sophie worried that this seemed a bit desperate, coming over to Win's and begging her for a day out she wasn't even sure she had the energy for. "About all of us, I mean."

"Even Ryan?"

Sophie pulled a face. "Maybe Ryan doesn't *have* to come."

"RYAN DOESN'T HAVE TO COME WHERE?" came a bellow from the stairs above and Sunny, towel wrapped round her, leaned over the edge of the bannister, hair dripping down the wall.

RYAN

Ryan woke with a heart full of Freya and a head full of fear.
Jesus. Freya couldn't possibly have phrased it worse than
she had. How was he going to talk Kellan down from *that*?

Still in yesterday's boxers, he stumbled down to the
kitchen where Jules was dressed like a photoshoot. Dragons
fought an embroidered battle across the shoulders of a silky-
looking thing that wasn't long enough to count as a dressing
gown, worn over a long white shirt and skinnies with the
cuffs turned up, knobbly ankles out on display.

"Looking sharp," Ryan said.

"I know you're being sarcastic."

"The only language I speak." Ryan inspected the ends
of the bread for mould before putting them in to toast.
Across the kitchen, Jules was drinking something fruity and
healthy-looking straight from the blender. "Mam out?"

Jules nodded. "She's started that running club,
remember?"

Neither Ryan nor Mam paid enough attention to know
what the other was up to.

"She'll be back soon." Jules looked at the clock on the
cooker that had run two hours and ten minutes ahead since
the last power cut. "So if you want a shower..."

"What are you saying, like?"

"That you stink like a wrestling ring." Ryan could feel
Jules looking as he mashed a lump of peanut butter onto his
toast. "What happened to your face?"

"Nothing. What happened to yours?"

"Have you been in a *fight?*"

Ryan shoved so much of his toast into his face there was no chance of answering. His jaw hurt as he tried to chew, the swollen skin on his face straining with every move. Raising his eyebrows at Jules, he pointed up to the bathroom to show where he was going.

When he checked his injuries, Ryan was disappointed that they weren't a little more dramatic. Sure, he was a little bruised round the jaw and there was a cut across the bridge of his nose, but beyond a bit of swelling, that was pretty much it. On the plus side, Mam probably wouldn't pick up on anything.

Like everyone else in this family, she thought Kellan was beyond perfect. If she found out the two of them had been fighting, her nephew wouldn't be the one she blamed. Not that giving her any context would help. Hard to blame the dynamite for blowing after the fuse has been lit.

The cold light of day – or rather the damp mist of the bathroom – gave Ryan no clearer idea of how he'd get out of this without Kellan landing another couple of hits to a face that was too sore to take them.

It's not like Sunny would be there to save him next time…

The only option Ryan had was to wait for his cousin's temper to cool to something a little less violent. Maybe try to explain over a string of texts or something … anything that didn't involve being in the same place at the same time.

Sound carried in this house and Ryan heard the murmur of voices from the kitchen as he crossed the landing.

Hopeful of cadging a little cash, he pulled on a pair of joggers and grabbed something clean off the pile (a tank top, as it turned out), hurrying down the stairs in bare feet ready to turn on the charm.

The kitchen door was open, framing Mam as she stood by the sink washing out the water bottles. Running club was all her own thing – instead of the usual Personal Trainer polo issued by the gym, she wore a violently bright racer-back vest that showed off tightly muscled shoulders and biceps to beware. When she turned to see him in the doorway, she raised a half-washed bottle in greeting, forearms all tanned skin and sinew.

"The kraken wakes." The closest Mam got to a joke.

"I've been up for—" his sentence stumbled as he stepped further into the room. "Hours."

Slouched against the corner of the counter was a third member of Ryan's family. One that didn't belong.

"Hey, Ry." Kellan's smile glittered with menace.

"Hi."

Ryan's eyes flitted to where Jules was standing in the corner furthest from Kellan, mug held close as they tried to become one with the fridge door. A flicker of understanding passed from one to the other. Jules got it.

Mam wouldn't.

"Pop the kettle on, Ry. Did you want something to eat, Kell?" Mam tipped the last bottle up to rest on the draining rack and turned to open the box of eggs on the side. "I'm making an omelette."

"I'm fine thanks, Auntie S. Just a cup of tea and I'm

grand." Kellan kept his eyes on Ryan as he was forced to venture close enough to fill the kettle up.

As long as they stayed in here, there wasn't much Kellan could do, but the kitchen was cosy at the best of times and with this many it was almost impossible to move without knocking into someone. Once Kellan got his tea, Mam would tell them to get out of her way.

Ryan didn't want to know what came next.

LUCAS

Within minutes of entering the kitchen, Lucas was subject to the same interrogation as he'd had from Alex, this time fired from all possible angles: the table, where Xen was threading beads onto pieces of elastic; the worktop, where Auntie Helena was preparing a tray to take up to Vas after his nightshift; even Kat, lying on the sofa in a hungover smear of make-up and last night's clothes, kept shouting questions through the door.

"I'm going to kill you." Lucas jabbed Alex in the side with the spoon he'd snatched from the drawer.

"You've only yourself to blame," Alex said with zero penitence. "Wet toilet paper holds up better than you."

His cousin had a point. Before he next saw Kellan, Lucas would have to make sure he knew exactly what he wanted to say about last night. A way to explain that the group of people he'd left with included Ryan and the girl who'd stopped Kellan from decking him…

"Oi. Space cake." Alex whipped him with the tea towel he'd been using to dry the pans and nodded to where Auntie Helena was holding out a plate of buttered toast.

"Take that through to Kat and then come back here and tell us all about this Sunny. I want to know everything – this one never breathes a word about his love life."

Alex gave a smug smile, lips pressed together, and mimed zipping his mouth shut.

When Kat saw the toast, she groaned in delight and shuffled into something like a sitting position so she could eat it. One set of false eyelashes had fallen off, but the other remained, giving her a dishevelled *Clockwork Orange* vibe.

"So this Sunny," she said, ignoring Lucas's eye roll. "Just a wild guess, but is she a bit taller than Mum, skinny, Chinese" – Kat looked a little like she wasn't sure that was what she should say, then moved swiftly on – "and with really long black hair?"

Lucas stared. He hadn't remembered telling Alex any of that.

Kat swallowed the nibble of toast she'd taken.

"Pre-school but make it fashion?"

"What... How..."

Kat nodded over his shoulder and Lucas turned to see Sunny marching up the front path, ponytail swinging with every exuberant step.

"I think she's here to see you," Kat said with a grin.

WIN

"I still think she should have warned him we were coming," Win said, leaning a little further forward to look across Sophie to where Sunny was standing in front of the third door along in a block of houses.

"Do you think she was worried he might have made an excuse?"

"What, like the fact it's two days until the most important exams of his life and he can't just go off on a jolly?"

"Ssh," Sophie hissed. "Denial is my happy place. Don't spoil it."

They watched as the bright blue door swung open and Lucas peered out, like a confused bear stirred from hibernation by a particularly tasty snack. On the doorstep, Sunny was flapping her arms about, pointing at him, the sky, the car.

Sophie and Win waved in unison when Lucas looked their way.

"Why does your sister look like she's desperate for a pee?"

"Nervous bladder," Win said, her grin matching Sophie's as she glanced back. This was nice. Much better than yesterday. If Win had been as bold as her sister, she might have suggested that she and Sophie drive off, leave the others to it…

But Sunny was already coming back to the car, grin as wide as the sky as she shouted, "He said yes!" with all the joy of someone who'd just had a marriage proposal accepted.

It didn't take long for Lucas to re-emerge – and for every single member of his family to line up at the window to see him off. As ever, Sunny's entire lack of shame had her waving back at them and, when she got out to let Lucas and Sunny in, so did Sophie.

"Don't encourage them," Lucas groaned as he folded himself into the car. Win watched him and her sister in the rear-view mirror – Lucas stealing glances at Sunny every other second, Sunny's dimple deepening each time. Envy twanged Win's heartstrings. To have someone want to look at her like that – to not feel like she should look away… After Riley, Win had found it easier than she'd thought: waiting. She'd been busy, and admiring girls from afar was about as much as she'd been able to manage.

Now one of them was sitting in her passenger seat – because Freya had engineered her to be there.

Win felt a stab of frustration. But then, this wasn't part of Freya's plan. They'd all heard Sophie's letter. There hadn't been anything in there about sharing herself with anyone, no veiled hints that Freya knew her better than she knew herself – only a trite little line that could have been cut and pasted from a Hallmark card.

Today, though, Sophie was here because she wanted to be.

"So." Sophie twisted round in her seat, dislodging a curl of hair that twisted forwards and directed all Win's attention to her lips. "Where *are* we going?"

Giddy at the freedom of a car, Win's passengers suggested everything from a picnic on the moors to a day trip to Newcastle, until Lucas asked how near the sea was and everyone – even Win, who'd had reservations about how far everyone wanted her to drive – cheered their approval.

And then Sunny killed the mood dead.

"So … are we going to call for Ryan?"

SOPHIE

When she'd snuck out of her house, Sophie hadn't thought further than getting to Win's. When Win and Sunny had agreed to a day out, she'd not thought further than getting to Lucas. Yesterday had taken a lot out of her and she didn't trust how much energy she had left – getting from one point to the next was about all Sophie could judge.

She'd not anticipated how her feelings would revolt at the thought of the next point being Ryan.

"Fine." She scowled her way through her words. "I think I know where he lives."

No one said anything, their silent concerns filling the car. But they didn't know. They'd only seen the worst of her, not the worst of him. Not by a long shot.

"Why do you hate him so much?" The question came from the back, but not from Sunny. When Sophie turned to look, Lucas was looking at her in a way that didn't make answering seem so hard.

"None of you know him at school. He's always been a bit of a dick – he used to wind Freya up all the time, but then she got with Kellan and the wind-ups became worse. Anything she said, anything she did, he was on her for it." She ground her teeth, remembering the worst: the blowjob joke in English; the day he kept playing a soundbite of a woman moaning on his phone any time Freya tried to talk; the way he'd see her talk to any of the lads in their year and make a joke that Kellan better not find out…

"Ask anyone in my year," she finished quietly. "They'd tell you the same."

"And Freya just took it?" Win looked troubled, like that didn't match up with the Freya she'd known.

It didn't match up with the Freya Sophie knew, either.

"Sometimes she gave as good as she got," Sophie said with a shrug. "Sometimes she ignored it. But she never did anything to change it."

You should tell Kellan.

About what?

About Ryan. He's his cousin, can't he stop him?

I'm aware of that. And I can fight my own battles, thanks.

And Sophie had backed down because it was easier than arguing. Guilt dropped like a rock into the well of Freya-related feelings. Always backing down wasn't the best way to support someone who needed propping up.

"One day it just stopped," Sophie said, staring out of the window. "A month before she left, maybe. Ryan came to school and acted like Freya didn't exist."

"You say that like it's a bad thing." Sunny sounded confused. "Surely that's *better*?"

But it hadn't been.

"She went to ask him something. Ryan didn't even look at her. Just turned around and walked off," Sophie said. "That was the first time he'd made her cry."

She turned to look at the three of them, at Sunny's confusion and Lucas's gentle frown, Win resting a hand on the wheel, waiting for Sophie to finish.

"If Ryan and Freya had something going on," she said, "then that makes the way he treated her worse, not better. So maybe hold off on sympathy concerto in A minor, OK?"

LUCAS

Ryan lived in a house a quarter of the size of Kellan's, set in a row of four with gently sloped roofs and Sixties cladding. An estate more like the one Lucas lived in, where nets masked ground-floor windows, stickers and toys suckered onto the ones above, a flat scrap of grass separating the road from the people who lived on it.

"I think it's this one…" Sophie frowned at the white plastic door before pressing the bell and stepping back onto Lucas's foot.

"Ow."

Sophie gave him a faint smile of an apology as footsteps thundered into existence, a shadow darkening the door's slim glass panels before it opened.

Ryan's hair sat in damp, dark tufts and the sting of citrus shower gel in Lucas's nostrils suggested Ryan had used half the bottle. "What the fuck are you doing here?"

He wasn't looking at the girls, but at Lucas – and he looked almost scared.

"Er…" Lucas hadn't expected to be the one to do the talking. "We're kind of going on a road trip—"

"To the sea!" Sunny put in.

"And we thought—"

"Yes." Ryan snapped his head round from where he'd been looking back into the house. "Yes I absolutely do want to come with you."

Lucas glanced at the others, all looking as surprised as he felt. He'd expected *some* resistance. Ryan snatched a pair of trainers from a heap next to the door, stepping out onto the path before he'd even put them on.

"We can wait while you get some socks…" Win began.

"Don't need them," Ryan said as he turned and pulled the door shut gently behind him so that it made almost no noise at all.

"Ryan, is everything—"

But before Sunny could finish her question, Ryan was chivvying them back to the car, still in bare feet, his hand jabbing Lucas in his lower back.

"Hurry it up, Big T."

Lucas frowned as he pulled open the car door, not sure he was so keen on being manhandled by anyone but Sunny. Clambering in first, Sunny followed, then Ryan. As soon as Win shut her door, Ryan started thumping a fist on the back of her seat.

"Drive!"

"Dial down the dramatics, 007," Win said with a calm that would have infuriated the patron saint of patience. "Has everyone got their belt on?"

"Just start the fucking car!" Ryan yelled with such force that every tendon stood out on his neck.

It did not have the desired effect.

"You can get out if you're going to talk like that, pal." Win arched her brows at the rear-view mirror.

Ryan huffed, hissed through his teeth and craned round Sunny to look at his front door.

"OK. I'm sorry. But unless you get a shift on, my cousin's going to walk out that door –"

Lucas would have hunched down to hide behind Sunny if he hadn't been so worried she'd think he was a coward.

"– and if I'm honest, I'd quite like to sit my exams with my face intact, so if you could—"

But Win had already let off the clutch, the car pulling swiftly away from the kerb to zoom off towards the end of the road. Although once she got there, she stopped at the junction and fixed Ryan with a glare in the rear-view mirror.

"I was serious about *everyone* putting their belt on."

RYAN

Ryan knew there must be nice places along the coast. He'd been to one when he and Jules were just kids, Dad the one holding the camera as they made sandcastles with Mam.

Dredging his memories, Ryan came up with beaches of soft golden sand and rock pools surrounded by gleaming slabs of stone. Harbours bobbing with fishing boats beneath a sky of soaring gulls. Crooked little alleyways crammed with shop fronts he didn't have enough money to look behind. A holiday of ice-cream parlours and mini golf and the Dracula Experience.

Nothing like this shit hole.

Killing the engine, Win announced, "We're here."

An apathetic "Hooray…" trailed from Sunny's lips as Ryan issued a more frank, "Looks like the arse end of Boro."

"You didn't have to come…" Sophie turned to say.

"And you could have just dropped me in town like I asked—"

"We're all supposed to be getting to know each other," Sunny said, with a fraction more enthusiasm than a moment ago.

"Give over." Ryan rolled his eyes. "This is just an excuse for you to get on biblical terms with Big T."

Lucas didn't like being called that, Sunny didn't like the implication, and Sophie hated him. If Ryan had the luxury of being able to make a quick exit out of the driver's seat like Win, he'd have taken it.

"Ry-an!" Sunny said it the same way Jules did when he'd

wound them up a bit too far. "Can't you at least pretend you want to be here?"

He wasn't sure he could. But then how was he supposed to explain to any of this lot that he never wanted to be anywhere. His whole miserable life was a series of trying to be somewhere other than wherever he was. Unless that "wherever" was with Freya...

"How about I pretend I want to be here and Sophie pretends that she doesn't wish I wasn't?" Ryan glared into the back of Sophie's skull, watched her shoulders rise and fall in a shrug before she turned to look at him.

"Fine. Let's see who breaks first."

And with that, she got out of the car.

The sun was warm and the wind cool. Not a bad combination for May – although Ryan wished he was wearing something a little more substantial than a muscle vest he hadn't the bulk to fill. Even though he'd dissed the place, the smooth, clean stretch of promenade looked new and nice, and when Sunny ran across it to go look at the sea, Ryan was happy enough to follow with the rest of them. Below the sea wall the sand stretched out towards the sea, the sea towards the sky, and Ryan tipped his head back to squint up into a blue that reminded him of his aunt's downstairs toilet.

No one else said anything as the five of them stared out into the sea, losing themselves in the glitter of the waves and the wheeling of the gulls.

Until Ryan's stomach let out an almighty gurgle.

"Bit peckish."

WIN

To absolutely no one's surprise, they couldn't agree on where to eat. Ryan had walked out of the house with nothing but change and favoured a meal of chocolate and crisps; Lucas had no opinion at all; Sunny was determined to inspect the menu outside every cafe they passed – all of which Sophie vetoed because "you can eat that stuff anywhere".

If someone didn't provide a solution, they'd still be bickering once the tide rolled in and the moon rose above the horizon.

Without putting it forward for discussion, Win turned through the door of a salubrious-looking fish shop: quintessential seaside food for Sophie; a limited menu to reduce Sunny's dithering time; a small portion of chips within Ryan's pocket-sized budget; and Lucas could sit there and look pretty for her sister.

Win didn't care about the cuisine. All she wanted was some peace.

The booth they settled in had seats that made a pleasing plastic squeak whenever someone moved, and Win found herself wedged into a corner with Ryan man-spreading in the middle between her and Lucas, while Sophie and Sunny luxuriated in acres of space opposite. At least she had the assurance that Ryan was clean. His hair had dried to chick-soft fuzz that she would have fluffed up if he'd been Felix.

She wondered if that was the sort of thing Freya would have done... Ryan didn't look like someone used to feeling anyone's affection.

"What's everyone having?" Sophie said. "You have to go up to the counter to order."

Everyone started speaking at once, money being pushed across the table in Sophie's direction – although she forgot to take any of it when she actually got up, intoning their order under her breath in a way that suggested no one should interrupt her.

"Go with her." Win nudged Sunny under the table and nodded at the money.

"I'm so pleased I'm not front of house," Lucas said, eyeing the two girls as Sunny joined Sophie up at the counter. "No worrying about orders and money."

"So what is it you do, like?" Ryan's interest wrong-footed both of them so much that he was met with silence. "What? Is it a fucking secret?"

"I work in the kitchen up at Rabscuttle, help with prep before service starts and after that I provide the very valuable service of putting the dirty plates in the dishwasher and taking the clean ones back for service."

"What's the money like?"

"OK, I guess." Lucas shrugged, biting the skin on the side of his thumb. "It's nice not to have to ask my aunt and uncle for money all the time, the way I had to with Justin."

"Justin?" Win said. Sunny's late-night word-vomit had contained various synonyms for sexy and no actual information.

"Stepdad."

Ryan raised his eyebrows, like Lucas had said something he was interested in, but then Sunny was back, flumping down onto the opposite seat. She released a handful of cash that clattered onto the table and looked suspiciously like the amount she'd left with.

"Sophie's put it all on her card."

"Class." Ryan reached across and pulled back the coins he'd handed over, ignoring the stink eye Win gave him.

"This is wrong; we can't let Sophie pay for us."

"Why not?" Sunny and Ryan startled each other by agreeing, with Sunny adding, "She offered."

"Oh my god, you really are a changeling," Win hissed. "When someone offers to pay you don't just *let* them." But before she could finish that particular lesson, she was interrupted by Lucas pushing a heap of money in her direction, the coins scraping across the surface of the table. "What are you doing?"

"I'm giving you my lunch money to cover mine and Sophie's share of the petrol."

"What? No! This is too much. It cost this much in total."

"Then Lucas has covered me and Sunny, too." Ryan raised his hand for her sister to high-five. Which she did.

Win stared at the money in despair. She didn't want someone else to pay for her lunch or the petrol. They might not want it, but it would mean Win owing them something, feeling an obligation towards people someone else had chosen for her. Sophie and Lucas and Ryan were *Freya's* friends, not Win's – much as she liked Sophie, she'd only exchanged a few sentences to either of the boys. Jury was out on Lucas-fisticuffs-Antoniou and Ryan was a verified blue-tick arsehole.

"What's up?" Sophie returned, tucking her card into her phone case.

"You can't pay for both me and Sunny. It's too much." Win tried to push the money back over to Sophie, like a gambler desperate to lay a stake on the next roll. "Please."

"Your money's no good here." Sophie made a barrier across the table with folded arms. "It's an apology and a thank you. For coming out with me today when you didn't have to."

"But you don't even have a job—"

"I get a lot of pocket money."

"How much?"

"Sunny!"

"What? Some of us need the bargaining power."

"I get a hundred pounds a month."

That silenced the chatter. Until Ryan muttered, "Of course you do."

"And by that you mean…?"

Unmoved, Ryan returned Sophie's glare with a look corroded by envy. "I mean you've always had everything you want."

Win exchanged another one of those brief, coded glances with her sister. They weren't exactly hard up – their parents gave them a decent allowance and Win topped hers up with babysitting and Patreon payments for her webcomic – but they'd both heard Sophie talk about dining in the restaurant that Lucas and Freya had worked at, and Win knew a posh road when she drove down one.

"You think I get this cash just because?" Sophie's voice

took on that same precise edge that came out when she talked about Freya, anger chiselling her face into something sharp and dangerous. "I get this money because five months ago I was diagnosed with lupus."

SOPHIE

Sophie hadn't meant to do this. But then, she'd not meant to tell anyone about Freya's five-month silence. Ryan had an amazing talent for annoying the truth out of her.

"Um. I don't…" Lucas was the one to say it. "What's lupus?"

She couldn't back out now, even if she didn't know how to say it – but when she opened her mouth, the words just came.

"It's a chronic illness. My body is attacking itself. And it hurts. *All* the time."

"What? Like right now?"

Sophie flicked a look across the table at Ryan. "What bit of 'all the time' confused you?"

Ryan scowled.

"Yes, Ryan. I hurt now, but I still want to do stuff. Sometimes I can. Sometimes I can't. But whatever I'm doing, wherever I am, I still have lupus and I'm still in pain. And it's never going away."

There was no way of Ryan knowing what she meant. Not really. She could tell him about the joint pain, muscle pain – that sometimes there was a pain that blistered down her forearm, tingling and terrifying, that she'd learned to recognise as nerve pain. But it was all just words. Pain wasn't something a person understood until they felt it. She hadn't. Now she could barely remember what it felt like to be without it.

Across the table Ryan's resting shit-face was sandwiched

between Lucas's thoughtful blink and Win's gentle concern. Three different varieties of listening face. The cushion bounced as Sunny wriggled on the seat next to her, silent for once.

"I'm *sixteen* and I feel like I've body-swapped with someone waiting for a telegram from the Queen. I'm never going to get better – and I'm scared and angry and sad and I'm exhausted from all of it. From battling my body and going to the hospital and trying to get on with my life, and I'm exhausted from hope. Because every morning I wake up and I hope that maybe today *something* will hurt less." One of them was going to give: tears or her temper. Sophie didn't have the strength to hold on to both. "My mum is trying everything she can to make my life that bit better, and some of those things actually make it worse – but that's what the money is. It's guilt and it's pity and it's better than nothing."

Her temper surged up the strongest – anger at what her life had turned into, sickening hatred of her own body and a rage that none of this was fair. For a few moments, the only sound was her breath flowing in and out as if in sync with the tide on the beach beyond.

"You were diagnosed five months ago?" Win said.

Sophie dragged her eyes up and met Win's gaze across the table.

"Sophie – did Freya know?"

Everything felt worse in the cold. Her hands and her shoulder and her knee. Her mood.

When Mum came to collect her early from school, Sophie put her headphones in and turned away to stare out of the passenger window, knowing that she could get away with it because they were on their way to the hospital.

Again.

She never thought she'd miss going to the doctor's, but having to go to Sandleford was so much worse. The drive took ages, then there was Mum's evergreen rant about private parking companies at the hospital taking advantage of the most vulnerable, the rabbit warren of corridors, and the sound her shoes made on the lino.

The TV was on in the waiting area, subtitles scrolling beneath a family agonising over which house to buy. Sophie watched them, headphones blasting the angriest tunes Spotify had to offer. Music that made her want to grind her teeth and punch a wall. Tunes to make her strong when she felt her weakest.

Mum's notebook lay open across her lap as she studied a diary of Sophie's symptoms. She'd started it after the school had called them in last year over Sophie's absences, not trusting anyone else's records but her own. After the glandular fever scare, she'd shown it to Dr Yoon who'd finally referred Sophie to a rheumatologist. That same day Mum had made Sophie go through every page, taking them back further to the Christmas before when the three of them – Mum and Sophie and Christopher – had gone to Mexico: a lavish spend on one last holiday before Sophie's exams turned serious and Christopher was completely lost to adulthood. A holiday spoiled by a heat rash under her arm and pains in her knees that her family had no sympathy for because she was the youngest.

Notes on the rash. The treatment for the rash. The run of weeks in which Sophie struggled with an infection that left her too wiped to manage more than a couple of days of school before she crashed again. The charming insomnia/tiredness combination that they'd put down to exam stress. The rash again. Different treatment for the rash. The "maybe it's anaemia" phase. Vague memories of aching joints that grew more specific when Mum pushed her to think harder. Then, after that, Mum would get her to report on her health every night – *everything* from persistent mouth ulcers to period pains, logging how much sleep she'd had and scoring her energy levels out of ten, like a player in an RPG incapable of finding a health pack.

Without the notebook, they wouldn't have been taken seriously.

Sophie hated the notebook.

Her rheumatologist was a man. Dr Seager. The first time her mother had laid eyes on him she'd murmured *"Talk about McDreamy"*, and watching them together was only marginally less cringey than when she talked to the postman.

That day, though, flirtation had been dialled down to a minimum.

"Right, Sophie, so we've been looking through the results from your blood test…" Her hand drew up to her arm, palm resting on the inside of her elbow as he talked about DNA and ANA and words that she was sure were supposed to mean something, but she was finding it hard to concentrate. Something she'd been asked to take a note of, which made her think of telling him to stop so she could get her mother to write it down…

Only Mum wasn't writing anything down. And she wasn't feasting on the eye candy of Dr Seager. She was looking at Sophie and she was very clearly trying not to cry – and failing.

"What? Why are you crying?"

Sophie looked from her mum to her doctor, and as ever the word "cancer" obliterated everything else in the world because that's where her brain kept going, even after she'd been told that wasn't what they were looking for.

"I wasn't…" She looked at Dr Seager and his handsome-I-guess face and his serious eyes. "Can you say that again?"

"The results from your tests are consistent with a condition called lupus."

"I don't know what that is…" Tears of frustration welled beneath the surface because she'd been given an answer that she didn't understand.

Dr Seager had been careful, quiet and patient. He had gone through her symptoms, explained the results of the blood tests – not just the most recent, but all of the ones she'd been told were for "monitoring" – and, all the time, her mum clamped her left hand tight around Sophie's, her right scribbling away in the notebook because it was the only way either of them were going to be able to process any of this after they left.

And it was utterly fucking terrifying.

All she could really comprehend was that she was being given a prescription that looked more like a shopping list...

Sophie had no recollection of leaving the hospital, although the second she was out, she turned her phone back on, too impatient to wait and see what notifications she might have. And she rang the one person she wanted to speak to.

"Hey there, it's me. Not answering right now. Don't bother with a message, I never check them."

But she left one anyway.

"Hi. It's me. Call me. Please. I'm serious."

SOPHIE

"And Freya never called you back?" Sunny's outrage was very loud, but Sophie didn't have it in her to reply to a question everyone else could answer.

Instead, she stared down at the patterns Ryan had been tracing in the sugar. She didn't want to look up. Didn't want anyone's pity. Didn't want to be here now that they knew the full extent of her misery. If she could have made a quick exit like she had last night, she would have done, but a lady turned up laden with a tray of drinks and asked who had ordered the black coffee – with the tone of someone who thought no one at a table full of kids had any business consuming something so adult.

"That's for me," Sophie said, wrapping her hands around the heat of the mug and shifting her attention to that rather than the sugar patterns.

This wasn't like it had been with Morgan and Georgia, when she'd just sort of translated the things her mum had learned from reading articles on the internet.

This felt as if she were finally talking to Freya.

"So you hurt. Is that it?"

"Ryan!" Sophie felt the thump of Win kicking him under the table – enjoyed his startled wince.

"*Ow!* I meant is there more stuff? I was trying to be nice!"

"Or you could do a Google instead of making Sophie spell it all out?"

"Left my phone at home, didn't I?"

Sophie smiled into her coffee at their bickering. She

could give Ryan a list of symptoms so long he'd grow bored by the end – who wanted to hear about aches and pains and flares and rashes and mouth ulcers and fatigue and brain fog? But then … who wanted to live it?

"Is there anything you want to tell us?" Win said, a tenderness in her voice that Sophie had to pretend she couldn't hear. "I mean, things we should know so we don't do something insensitive?"

Sophie swallowed while she considered the question.

"Well. Try not to bump into me or grab me. It can hurt."

Sunny edged further along the booth until she was squashed up against the window and Win rolled her eyes in a way that made Sophie smile.

"And I get fatigue."

"You get tired?"

God. Sunny sounded so much like Freya at times. That *so what* tone permeating what was clearly intended as a sympathetic question.

"I get fatigue. Not the same." Sophie had spent so long thinking about how she might explain this, never thinking that it would be to a bunch of strangers. "Tired is something you can get rid of, OK? You sleep, you regenerate, you feel awake. That's not fatigue. It's like your energy is being drained away before you even start using any. And it doesn't matter if you don't have any to begin with – it *still* keeps on at you."

She could hear the fear in her voice. Felt it, because she was already paying for yesterday's exertion. She'd woken into that wading feeling, everything taking that much more

261

effort – thinking, moving, existing. It would have been better to stay home and do nothing than try for another day of activity, but she'd wanted something more. Now here she was, paying for it.

"So, what do you do, like? Just grin and bear it?" Ryan's outrage *almost* sounded sympathetic.

Sophie shrugged. Winced, really. "Sometimes I have to stay home from school, bored out of my brain stressing out that I'll have to re-sit my GCSEs."

"But today you're OK?" Lucas looked a little alarmed, and Sophie thought better of telling him that "OK" was a relative term. By his standards, she probably wasn't.

"I need to go carefully. Last night…" Sophie closed her eyes a moment, remembering. "I went too hard. Stayed out too long, tried to do too much."

There was so much more she could tell them, but this was all she had stamina for. Explaining herself was hard work.

"Can we change the subject?"

"Of course." Win stretched across the table and cupped her hands gently around Sophie's. She wore a stack of three green rings on her thumb. Sophie wanted to run her finger across them, feel the smooth green surface of each ring and the grooves between them, but then Sunny laid her hand over Win's, then Lucas over Sunny's.

Ryan gave the lot of them a repulsed curl of the lip.

"I'm sorry, are we the three fucking musketeers?"

A second later they all pulled back to make room for plates of battered fish and steaming chips and Sophie felt an urge to snatch Win's hands back, to hold on to a comfort no one else had given her. As they ate, Sophie caught Win looking at her across the table, thoughts hidden behind an artfully blank expression that creased into a warm smile.

For all the things Freya had got wrong, Win Su was something she'd got very right.

RYAN

Going with them was supposed to be an easy getaway, not a guilt trip.

All those times Freya had grumbled about Sophie flaking out on her, how she never wanted to do anything fun any more…

Shit.

Ryan looked across the table. Sophie was a stone-cold bitch who liked him about as much as he liked her. Still. What she'd said about her illness sucked. Pain wasn't something you could climb into a car and drive away from.

Not like Freya had done. She'd left everything behind her when she went – her problems and the people that went with them. She'd said she needed to get away from everyone. He guessed that included Sophie and him and Lucas and … Win? Didn't seem likely, did it? That girl solved problems, not created them.

"Beach or amusements?" Lucas nudged him in the side. "You're the deciding vote."

Across from him Sunny very clearly mouthed *"Amusements."*

"Amusements," Ryan said. "See if I can double my money on the penny falls."

SOPHIE

The amusement arcade was Too Much for someone who wanted to have a rest and not have to talk or think or be.

"You OK?" Win appeared in the periphery of Sophie's vision. "You look…"

If she said tired, Sophie was going to thump her.

"…like you need to sit quietly for a bit?"

Words so familiar that Sophie wondered where she'd heard them before.

Win's smile was as subtle as everything else about her. "That's what you said, last night in the garden."

There were so many ways for someone to listen, but Sophie liked Win's way best. It wasn't the prove-yourself variety like Morgan, who only showed she was listening if someone tested her, or Georgia, whose attention had to be caught and held cupped in your hands before it escaped.

And Freya… Well that was something Sophie was starting to think hadn't worked in either direction. Sophie had only listened for the things she expected to hear and Freya for the things she could fix. She'd never had patience for Sophie's rash issues, or how tired she felt. Never asked about the doctor's appointments because she'd not listened when Sophie said she was going. Like every healthy person in the world, Freya had assumed treating an illness was enough to make it go away.

But Sophie shouldn't have tested her, either. She'd been playing chicken with the truth against someone unaware of the game.

With Win though… Sophie had a feeling that if they'd been friends, Win would have asked.

The two of them sat squashed together on a seat for one of the driving games, legs over the side so they could watch the others. Ryan was at the penny falls, all the money he'd saved from lunch turned copper as he doggedly fed two-pence pieces into the machine, eyes on a five-pound note that quivered with promise at the furthest reaches of the fall.

"Do you think he'll win?" Sophie asked.

"I'm not sure winning's in Ryan's nature," Win replied, watching him with a quiet kind of interest that encouraged the same from Sophie.

She knew Ryan so well that sometimes it was hard to see him. They'd been in the same form since they started at Buckthorn. Memories of him pissing her off came more easily to mind than half the things she was supposed to know for her exams. He did all the same stuff as the rest of the rowdy lads and the girls that thought equality came in the form of lowering themselves to the same level of gross-out humour and devil's advocacy. But Ryan was someone who took it too far. The kind of person that got yelled at by the teachers for real.

Maybe he hadn't been *all* bad *all* summer. There had been moments when he'd made her laugh. And there were times, when it had been just him and the Buckthorn lot, when she'd almost thought he was all right. Moments when Kellan wasn't there for him to compete with.

"He won Freya," she said, mood buckling beneath a weight of sorrow brought on by the thought of how close her best friend had got to someone else without Sophie having a clue.

"People aren't prizes," Win said, switching her attention from Ryan to Sophie. "And even if they were, do you really think it's winning to have someone you care so much about keep you a secret and then leave without a word?"

WIN

Only as Sophie sat up a little straighter did Win realise how she'd been leaning her weight against Win's side. It hadn't been a problem.

"Your sister and Lucas are adorable," Sophie said.

A change of subject Win could permit.

Those two were playing a dancing game against each other, only Sunny kept nudging and bumping and shoving him, constant contact under the guise of cheating. As Win watched, Lucas wrapped his arms around Sunny and lifted her high enough that her feet couldn't make contact with the dance pad. The squares lit up beneath her as she squealed and kicked and made like she wanted him to put her down.

"You know him better than me," Win said. She liked what she'd seen of Lucas; not so much the things she'd heard. Sophie had known him longer, seen him out and about with Kellan. "Should I be worried? Go full scary big sister on him?"

"I *thought* I knew him."

"I think you do," Win said. She heard the melancholy dip in Sophie's voice and felt frustrated that a question about Lucas had invoked Freya. She really *did* want to know more about Lucas. "Lucas and Big T are different in name only. Not everyone's hiding something. Or, at least, they're not hiding it from you."

"Maybe."

"*Definitely*. If there's any hiding Lucas is doing, it's from his friend Kellan."

Sophie didn't reply immediately, and Win turned to look at her.

"I guess." She sighed. "I'm not so sure I'm all that good at knowing people, Win. I liked Kellan just fine – I'd stick up for him when Freya was being all emo about him because I thought it was just her being dramatic. Now she's gone, I can't help thinking that was part of the problem, that I never actually listened…"

"Funny how every conversation comes back to Freya, even when it's about someone else," Win said, ducking her head down so that her hair fell forward, the ends of her bob tickling the hollows of her cheeks. A second later, she turned to look at Sophie. "She's *very* good at being the centre of attention."

"Maybe at some point I'll notice other people exist for longer than twenty seconds?"

"I can wait," Win said.

LUCAS

"Tell them you need to go and get some money from the cashpoint," Sunny whispered, eyes full of stars and promise.

So that's what he did. Even though he had ten pounds in his wallet.

No one fell for it. Win gave him a look that threatened castration and Ryan muttered that the public toilets looked spacious. Sophie made no comment, but she was smiling. A lot.

As soon as they stepped beyond the beeps and bloops of the arcade, Sunny fisted her hand in the front of his T-shirt and pulled him over the road towards a promenade swept clean by the sun. A wide-open world, when Lucas would have preferred somewhere more private. Ryan's comment about the public toilets came to mind, making Lucas feel dirty and guilty, as if wanting to be alone with Sunny was something to be ashamed of.

But that was what he wanted. To have her all to himself. Preferably with her hands somewhere on his body – maybe around his neck, or curled around his sides – and her face so close that kissing was the only option. Every glance, every touch, every moment he couldn't kiss her was the worst. Yesterday, the thought of having her this close would have been enough, but after last night, after they'd kissed…

All he wanted was for it to happen again.

At the railings, Sunny bounced up to sit facing him on the sea wall. Sun glinted off the stud through the nub of her right ear and a single pink gemstone glittered in her lobe.

"This is better," she said, her head exactly the height of his. Lucas took in the way she moved her eyebrows and the curve of her eyes, the line of her neck and…

"Are you wearing a Peppa Pig T-shirt?"

Sunny looked down, scandalised. "How dare you! This is *Daddy* Pig. Peppa's a horrid little nugget."

She was too much. He wanted to laugh with her and hold her and kiss her – he wanted to scoop her up in his arms and press his face into the curve of her neck and grin into her skin as he kissed it.

"What? Why are you looking at me like that?" But even her self-consciousness shone with laughter.

"I like looking at you." For a moment, Lucas's attention wavered between her eyes and her lips. "Especially when you've got this smile going on."

"I have others?"

"So far I've seen this one…" He reached out and traced his finger lightly along the line of her lower lip. "It only comes out when you think someone's looking. I like it a lot."

Helpless in the face of a compliment, Sunny's other smile broke free, soaring on the sea breeze.

"But this one's got the edge. You get this, here." He waved across the bridge of his own nose, the place where Sunny's skin scrunched up as she wrinkled nose and eyes and brows in delight. "And there's a dimple. Here." Lucas touched his thumb to her skin, filling the hollow of her dimple.

Sunny's teeth, set free by her smile, nipped at her lip.

"That one's new," he murmured, leaning so close into her that looking at her lips turned into kissing them, Sunny sighing into him, like she'd been longing for this moment as much as he had. He lifted his arms up to cradle her head lightly in his hands, fingers in her hair, and Sunny twined her arms around his neck, leaning so far into him that she slithered off the wall to stand on her tiptoes, not breaking contact.

The kiss flooded his senses. The hesitant touch of her tongue on his, her breath on his cheek, every curve and bump and plane of her body as she pressed against him...

"Wait." Sunny broke away with an urgency that startled him. "I need to check something."

The way she said it, the look she was giving him – both were so earnest that Lucas felt a pang of fear that she was about to ask him what he was going to do about Kellan, which was the last thing he wanted to think about.

"Which Avenger would you be?"

But Lucas couldn't answer for grinning.

Sunny thumped him on the chest. "I'm serious! It's important."

"Yes. Very important. You couldn't possibly kiss me if I said the wrong one..." Except that she did kiss him. A little.

"Should I tell you which one I am?" she said.

"You're Spider-Man," Lucas said without hesitation. "Because you're little and run into fights you didn't start."

"I'm not *that* little!" Sunny objected, even as she grinned that same soaring smile as before, all teeth and braces and no inhibitions.

"Compared to me you are," Lucas said, kissing her nose.

272

"So what about you?"

"I'm the big guy who ends up in fights because I swing before I think." A confession as much as an answer. "I'm the Hulk."

An answer he'd worried might disappoint had the opposite effect, delight fizzing up and exploding out of her faster than Mentos dropped in Coke.

"Oh my God, would it be weird if I told you I had a major crush on Hulk?"

WIN

Win left it as long as seemed reasonable – long enough for Ryan to win his prize fiver and a Maoam, and for Sophie to find a little more energy for whatever came next. Inevitably, Win saw her sister and Lucas across the road, the two of them wrapped around each other tighter than a double helix.

"Not in front of the children!" Ryan bellowed loud enough to startle the gulls who'd been feasting on a discarded box of chips. As Lucas and Sunny sprang apart, Ryan flashed a complacent smirk at Win. "You're welcome."

"You're a dick," Sophie said, peeling away in the direction of the public loos and saying something about needing to put on sunscreen, Ryan and Sunny following suit, leaving Win with the perfect opportunity to intimidate Lucas.

"Upset my sister and I will destroy you."

Lucas recoiled with such sincerity that Win thought she might have gone in a bit too hard. He might be a small mountain, but Lucas was soft.

"OK. I won't."

"She's not as tough as she seems."

"Neither am I." A smile nudged the corner of his mouth, but when he saw the way Win was looking at him, it disappeared. She was thinking about last night, about the blood on Ryan's face and the worry in Sunny's eyes when she'd been standing on the driveway, looking back at what had happened in the house. Lucas might have been able to win Sunny over with a promise and a kiss, but Win was here to hold him to it.

"Last night she seemed to think you were going to talk to Kellan?"

"I am. I will. I promise. I'm not going to get into any more fights; not even going to risk breaking them up." Lucas raised his hands as if surrendering to all the fights that ever would be, and Win grinned.

"Good to know that you won't fight back in the you-upset-Sunny-and-I-destroy-you scenario."

Lucas shrugged, like he only half thought this was a joke, then squinted out towards the sea, before twisting back to look at the clock that towered over the toilets behind them.

"How's Sophie?"

"Sad? Confused? In quite a lot of pain?" All guesses, but Win suspected accurate ones.

"That was rough, about Freya leaving just before she got sick."

Win didn't correct him on the technicality – an illness like that didn't spring into existence the day it was diagnosed. Sophie had been ill long before Freya left.

She sighed and glanced across and, as she had done every time she looked at Lucas, admired his hair. "I don't feel like Freya owed me a goodbye, or even a letter. You?"

Lucas shook his head.

"But those two…"

They stood with their backs to the beach and watched the others emerge – the slouch of Ryan's shoulders and the stiffness whenever Sophie put any weight on her left hand side.

"How about I see if Ryan wants to talk about it?" Lucas said, his voice low.

Win nodded, her hand resting on the solid little lump of Freya's letter, still in the pocket of her jeans.

"I'll talk to Sophie."

The sand on the beach was soft and slippery and, next to her, Sophie lost her balance and flung a hand out to catch Win's shoulder.

"Ow." Sophie hissed the word out through her teeth, but when Win glanced at her, Sophie gave a tight little shake of her head to silence any concern. As soon as she regained her balance, she let go.

As they reached a band the tide had touched, Win watched Lucas scoop up a handful of sand and drop it down the back of Ryan's shirt. He was already sprinting away towards the sea as Ryan yelled a swear-riddled promise of vengeance and set off in pursuit, Sunny immediately taking off with him, yelling that she'd race them to the water.

"They're like dogs," Win said mildly, looking from their friends to a couple of yapping, bouncing, joyful dogs who'd been riled up by all the action. The person with them looked more riled up by Ryan's profanity.

"Puppies," Sophie corrected her, eyes warm with good humour. Then she added, "I'm not up for running."

The two of them walked in step over sea-soft pebbles that pressed through the rubber of Win's shoes. She stayed silent, feeling the conversation hanging between them now that they were under wide open sky with space enough for scary truths and overwhelming feelings.

Sophie was the one to start it. "Freya and I went to the

beach last summer. Just us. No Morgan and Georgia. No Kellan and his hangers-on."

Win said nothing, letting her talk.

"We brought a rug and a windbreak and a picnic. Tried to make sandcastles with the empty yogurt pots."

"Did it work?"

"They were very small sandcastles," Sophie admitted. "After that we tried going in the water."

Win looked at her then, eyebrows flashing up.

"I made it as far as my thighs." Sophie peered ahead to where the water was folding over itself in crisp white waves. "Freya went right the way in. Dived into the surf like we were somewhere hot."

Win's mind conjured an image as clear as a snapshot, of Freya emerging from the surf – flesh goose-pimpled all over, water sparkling on her skin – before realising that she'd seen it on her Instagram: a shot staged by Freya and snapped by Sophie. Those two had seemed so close, lives knotted so tightly together that Win had felt sad that her best friend was a boy who lived a three hour drive away and could only hang out through the phone.

The shock of going from what Sophie had with Freya to having nothing at all – not even *email* – must have been devastating.

As they reached the sandbreak Win suggested they sit. She'd listened when Sophie'd said about going carefully and the tide was a long way out.

For a moment, Sophie looked like she might refuse on some kind of principle, but when Win perched down

277

lightly – hoping the green algae that fuzzed the edges of the wood wouldn't stain her jeans – Sophie did the same, both angled towards the sea. Down at the water's edge there was a smudge of shoes left on the sand, then further along Sunny and Lucas and Ryan splashing around in the shallows, trousers and leggings rolled up above the knee. Sunny's shrieks – louder than any of the gulls' – kept time with the flow of the tide.

"If you asked me back then I'd have said we'd be friends for life," Sophie said, a finger tucking under the silver bracelet that Win had been careful not to mention, or so much as look at, all day. "When people called her my BFF, I'd always thought 'yeah, you're right'. But then she left and I just carried on pretending that we'd been perfect pals – not just to everyone else. I think I was pretending to myself."

"You guys *were* close."

"We were, but close isn't perfect, is it?"

Win shook her head.

"I wish I'd told her I was ill. God. There were so many doctor's appointments – I spent half of August convinced I had skin cancer because of that stupid rash." The hand that had been fiddling with the bracelet slid up past her elbow and clamped tightly around the top of her arm. There were freckles there, too. "I thought she'd notice, but she never did. And I never just said, *'ask me'*."

Ask me. It wasn't in the telling, it was in feeling important enough to be seen.

"But then..." Sophie's voice dropped. "It's not like I ever asked her, is it? She probably thought there wasn't anything to ask about, same as me, while both of us were there, struggling along with problems we wanted the other to notice." Her eyes misted over as she sniffed, before the weight of her sadness dragged her gaze down from the horizon and she sank into her hands. Reaching out, Win rested a hand on her shoulder. When Sophie leaned in, she pulled her into a gentle hug, wary of putting any pressure on her.

"I'm so sorry," Win whispered, but Sophie was shaking her head. When she sat back up, her eyes were bright with tears and she dabbed at her nose with the heel of her hand.

"I never used to cry this much."

"Maybe you never had this much to cry about?" Win laid her hands over Sophie's. "Sophie. I'm not going to pretend I have the first clue what lupus really is" – as she'd told Ryan, she'd Google it – "but from what you said before it sounds like you've been sick on and off without knowing why, then Freya disappeared without telling you she was going *the same week* you found out you had a chronic illness, which, FYI has happened right in the middle of your GCSE year—"

"Oh God, *don't*..." But she was smiling through the tears. "Plausible deniability, Win – they're not happening."

"Well then I won't offer you my somewhat stellar revision notes."

"How stellar?"

Win felt a little awkward, but she channelled a little of Sunny's boastfulness. "I mean, good enough that my results got a mention in the local paper. Which you probably wouldn't have seen because Mama bought up every copy in the region to send to her family."

"I am *very* pleased I had no idea how cool and clever you were before I had to deliver your parcel."

"Shut up." Win nudged her gently and ducked her head to hide just how much she was smiling, but when she stole another glance at Sophie she was crying again. Shuffling closer, she pulled Sophie in for another hug. A little tighter this time, the kind of hug that can hold a person together as they threaten to fall apart.

Sophie's shoulder notched neatly under Win's chin and she felt the faint shake of sobs caught deep in the other girl's chest. Red hair tickled her face and, just for a moment, Win closed her eyes and sank into the feeling of having her so close.

"I miss her," Sophie whispered.

Slowly, Win eased away. "I know."

"I've spent five months being angry and calling it sad and now, I just … I just feel sad."

"That's allowed."

"I think the parcel broke me." Sophie huffed a rueful laugh. "Snatched back more hope than it gave me." She lifted her hands to her face, wiping away the tears, shaking her head all the while like it had been foolish to have any hope.

Win thought of the letter in her pocket, the lines threaded between all the ones that had annoyed her so much, lines that provided an explanation Win hadn't been looking for, that Sophie craved so much. Stretching her leg out, Win dug around in her pocket, pulling out the paper she'd folded so many times it could barely keep its shape. She looked at it for a moment, weighing up what she was going to do with it.

Then, carefully, she held the paper out for Sophie to take. "I think you should read this."

RYAN

The water was too cold to stand in for any length of time. Further along the tideline, Sunny had ventured up onto the sand, searching for stones suitable for skimming, but Lucas showed no signs of moving, which meant Ryan couldn't move either. Not without looking soft.

The two of them were hurling pebbles as far as they could into the sea.

"Mine," Lucas said, claiming his third win in a row.

"Whatever." Ryan flung a handful of shrapnel into the water and dusted his palm on his joggers. The waves at his ankles had licked away any sensation below the waterline and his feet had turned a cadaverous white. Picking up a bit of driftwood from the shallows, he waded out a little further to poke at some seaweed, trying to lift it up so he could flick it at Lucas, who'd been foolish enough to follow him.

"Have you thought about the order?"

"You what?" Ryan wasn't really paying attention, busy with the seaweed plan.

"The order the parcel went in. All of it led to you."

"And look where that got me."

"Freya trusted you…" Lucas didn't seem to hear the warning note in Ryan's voice, and had walked that bit further out, eyes on the horizon so that he couldn't see the scowl being levelled at his back. "With the letters I mean."

"Don't start. She baited Sophie with the promise of treasure at the end of the trail, knowing she'd bite. I was just the hook." Ryan scowled at the sky and the sea and himself. "Not that being baited for such a headfuck of a letdown sounds any better."

Ryan turned away, walking fast enough that the waves splashed up his calves to splatter his joggers, rolled up beyond his knees. Stick in hand, he poked at another frond of splayed seaweed swaying beneath the surface, hoping Lucas might take the hint and leave him be.

"Ryan."

Ryan ground his teeth and jabbed at the water. "What?" He spun round, tracing an arc in the water with the end of his stick. "What are you trying to do? Spy for my cousin? Get something you can use to buy your way back into Kellan's good books?"

"Like what?"

"Like what happened."

"Doesn't he already know that? From the letter?"

"Fuck off." Ryan threw his stick out to sea with such force that he could hear the whip of it as it spun through the air, wondering how far he'd have to fling himself into the water to be swept away with the rest of the crap the waves had washed from the beach.

"What was she to you?" Lucas said, voice only a little louder than the water they were standing in.

Freya had been a secret.

A friend.

A need Ryan hadn't known existed.

"Nothing. Same as I was to her. A one-time mistake and a crapload of regret."

"That's not true."

"Isn't it?" Ryan turned on him. If he'd still had his stick he'd not have thought twice about swinging it round to smack Lucas in the arm as the anger rose up, the way it always did when people got too familiar. "How would you know, Big T?"

But Lucas didn't react to the snarl of Ryan's voice or the scowl on his face. He just looked at him, like he could see something Ryan had hidden so successfully he'd forgotten it existed.

"I can see it," Lucas said. "How much you miss her—"

Before he'd even finished his sentence, Ryan was shouting, "You don't see shit."

He tried to force Lucas away, to create some space between them, but Lucas only took a single step back, edging further into the water – still upright, still there.

"I see you miss her more than I do, more than Win does."

Sophie's name hung between them a second before Ryan trampled over it. "I don't miss her at all."

But Lucas's mouth twisted into a smile that spoke of disbelief and Ryan didn't know what would happen if Lucas pushed further. If this great bloody lump was going to be the one to get him to talk – to feel…

"I don't believe you, Ryan."

"You calling me a liar?" A battle cry Ryan knew how to sound, face contorting to match the anger of his words as he shoved Lucas in the chest, hard enough for him to stagger back deeper into the water. If Lucas didn't shut up, Ryan would make him.

"Well…"

"Are you?" Another shove, harder than the last and Lucas still just stepped back, taking it.

"Yes. You're lying to yourself—"

And Ryan flew at him, a storm of ill will too wild to keep contained. Anger for letting himself care. Hurt that she'd gone and that stupid parcel was the only way she dared to come back. And guilt.

Guilt for what they'd done, for what they hadn't, for the fact that he'd pushed her away when she needed someone to hold her close...

...that month we didn't talk ... was actually what I needed...

G-force feelings that came out through his fists, pummelling Lucas in the chest, then smacking, shoving – anything to get him to fight back because it would be better to fight Lucas than to keep on endlessly, endlessly fighting himself. Only Lucas kept taking it, edging back further into the sea, and Ryan grew desperate, fists flailing harder and higher, until he caught Lucas in the face and felt a surge of triumph as he anticipated the comeback...

One that didn't come, as Lucas windmilled a second before he slapped down in a spray of sea water.

Ryan stood, braced for Lucas to surge back up looking for vengeance.

He didn't.

There was a fever of water in front of him, Lucas still beneath the surface, and Ryan realised with a deep chill of horror how far the sea reached up his thighs.

"Shit!" He thrust an arm below the water, grabbing for

anything he could. "Get the fuck up!"

His fingers caught on something solid, closing tightly around Lucas's arm – wrist? – and Ryan hauled up with a strength greater than the force that had powered his punch.

Lucas struggled to stand, his free hand grasping at Ryan's clothes to help him up, sea churning white with the effort, until eventually he was up, bending double and spitting out mouthfuls of water.

Turning his head to the side, Ryan was surprised to see that he was grinning.

"Should maybe have warned you" – he coughed again – "that I am officially no longer getting in any fights."

LUCAS

Lucas stood dripping onto the pavement, the sting of salt lingering on his lips as he looked up at the peeling cursive of Louisa's Cleaners. One side was lined with washing machines, the other with tumble dryers; customer desk nestled in the shadows at the back.

When Sunny had knocked on his door this morning, he'd not imagined that it would lead to this.

"So, does anyone have change for the machines?" he asked, pulling out a handful of wet shrapnel from his own pocket. Most of it was in copper from the arcade, same as Ryan's and Sunny's. Win scooped the lot into her hand and jogged along to where there was a newsagent with faded plastic buckets and spades hanging down either side of the door.

"Do you think they'll let the two of you sit there naked while your clothes dry?" Sunny flushed as she said it and wouldn't look Lucas in the eye.

"I have a towel." Lucas held up Mrs Su's hibiscus-print swimming bag that Win had unearthed from the boot of her car, while Ryan cast a filthy look at the black bin bag he'd been offered. Given how angry Win had been with him – more so than either of the other girls – Ryan was lucky that she hadn't wrapped him up in it and thrown him back in the sea.

"I saw a charity shop on the corner," Sophie said, half turning in the direction they'd come. "If we got you some clothes we could go grab a drink or something while your stuff dries." Ryan glowered a moment, then, to everyone's surprise, he dug in his pocket and handed over the fiver he'd coaxed from the penny falls. Wet, but spendable. "See how far that gets you."

Sophie took it with the air of someone who thought it was the least he could do, but five pounds meant more to Ryan than it could to her – or for Win or Sunny.

"I'll pay you back," Lucas said after the girls had gone.

"Might not want to once you see what they get for it," Ryan grunted, shoving the door open and dripping across the threshold.

But Lucas knew that wasn't a "no".

"What you gonna do about your boxers?" Lucas asked, pulling his own off under the safety of a candy-striped towel that was as soft as a cloud and smelled like Sunny's T-shirt. The man at the desk wasn't too impressed with them putting sea-water-soaked clothes straight into the dryer and had set up one of the washing machines for a rinse.

"Wear this like a giant nappy?" Ryan said, brandishing his bin bag before tucking it into his pocket and pulling off his vest to expose a pale expanse of radiator ribs and a concave stomach. A lad built like that had no business trying to start on Lucas.

Once the rinse was on, the two of them sat on the bench, watching their clothes flop round in the drum, Ryan rustling as he tried to get comfy.

Lucas cast him a sideways glance, aware of how little thought he'd ever given Kellan's annoying cousin. Until today, he'd assumed Ryan was loaded too, but people with money didn't live in houses like Ryan's, and Lucas realised that he'd always been vaguely aware of the times Ryan had showed up at Kellan's, holes in his socks, and an absence of branding on his clothes.

Stuff Lucas worried about less now Uncle Vas was the one asking Justin for money to help pay for the things his stepson needed.

There were still days when something slipped out amongst his friends that reminded Lucas of the differences between them, and for all the time he spent round Kellan's, he'd never felt comfortable enough to ask Kellan back to his. He wasn't sure he ever would.

With Ryan he wouldn't worry.

Next to him, Ryan stared between his feet. Every expression he possessed was a variation on the theme of hostile – even now, it looked like he was about to start a fight with the floor…

"Sorry."

Lucas stilled, not sure he'd heard right. Only then Ryan said, "You know. For what happened."

"For trying to drown me in the sea?"

"Don't be such a fucking drama queen. You fell."

"Because you punched me." Lucas rubbed his jaw where the memory of Ryan's fist promised a bruise.

"And you went down faster than Neymar."

"Not used to apologising, are you?" Lucas was grinning though. An apology from someone who never gave them was worth treasuring, even if that someone was a complete and utter dickhead. Maybe *especially* because of that. After a second, Ryan twitched back what might have been a grin.

There was a lull then, before Ryan said, "You know you were supposed to hit me back, right?"

"I'm not doing that any more. Not after last night."

Ryan's eyes darted up to Lucas for a second. "Call it even?"

And he held out a fist for Lucas to tap.

RYAN

Ryan's hand returned to the sticker on the bench that he'd been worrying at with his thumbnail, nipping again at a corner where he'd already peeled some away. What was left of the print suggested it was one of those freebies you get at the dentist for not biting their fingers off.

"This has got me thinking," Lucas started up.

"Bit dangerous." Because all this had got Ryan thinking – about Freya, mostly.

Lucas ignored him. "I know I started out mates with Kellan, but … if you ever wanted to hang out—"

Ryan's "Fuck off" was reflexive.

"I'm serious."

"Why?"

"Because that's what Freya said, in my letter. Thinks I need someone around who won't put up with Kellan's bullshit."

The progress Ryan had made on the sticker slowed a little. That last line of his letter wasn't so different. About him needing friends… Anger came and went, but missing her was a hunger that wasn't going anywhere and the only way to feed it was with her words. Hating himself for it, he said, "She say anything else about me?"

"That you'd never demand too much from me."

Hearing that was a pain Ryan couldn't bear. One that squeezed his heart and wound its way from his chest to his throat, wrapping itself around each burning breath.

"Of course she fucking did."

Outside the light had dimmed from day to dusk to dark, the glow of the streetlight falling unevenly over the arm of the chair and the wall behind.

Ryan had thought about getting up to turn the main light on, but Freya had slumped slowly against him during whatever reality re-run they were watching so that now her head had fallen to rest on his shoulder.

"Plastic surgery looks painful," Freya said. Half at the TV, half to Ryan.

"Great observation, Captain Obvious."

"I just mean that I'm not sure I could do it. Go through the pain."

"Then don't."

There were kinder things he could have said. Like the fact that she'd never need to because she was the most gorgeous person he'd ever seen. But you don't say shit like that to the girl who'd been boning your cousin since August.

"Maybe there are some things that bring you a different kind of pain," Freya carried on, "so that an operation doesn't seem so bad?"

Ryan thought about all the names he'd been called as a kid and wondered what that pain was worth.

"Still costs a tonne of money though – I'd rather keep the cash and not have people know I cared that much about how I looked."

He felt her shift against him, her attention no longer on

the TV, but on him, head still on his shoulder, but tipped back a little.

"What if it was free? And it didn't hurt too much. Like an injection. And no one would remember what you were like before. Would you do it? Change how you look?"

"No," Ryan lied.

There were times, on the rare occasions he actually washed his face and looked in the mirror – when his reflection was collarbones and shoulders and neck, his body small beneath his head – that he would lift his fingers up to push his ears closer to his skull. He'd imagine them small and neat and completely unnoticeable.

He turned his head just enough to meet Freya's gaze. "What about you?"

Freya reached across, traced her finger down the edge of his left ear, her thumb nipping gently at the soft skin of his lobe. He expected her to stop there, to make a joke, but her touch followed the line of his scar from his ear and along his jaw.

"No, Ryan," she said. "I wouldn't change how you look."

"Stop that." Ryan pushed her hand away and stood up from the sofa. They shouldn't be sitting like this, but it had been happening more these last couple of times she'd been over, the two of them getting far too comfortable with being so close. "Do you want a drink?"

He didn't wait for her to answer, just went through to the kitchen and opened the fridge, pulling the door open so hard that the jars rattled and the up-ended ketchup toppled out. Ryan darted out a hand to catch it, feeling smug when he succeeded and disappointed that Freya hadn't seen him.

No. That was a stupid thing for him to feel. Dangerous. Ryan wasn't supposed to want Freya Newmarch to find him impressive.

Forgetting why he'd opened it, Ryan shut the fridge to find that Freya had followed him in and was resting against the doorframe.

"Why'd you run off just then?"

"Needed a drink."

They both looked at his empty hands.

"I think you might be the person I like best in the world right now," Freya said, looking up from his hands to meet his eyes.

"You have shit taste, then."

"Shut up." She shifted off the frame and stepped so close she could put her hand over his mouth, her fingers moulding to his lips. When he half raised his hand to push hers away, she shook her head. "Just. You don't have to fight everyone all the time."

And instead of pushing her away, Ryan's hand came to rest lightly on her forearm where the sleeve of her shirt had been rolled back far enough to read the homework she'd written along her arm. His thumb grazed the hairs on her skin and he felt his own rise up in response.

"Do you know why I like you?"

Ryan shook his head, her hand moving with it.

"I like you because you *never* try to say something just because I want to hear it. It means that when you do tell me something I want to hear, I can trust that it's not because you're trying to make me feel better."

Ryan frowned and gently pulled her hand away. "Have I ever said something you want to hear?"

She laughed, falling forward to bump her head lightly on his chest. "Like maybe once or twice."

When she straightened up, she'd slid her hand into his, holding him so he couldn't get away.

"You might be brutal, Ry, but you're honest." Everything about her softened a moment. "I wish I could be as straight with myself as you are."

Ryan knew he should stop staring at her. All those times he'd taken the piss, pushed her away with insults and filthy jokes – all safe, safe, safe. She couldn't like him back because he'd made himself unlikeable.

"I want to hear something true," she said. "Something I'll like hearing from you."

Her hair was scruffed up from leaning on him earlier, lips slightly parted as she breathed through her mouth. He wanted to tell her she was perfect, but they'd talked enough for him to know she hated that word. Felt trapped by it.

"You're my best friend," Ryan said, lifting his hand up to scratch the back of his head, to give him something to do. "My only one, actually."

The way she looked at him blew him apart completely. She was nothing but wide, awed eyes and the smallest of gasps came out – and then she kissed him.

Not a platonic peck, but a firm, hungry kiss, aimed at his lips. When he breathed in, she drew closer and then his lips had parted and they were kissing for real, messy and soft, the kind of kiss that forced his hand into a fist around the material of her shirt, pulling her tight towards him.

He'd kissed people before. Girls who didn't know him well enough to think he was a dick, or friends giggly enough on gas to make out just for fun. Kisses without consequence.

Nothing like this.

His hands were on her body, her fingers raking against the soft buzz of hair up the back of his head in a way that made his skin prickle from head to toe, and he wanted her so much…

"*Shit.*" He pushed himself back from her with enough force to propel him all the way to the sink. "What the fuck are we doing?"

"What do you think?" But for all she was smiling, she kept her distance, like she was well aware of how terrible this idea was.

"You're going out with my cousin."

"Am I?"

He couldn't tell if she was being sarcastic. "*Yes.*"

She looked at him for a long moment and then, "I want to be with you, Ryan. Or are you really so dense that you haven't noticed that you're the person I keep coming back to?"

"Well you can't!" The words came out before he'd had a chance to check if they were the ones he was looking for. "Kellan's family."

"You hate him!"

"Like that matters!" he snarled back, furious that they were fighting about this, that the best thing in his utterly miserable life had been ruined in the space of a single kiss.

Because this was it, wasn't it? She'd never come back now. They couldn't be friends. The longer he stayed here, with Freya, the harder it would be to keep to his word. Even as he was yelling at her all he could think about was giving in and letting it happen again. Seeing where it led to.

For one moment he thought about it. Teetered on an impulse, and then he spun away, went for the back door. Ignored Freya calling after him, just walked out in his socks. Out the back gate and into the alley, away from his house and the girl he should never have invited inside. He'd kept her secret, but if he gave Freya what she asked for now, it would destroy him.

He had *some* fucking honour.

Not much, but enough worth keeping.

He stayed out so long that everyone else was home when he got back, Mam as riled up as a box of badgers because he'd gone without locking up, lights and telly left on, burning up the electricity. There was no trace of Freya. No note, no messages on his phone. She'd walked out the same as him.

The next day at school, when he saw her approach, Ryan turned away.

When she said his name, he pretended not to hear it.

He couldn't face her, couldn't face himself. Kellan was his cousin and family came first.

WIN

No one would have blamed Win for being angry with Ryan. It was straightforward cause and effect, but not all of her frustration stemmed from him starting a fight – most of it was in the timing.

Because Sophie had read her letter.

For one second, she had looked Win right in the eye. Everything around them – the sky, the sea and the sand, the cool caress of the wind, all of it – had faded to nothing. All Win could take in was Sophie. Red hair blown forward, wisps breaking up the smooth pale heart of her face, those fine, elegant eyebrows tipping up in realisation, the line of freckles along her lip hinting at a curve that might have turned into a smile...

And her eyes. Bronzed and bold as if she finally saw Win for who she was.

A second split apart by a shriek from the water's edge and the two of them leapt away from their own private revelation and into Ryan Krikler's drama. Again.

That boy was a lot more effort than he was worth – but then, Win was starting to think that was his problem. Ryan believed he was worth no effort at all. If he could settle halfway between the two, that would be a start.

Win couldn't imagine engineering another moment like the one on the beach, one just for her and Sophie. But she could buy it. As Sophie drifted towards the men's clothes at the back of the shop, Win pressed a five pound note into Sunny's hand.

"Rang wo he Sophie dai wu fen zhong."

Sunny hunted for a clue by scanning her face. And as ever, Win played it poker straight.

"Wu fen zhong?"

Win nodded. Five minutes was all she needed.

Turning towards the back of the shop, Win felt that familiar swoop of fear tempered by nerves of a different nature as her gaze settled on the back of Sophie's head, the churn of her curls as they spilled from her ponytail and the freckles dappling the skin of her neck.

Win had already plunged beneath the surface, all she could do now was hold her breath and see if she resurfaced.

From behind came the screech of a rail's worth of wire hangers being scraped to one side of the rack so that Sunny could go along the row from left to right, giving each item careful consideration.

"Does Sunny know that's the kids' rail?" Sophie said, looking over with a frown.

"That's where you find the bargains."

"Not much of a bargain if it doesn't fit."

"Depends who you're buying for." Win glanced back at her sister. "Pretty sure half Sunny's wardrobe comes from the kids' section."

But the way Sophie nodded was the chin dip of someone aware that they were in a conversation without having heard the words.

Rather than force her attention, Win came to stand next to her, nudging the hangers along, going through an exercise her father had taught her, of going through her body, muscle by muscle, brow to toe, concentrating on relaxing each and every atom of her being, ironing the tension from her body. It was all about putting faith in stillness, in trusting that whatever might happen next, there was no need to be ready to run or to fight.

Freya had said Sophie was someone she could trust – but it wasn't always a question of trust. Sometimes it was a declaration.

"I should give you this back." Sophie reached into her little biscuit bag and held the letter out for Win to take. "Thank you for letting me read it."

"Did it help?"

Sophie sighed. "Maybe if she'd written it to me instead of you..."

"Oh." Win felt foolish. "You can forget I ever gave it to you, then. If you want."

"I don't want." A pair of trousers slithered from the hanger and onto the floor. Neither made a move to pick them up. They stood, half turned to each other as Sophie said with quiet fervour, "I don't want that at all."

Win glanced down at the trousers, then bent quickly and picked them up, reaching for the hanger, needing something to do other than stare at Sophie.

"Win. The best thing about the letter wasn't what Freya *wrote*, it was what it said about you. And I don't want to forget that." Sophie reached for her, fingers curling over her hand and stilling Win's attempts to stuff the trouser legs through the slot in the hanger. "When I said thank you for letting me read your letter, what I meant was thank you for coming out to me. For inviting me in. I know it's a big deal."

In that moment, when Sophie looked at her, Win understood what it was that Freya meant about seeing her at Pride, how she looked "glorious". Win *felt* glorious. Here, now, in a dingy charity shop just off the sea front, as all the parts of herself overlapped long enough for Sophie to see her through a single lens.

A moment of indecision, from both of them, then they were reaching out to envelop each other in a hug. The kind of hug that only came from – and could be given to – someone important enough to keep around.

The trousers slithered off the hanger and back onto the floor once more.

SOPHIE

The three of them drifted back towards the laundrette, too many to fit on the footpath so that Sunny spilled off the edge to walk in the road once they passed the one-way sign. Sophie was pleased to stay on the pavement: the whole of her left side was starting to go and she wasn't sure she'd be able to leap out of the way if a car came along.

"Do you think he'll like them?" Win held up the shorts they'd found for Ryan, the pattern so lurid that when the material caught a flash of sun between the houses, it burned into Sophie's retina.

"I think he'll hate them," she said with a gleeful grin. But not as much as he would hate the slithery nylon shirt they'd bought to clash. For Lucas, they'd found a pair of soft, grey tracksuit bottoms and a black T-shirt with a faded print of a skull on the front.

"What do you think happened back there? In the sea?" Sunny asked.

"Ryan acting entirely on brand and behaving like an absolute tool," Sophie suggested.

"He's not been *that* bad. Today, I mean."

"I thought a character redemption arc didn't make up for … what was it?"

"A history of being an asshole?" Win suggested with a glint in her eye.

"Anyway," Sophie carried on before Sunny could start up on Tony Stark, "I'd've thought you'd have changed your tune now he's decked your boyfriend?"

"Lucas isn't my boyfriend!" A protest that carried the vehemence of someone who wished that he was.

"Please please please don't tell our parents without me there to watch." Win was grinning almost as wide as her sister, although it faded a little as she added, "Actually, scratch that, you'll have to record it because I plan on being very far away so I don't get the blame for you losing your focus on school."

The two of them cackled in a joke that seemed funnier to them than it did to Sophie. She wished she knew Win better. She wanted to know everything… So far she liked all the things she'd learned. Win was funny and kind and tough. And she was into girls.

Sophie stole another look. They were still talking about their parents.

"You know they'll say he's too old."

"He's only in the year above!"

"I'm not the one who sets the rules." Win lifted her hands, freeing herself from association. "Remember when Mama found a picture of Tom Holland on your lockscreen and gave you a lecture about dating older boys?"

That was it. Sophie wanted in. "Why did you have a picture of Tom Holland?"

"I had a picture of Spider-Man. Then I saw *Into the Spider-Verse* and changed it." She held her phone out to show Sophie the screen.

"Is that a still from the film?" Spider Gwen leapt across Sunny's lockscreen, limbs stretching from one corner to the other, torso, legs and toes flowing in a single smooth sweep.

"No!" Sunny's voice rose to a squeak. "Win did it! She's amazing."

As Sunny tapped through for more pictures, Sophie's attention glided up from the screen to settle on Win. "She is…"

She liked the way that Win pressed her lips together and looked away. Maybe modest, maybe flattered.

"Look. She's done loads…" Sunny shoved her phone so close that it was practically up Sophie's nose, scrolling through an Instagram account that Sophie committed to memory for when she was reunited with her phone. Pages of sketches and full-colour artwork. Superhero outfits on diverse bodies and a series of familiar (and less familiar) Marvel characters against different flags – bi and trans and gay, and others Sophie didn't know – all holding a sign saying "Make it canon, you cowards".

"You guys really like Marvel, huh?"

"More than anything," Sunny declared without hesitation.

"More than Lucas?" *This or that?* had been an old favourite game with Freya.

The thought struck Sunny temporarily silent, as if this really were a question to take seriously. "Marvel love is for life," Sunny said, with a somewhat pained expression, but then, as she turned to look through the glass to where Lucas was standing with a candy-striped towel wrapped round his waist, chest bare and hair drying in curls crusted with sea salt, she made a low, strained, *hnnng* sort of sound in her throat. "Scratch that. I pick Lucas."

As they walked in, Sophie passed close to Win's body as she held the door.

"What about you?"

Win smiled and shook her head. "I don't like these games. If I can have all the things that make me happy, why would I choose? I want them all."

LUCAS

Lucas liked how his new clothes *looked*, but he wasn't so sure of the smell.

"I smell like a foot," he murmured to Sunny, who surprised him by pressing her entire face into his chest and inhaling dramatically.

When she pulled away her face was screwed up and she eyed him uncertainly. "Yeah. I think that's being generous. You smell like a foot that's been chopped off its body and buried in a damp cardboard box in the garden." Her whole face lit up. "But you still look pretty."

No one had ever accused Lucas of being pretty before Sunny.

"Oi. Vomit emojis. Are you getting an ice cream or not?" Ryan shouted from where they'd finally reached the front of the queue.

There was a lot of indecision, until Lucas asked what a lemon top was and Sophie and Ryan reacted with perfectly harmonised gasps of horror. When Win and Sunny looked equally blank, that settled it. Apparently it was law to try a lemon top at least once.

"Not for Win!" Sunny exclaimed. "Lactose!"

As Win buried her head in her hands and murmured something that sounded a lot like a death threat, Sophie changed her order, handing Win a cone that was all lemon top and no bottom.

"At least you've got an excuse," Sophie said, nodding at Lucas as the five of them settled in a line, sitting along the sea wall – Ryan and Lucas and Sunny and Win and Sophie – facing the beach so the breeze blew Lucas's fringe out of his ice cream. "You're from the south. They don't have the good stuff down there, but *you*." She bumped Win gently and looked across at Sunny. "You've lived here how long?"

"Whole life." Sunny had stopped speaking in sentences – words would have interfered too much with her attempt to devour her ice cream in less than twenty seconds.

When Ryan caught him watching her, he gave Lucas the slyest of smiles and came *very* close to being pushed off the wall and onto the sand.

Predictably, given that she'd made it her mission, Sunny finished first, everyone else taking time to savour what they'd paid for. As she brushed the crumbs of her cone onto the thighs of her leggings, then down onto the sand below, she took a short, in-out breath.

"So – and I know you're all going to hate me for this – but are you lot ever *actually* going to talk about Freya?"

WIN

Of course it would be Sunny who brought her up – just when Sophie had stopped.

"She has a point," Lucas said, backing up Sunny automatically because the two of them *were* adorable. "Last night we were all yelling at each other—"

"Or hitting," Ryan stuck in, but Win arched her brows in his direction and hissed, "You dunked him in the sea. Let it go."

"All because of Freya's parcel," Lucas pressed on. "Then we read our letters and we're here. Together."

Before he'd even finished, everyone other than Sunny was shaking their head, objecting to the Disney-movie spin Lucas was giving this.

"No." Win's voice was loudest and firmest, because that's exactly how she felt. "I'm not here because Freya told me that I could trust you." She noticed Ryan and Lucas pass a furtive look and wondered what they'd talked about in the laundrette. "I'm here because yesterday ended pretty badly. I don't just mean for Sophie, up by the church, but when I finally got to read my letter, it made me cross."

"How so?" Lucas asked, but it was Sunny who was looking at her the most intently. Sunny, who was always the first person Win shared anything with, who'd not heard a peep about what had been in Freya's letter.

"There's things I don't want to talk about just yet with you guys." Win felt Sophie lay her hand gently over her fingers, hidden from view by everyone else. "But Freya said a lot of stuff that made me feel like she thought she knew me better than she did. I felt … manipulated by what she said, by what she did with the parcel. So, although some of what she said turns out to have been right, that maybe I *have* enjoyed hanging out with you" – when she gave Ryan a slightly disapproving smile, he *almost* returned it – "I don't like the idea that I'm only here because she wanted me to be. I'm here because *I* want to be."

She sighed.

"Also, she said I was intimidating and—"

"You are."

"Totally."

"I'm actually a bit scared of you."

"You should be. This one time, when we were eight—"

Win rolled her eyes as Sunny started misquoting *Ragnarok*. "Oh my God, if one of us was Thor it would *not* be you."

Sophie leaned in and quietly said, "Surely you'd be Valkyrie?" And Win thought she might die from joy.

SOPHIE

Making Win smile was a reprieve. What Sophie needed to do was to stop avoiding the subject and meet it face on. Telling this lot about her lupus, talking to Win on the beach – all of it made Sophie feel stronger, like she wasn't in this alone any more.

"What was in your letter, Lucas, that makes you think this is what she wanted?" Sophie said. "I can't see any answer in mine."

"There is, though," Lucas said. "She thanked you for trusting her, said she missed you. That's pretty much all she said in mine."

But Sophie was shaking her head. She was done reaching for the answers she wanted when the truth was closer to hand.

"I've been sending her a message every day since she left." She felt the ripple of revelation pass along the wall. "If she really missed me all she had to do was reply. As for trust… I thought she wanted me to deliver that parcel and follow her trail because I was going to get an explanation for why she left." She looked across at Ryan and felt an unfamiliar pang of guilt. "Something that meant I could stop blaming myself or…"

"Me?" Ryan said and Sophie shrugged.

"You kind of set yourself up for it." She wanted to ask him what had happened. Whether he and Freya had been something more than a one-off mistake. She'd known him for years, but she felt now like she didn't know him at all. Much the same as Freya.

"Maybe that's the problem?" Lucas said, frowning into the sand. "You think it's something one of you did. I don't think that it was. I think the only person Freya made the decision for was her. Not in a selfish way…"

He broke off with a sigh, like he was impatient with the words and Sophie swore she could see Sunny's pupils turn to love hearts.

"I'm not saying this right."

"Do you mean that leaving is something Freya needed to do for herself?" Win offered.

"I do." Lucas cast her a grateful look. "She always talked like she was thinking of how everyone else would react. In my letter she apologised for never letting us be friends because she'd worried how Kellan would react."

There was a poignant pause as everyone looked at Ryan, but his gaze was fixed on the horizon.

"That does sound like Freya," Sophie said, quietly.

All of a sudden Ryan turned away from the sea to look across at them.

"Lucas is right. That's why Freya kept coming over, only wanting to know me out of school, when it was just us. She said she never felt like she had to perform."

A revelation that broke Sophie's heart just that little bit further because she knew now, for sure, that Freya had performed for her. They both had. A vicious circle of behaving the way each thought the other wanted to see.

This was why she'd never known about Ryan. Because Freya had pretended to hate him and Sophie had taken on the role of supportive friend.

For a while I worried Morgan was right, that Ryan had a thing for you.

Worried?

You'd have ended up with the wrong cousin.

Maybe she had.

Ryan shifted position on the wall, shirt falling open because they'd forgotten to check if it had any buttons. With the shorts and that shirt, hair crusted with salt from the sea, he looked like an extra from *Romeo + Juliet* that they'd watched at the end of Year 8.

Actually, from this angle, maybe if he had longer hair and less obvious ears, Ryan's weasely little face had a smidge of Leonardo DiCaprio-ness. The squinty eyes and slappable mouth maybe.

Sophie couldn't help herself. "Why you, Ryan?"

Ryan didn't know how to answer Sophie's question. It wasn't like he'd ever made himself worthy of Freya's attention. Except that had been the point, hadn't it?

"She saw through my bullshit. Looked harder than anyone else ever did." He scuffed the heel of his shoes against the wall. "Liked what she saw for some reason."

He knew they were all looking at him. All listening. Having started the conversation, Sunny was now nothing but wide eyes and flapping lugholes.

What came next was the truth. All the stuff he'd kept to himself – if he was ever going to share it, it had to be now.

"She came over to mine every Wednesday. Started in, like … October. Wasn't anything dodgy. She'd come back to mine after school because my mam and Jules would be out and we'd hang out, play a bit of *Mario Kart*, watch TV. Talk shit and waste time." He levered his foot wrong and his whole shoe nearly dropped off. Ryan lifted it up swiftly to pull it back on, still not looking to his right where he'd have to face the rest of them. "But Kellan couldn't know, could he?"

"No," Lucas said, voice little more than a murmur. Ryan caught a glimpse of Sophie nodding like she understood. He knew this was killing her though, the way it had killed him when he thought she was the one Freya still talked to. But same as he wished he'd known the truth about that, Sophie needed to know the truth about this.

"We kept it secret because of him, mostly, but I think

part of that was because she was trying to blow up a little bubble around us. Freya wanted something secret." Ryan sighed. "Then at the start of December, she kissed me. Just one kiss. Ruined everything, the dickhead. And after that I knew I couldn't see her. We fell out for real."

"I thought—" Sophie began.

"Yeah. I know you all thought. I know what Kellan read in that letter. Freya said we had sex, but she regretted the timing." He lifted a hand up and rubbed his eyes, still not knowing how the hell he was ever going to fix this. "I was half in love with her for months and I never did anything about it. It happened after she and Kellan broke up. At his sister's wedding."

"Was that...?" Lucas started the question even though he knew the answer.

"New Year's Eve. Up at bloody Rabscuttle Hall." Ryan opened his eyes and finally looked at the rest of them. "Freya and I had sex, then she left the next fucking morning and never spoke to me again."

December – 1 day before Freya left

Mam fussed over them before they went in, adjusting a grip in Jules' hair, making sure Ryan's buttonhole had been pinned on properly.

"I'll not have anyone say I don't take care of you," she muttered, cracking Ryan across the face with a rock-hard look. "And don't you cause any trouble."

"Why me? What about them?" Ryan flung his arm at where Jules was standing by the church gate looking angelic, but Mam pursed her lips.

"Not today, Ryan. I mean it."

Catholic weddings were long, although the audience participation kept Ryan on his toes (and his knees, and back up again), but he would have stayed there till midnight rather than go up to Rabscuttle for the reception.

The prospect of seeing Freya bubbled unpleasantly through his stomach. Although surely she had better things to do on New Year's Eve than serve tables at her ex-boyfriend's sister's wedding? Maybe if he hadn't cut her out completely he could have sent her a message to ask.

It had been the only thing he could think of, though. Make it so she'd never want to be alone with him again, because if Freya Newmarch had come knocking at his door after that kiss, well, it wasn't as if he'd ever said no to her before.

"This place is posh," Jules muttered as they pulled up outside the hotel.

Ryan grunted. The only way he and Jules and Mam could ever be in a place like this was if someone else was paying.

He hated it.

As Mam paced ahead, her children hung back, the sequins that glimmered on the lapels of Jules' jacket at odds with their mood. A family occasion like this was their worst nightmare – trapped with people whose idea of them lay in the past, not the present, as if a snapshot from the last big Christmas was all a person could ever be.

Ryan had always been the one to get the funny looks – his

reputation for trouble a rumour that travelled to every branch, twig and tiny little bud of the family tree. Now it was Jules, Ryan wished the two of them could swap.

The best he could do was keep his word from last night.

I'll stay close, if you want.

Thanks, but … if someone says anything, just correct them and move on. Sometimes making a big deal makes it worse, Ry.

You sound like Mam.

I'm serious.

So Ryan had promised. Which meant it was best to go for an orange juice instead of the flutes of champagne weaving their way round the room on perfectly balanced silver trays.

When Ryan looked for Freya, he found her. Her tray was full of empties and her hair was pulled back in a high ponytail, her face bland and professional and beautiful. She moved with practised grace, black waistcoat sculpting her into something slimmer than the school uniform he was so familiar with.

"Maybe stop ogling Kellan's ex quite so obviously?" Jules said with a grin. They knew that Freya and Ryan had been friends, but not about the kiss. Jules felt anxious enough around Kellan without having to keep that kind of secret.

"Yeah, umm, actually, I think I need the loo." Ryan watched as Freya took her tray full of empties across the far side of the room. "If you don't need me?"

Jules rolled their eyes and glanced to where Mam was standing with some of the groom's side of the family.

"I'll be fine."

Ryan shoved his orange juice at his sibling and slipped through the crowd, aware that this was the best time to catch Freya, while his cousin had been called away for photos.

The corridor she'd turned down was long and empty and she was almost at the end.

"Freya!"

She stopped, her shoulders dropping in a sigh before she turned.

"So you're talking to me now?"

Ryan didn't know how he got so close so fast. Too little time for the words to surface from the sea of shame swimming inside him – all he could do was look at her and think how utterly ridiculous he'd been to push her away.

"I'm sorry."

"For what?" Freya glanced round, saw a side table with a vase of gold-sprayed sticks poking out of it and set her tray down.

"For blanking you. After we – when…" He swallowed.

"The word you're looking for is 'kissed'." The way she lifted her chin as she said it, made him feel like a coward. "And you *should* be sorry because it was a shitty thing to do."

"I know, I…" He ran his hand up the back of his head against the bristles of the number one he'd had round the back and sides in preparation for the wedding. He wished he'd prepared for this. His hand dropped to his side where it ached to reach out and touch the girl in front of him. "Look. I thought it was best if we didn't risk it happening again and I – maybe I took it too far."

"When do you not?" She sighed and looked down as she twisted the cuff of her shirt round, avoiding his eye. "It doesn't matter now anyway. It's done. We're done."

"I don't want to be."

"But you *did* and…" her words faded out and she finally met his eye. The look on her face nearly broke him. "I missed us."

Then she was gone, through the doors marked STAFF ONLY, the tray of empty glasses left to stand on the side table.

Ryan and Jules and Mam were on the second-to-top table, where Auntie Lou could keep darting over to gossip with Mam. The three of them, along with Kellan, were clustered at the middle of the table, book-ended by crepey-faced family members, with a couple of the groom's best friends at either end.

After the mains, the floor manager directed Freya to clear the next table over and Ryan watched her, wishing it was their table she'd been sent to. Although maybe not, since someone had brought up the story of another wedding, long ago, when Kellan had dared him to run onstage and moon the audience halfway through the best man's speech.

A memory that neither Mam nor Ryan wanted to relive, but that Auntie Lou – who'd pulled a chair up and stage-whispered that the top table was a drag – had cackled at.

"Bless our Ry," she said, giving him a fond look. "Never been one for behaving, have you, pet?"

Ryan tried on a smile and watched as Freya added a

third plate to the stack balanced on her arm.

"It's a shame he can't go to Campion Boys'." From Uncle Tim's sister, who'd been sitting on his right and ignoring him all meal.

"We're not Catholic, Karen," Mam replied.

In spite of himself, Ryan exchanged a twitch of a smile with Kellan, who was as Catholic as a bear shitting on the Pope.

"But it's such a good school and excellent on discipline. My two flourished – and look at Kellan, doing so well."

Ryan coughed a "bollocks" that wasn't subtle enough to go undetected. Arching wafer-thin eyebrows at him, Karen said, "Swear words are for people too illiterate to use proper ones."

"What if I use sign language, Auntie Karen?" Ryan's hands flew up, both middle fingers in full view.

Jules folded forward until their head rested on the tablecloth as Mam whipped her arm across the table to slap her son's hands.

"Ryan! Apologise at once!"

"Apolo-what? That's too long a word for me." Ryan pushed his chair back abruptly and walked off, not caring about whatever scandal he'd left behind.

Auntie Karen was a dick.

The toilets were a better place to be than the dinner table and Ryan locked himself comfortably in one of the cubicles, burning through what little battery he had left on his phone until a message came through from Jules.

Did you drown, like?

He should go back. *Sorry for ditching you.*

It's fine. Everyone's being really nice to me – they pity me for having you as a brother.

Bet they think you'd be better off with Kellan.

They'd be very wrong then, wouldn't they?

Sighing, Ryan gave up his peace and returned to the Speedwell Suite, where the tables had been rearranged to make room for a dancefloor and a buffet table of desserts, the centrepiece of which was a chocolate fountain surrounded by swirls of chopped fruit and marshmallows. Ryan had already helped himself to several handfuls of exclusively white marshmallows when Kellan found him.

"Excellent work at dinner, mate." He did a chef's kiss, blowing traces of alcohol into the air. "Made me look like a saint."

When Kellan took a marshmallow from Ryan's plate, he held it under the chocolate, then wiped a smear of it on Ryan's cheek. Didn't work when Ryan tried to do it with his finger.

The two of them stood together, watching the room, Kellan fit to walk the red carpet while Ryan looked as if he'd come dressed as his butler.

The fact that his aunt had paid for his outfit didn't help matters.

"Jules is looking very sparkly tonight," Kellan said out of nowhere, eyes narrowed as he stared at where Jules was dancing with Heather and a couple of her university friends, flailing around, taking the piss out of the adults.

Alcohol made Kellan more of himself. More confident,

more charming, more cutting – innocent words were anything but when Ryan's cousin smiled like that.

"Don't start." Ryan ground his teeth, his promise to Jules the only thing keeping his fists locked safely away in his pockets. "I'm not in the mood."

Kellan cocked his head, eyes like ice-chips in the cool blue light over the dancefloor. Then he shrugged and reached out to hold a strawberry under the fountain.

"You know what I am in the mood for?" he said, looking round the room with interest. "Sex with my ex."

Ryan thought about saying nothing. Ignored his own advice.

"Leave her alone, Kellan. She's working."

"So?"

"So shagging one of the wedding guests on her break might get her fired." He should leave it there… "Assuming she'd even want to."

Kellan laughed, loud and cruel. "Of course she'd want to. She always does when I'm the one asking, she's—"

"Shut up."

Kellan's grin only grew wider – like he'd found what he'd been hunting for in a place he'd not expected.

"I'll talk about her however I like."

Ryan's hand flashed out to grip his cousin's jaw, squeezing it tight enough that he could feel Kellan's teeth through his cheek.

"Rethink what you're saying."

Beyond them, the dancefloor was a frenzy of movement, of arms in the air, people singing along, too absorbed in the music to notice what was happening by the dessert table.

Ryan held Kellan there a moment, not knowing what would come next until it happened. Until he had enough control to let go and lower his hand.

Only Kellan had to push. Had to lean in and whisper what would happen when he got Freya alone...

He only had himself to blame for making it all too easy for Ryan to shove his smug head into the chocolate fountain.

Mam could (and did) blame Ryan's dad for a lot of his worst failings, but his temper came from her. Rage was what drove her, made her bloody-minded and bold.

Not a force to be reckoned with so much as flattened by.

Being out in the corridor with her was terrifying and Ryan pressed his back against the wall, feeling an intense pity for all the people who paid her to yell at them as they sobbed through their sit-ups.

"Every time – like you can't help ruining everything." Ryan set his jaw and avoided her eye. "Could you maybe think of *anyone* other than yourself? Kellan's family, he's your cousin, my sister's son—"

"Oh my God! Kellan this, Kellan that – why can no one else see that he's an absolute tool?"

"Because he's not the one who gave an old woman the finger and tried to drown *the bride's brother* in a chocolate fountain!" she screamed back at him, face contorted so that if she hadn't been shouting, Ryan would have thought she was crying.

"Maybe I had a good reason—"

"I. Don't. Care." She brought her hands up to her head, nails scraping into her scalp. The hair she'd spent so long styling coming loose with frustration. "All I want is for you to stop being such an absolute arsehole at every possible opportunity."

"Tell that to Kellan!"

"Kellan isn't my son—"

"*Bet you wish he fucking was!*" The words tore out of him, louder and more violent than all the others, his throat ripping with the force of it.

Mam looked at him, mouth still twisted down in disgust.

"Right now I just wish you weren't mine."

She opened the little clutch bag she'd brought, not even looking at him as she took out a ten pound note and handed it to him. "Reception can call you a taxi and you'll pay me back for the fare."

Ryan waited until she left, then went and sat on the stairs. The taxi could wait. He'd rather remain hidden and alone. Sinking forwards, he rested his head on his forearm, hate towing him under.

Hate for his mam, but mostly for Kellan for always being there to make him look worse. The golden boy who got away with murder because no one ever caught him holding the weapon.

His phone went – a message from Jules.

What happened to not causing a scene???

He was going on about Freya and I lost it. Then Ryan added: *Mam's told me to go home but I can stay if you need?*

Jules replied with a selfie of them with someone Ryan recognised from across the aisle in the church. Both of them were grinning into the camera, Jules' arm slung round the other person's shoulder.

Ally ran a protest when their school banned an LGBTQ+ book from the library. I have found my people. And honestly, Ry, maybe don't piss Mam off any more?

That hurt. He was always on Jules' side, for everything, but Jules couldn't be on his?

Too pissed off to reply, Ryan got up from the stairs and hurried past the doors to the Speedwell Suite. The band was playing "All Star" and Ryan wished he was the kind of person who could ever just enjoy something like this; dance around like a twat and sing along to a song without thinking that it would lead to some crashing downfall.

As he turned the corner into reception, he saw Freya. She was sitting on the window seat by one of the front windows, one ankle hooked up over the other knee, scarf on, jacket across her lap as she looked out into the night.

She looked too sad, too alone, too much like how he felt for him not to talk to her.

She must have seen his reflection because she turned just before he could speak.

"Hey you."

"Hi." He pulled his coat on awkwardly over his suit.

"Going home so soon?" she asked.

"I've been kicked out for bad behaviour."

"Shocker." The way she smiled suggested she'd not heard what he'd done, which was for the best.

"You?"

"I've behaved perfectly well, thanks." She stood up and slipped her jacket on. "But some of us never wanted to be here in the first place."

"Ah, well next time they ask you to work a shift when your ex is there you'll know not to accept."

"There won't be a next time." Her voice, the look on her face, everything about her sounded final.

And Ryan realised his mistake. The one he'd made back when Kellan had first demanded that Ryan introduce him to that fit blonde girl he'd been talking to.

From the beginning, he'd assumed that Freya belonged to Kellan, same as everyone else. But she didn't.

Freya belonged to no one.

But if she wanted, then he could belong to her.

"Come on." Freya hopped off the window seat and handed him her phone. "I want a photo of me leaving this place."

She stage-directed herself and made him take more shots than he would have thought necessary – as far as Ryan was concerned she looked amazing in all of them, but he watched as she tutted and deleted and whittled them all away to one that she murmured something about posting after midnight.

Then she glanced round at the reception desk and the few guests that were sitting on the sofas by the fire, then at Ryan before she slid her hand into his and pulled him out of the door she'd just been posing in front of, out into the night where no one would see them, because alone was the only way they worked.

"About before," Ryan began, wanting to say something,

anything, that might give him a chance to explain himself.

Only the words dried up as he looked at her, lit only by the glow of the moon and the lights angled away from them towards the hall, her face all planes and shadows but for the pools of her eyes and the swell of her lips.

"I missed us too," Ryan said. "That's all."

She looked furious with him, but the hand that wasn't in his ran down the length of his arm as she frowned at his tie and then, without any warning, she was holding him, arms wrapped around him, face pressed into his shoulder so that his nose was pressed into her hair, breathing her in like he had when they were sitting on his sofa watching TV.

"God, you're such a dick," she whispered.

"Yeah, sorry about that," Ryan murmured into the top of her head.

"I don't care though. Not tonight." And she leaned back, her eyes all over his face, searching for something he wasn't sure she would find.

So he kissed her. In case that was it.

She didn't hesitate, didn't push him away, but pulled him closer, kissed him so deeply that it took his breath away and he had to break the surface just to stay alive.

"Freya—"

"Shut up." She kissed him, just briefly. "You have a knack for saying the wrong things and right now I'd rather concentrate on *doing* the wrong things."

"What do you—"

There came the crunch of gravel and headlights swung across them as a taxi turned into the forecourt.

"That's for me." Freya glanced at the car, then looked at him as she said, "My mum's out all night."

Ryan said nothing, needing to hear the words before he could trust what he thought might be happening.

"Come home with me." Freya looked as raw and vulnerable as she had the night she'd first knocked on his door. "I don't want to be alone by myself – I want to be alone with you."

He wanted to go with her. *God* did he want to. But the thought scared him. Not of what would happen if Kellan ever found out – guilt could wait till tomorrow – but of what would happen with Freya.

He couldn't lose her again.

"I want to." He couldn't resist kissing her, just quickly, his next words whispered into her mouth. "But shouldn't we take this slower?"

Only Freya was shaking her head and for a moment he thought she might be crying, until she kissed him again, her hands fisted in his coat and pulling him close.

"It's now or never, Ryan."

SOPHIE

Sunny blurted out, "But the letter! The way Kellan went on I thought this happened when him and Freya were together?" and Sophie exchanged a look with Lucas. That letter could have been worded with the accuracy of a legally binding contract and Kellan wouldn't have taken it any better.

When the alarm went off on Win's phone, the rest of them jumped off the wall as Sophie slithered off in the least elegant manner possible. Elegance required enough energy to care. As it was, Sophie barely had enough to make it back to the car. Every move she made conjured a throb or a stab of some form of pain: in her left side, the promise of a migraine swelling behind her eye socket, even the impact of landing on the pavement echoed from the soles of her feet to the inside of her mouth where a row of ulcers were emerging along her lower lip.

"Can I stay here while you guys get their stuff?" They all went into a frenzy of concerned nodding, but as Win took a step back, the offer of keeping Sophie company yet to make it as far as words, Sophie shook her head. "I'd like to talk to Ryan."

Once they'd gone, Ryan turned to look at her with a familiar wariness, like she was about to confirm his suspicions that the world was out to get him. Back at the amusements Win might have said that winning wasn't in his nature, but Ryan was a strong contender for that undesirable prize of who hurt the most.

"What?"

"I just wanted to say sorry. For how it's been with us – since she left, and maybe before too." Sophie searched his expression, a cliff face on which she was trying to find purchase. "I might have got a few things wrong about you."

"A few." Something in him shifted, like he wanted her to make the climb. "But she was your best mate and I didn't treat her well—"

"She didn't treat you well, either."

All he did was shrug, like that was something he could forgive more easily than he could forgive himself.

"Maybe not," he said. "Maybe she had her reasons. I thought I knew what those were, but I'm as good at getting things wrong as you are."

Sophie turned to look out at the sea, the way she had with Win on the beach before she read her letter, thinking of all the things everyone else had said just now, what Freya had been trying to say with all of this.

"I think Freya got a lot of things wrong as well," she said, tucking her hair back behind her ear from where the breeze was trying to blow it across her lips. "But I think she got us right."

"What do you mean?"

Sophie looked at him once more, tried to see him beyond the filter of all the things she thought she knew.

"I think Freya might actually have figured out what we need. Not then, but now." Sophie took her hand from her pocket and held it out. "We can't start over, but I think we could build on what we've got a little better than before."

Ryan looked at her for a long moment, eyes narrowed to

nothing against the sun, before he reached out to shake on it – his clasp firm without being too tight. Like he knew he needed to be careful.

"I think we could."

RYAN

Ryan had been sitting on an ever-swelling bladder for the last half hour of the journey. Before Win even put the handbrake on outside Lucas's house, he thumped the back of Sophie's seat and demanded she get out.

"I need a piss."

Lucas showed no such urgency. As Ryan danced a desperate jig on the pavement, Lucas snuggled a sleepy Sunny on the backseat, the two of them making promises to see each other the next day...

Ryan rapped a knuckle on the window and threatened to piss on Lucas's door if he didn't get a shift on. If they were seeing each other tomorrow, they didn't need to drag out their goodbyes now, did they?

Lucas's home wasn't so different to Ryan's. Cosier and cleaner, mind, with a stairwell of family pictures that Ryan would have nosied a bit if he hadn't been sprinting up the stairs and heading for the sweet release of the second door on the right. The place was empty, but Lucas had warned him that his uncle would be sleeping off his nightshift and not to flush.

One swift pass round the bathroom – taps free from the crust of limescale, and more toiletries than crowded the tills at TK Maxx – and Ryan sauntered back on out, taking his time as he studied the pictures down the stairs.

"Are you even in any of these?" Ryan said when he got to the bottom, where Lucas was standing in the door through to the lounge, dead phone transferred from pocket to hand and looking no more lively.

"Not on the stairs. There's a couple in the lounge."

Ryan thought back to when he'd lived in his cousin's house – how he'd never felt like he'd ever be able to call it home – and wondered whether it was like that for Lucas. Probably not. He didn't have Kellan as a cousin for a start.

Ryan stopped on the doormat, not sure he actually wanted to leave. Back home all he had to look forward to was revision he had no intention of doing and questions from Mam about why he'd run off.

"Lucas?" It was the first time he'd called him anything other than Big T and they both took a second to acknowledge that. "It's been all right, hanging out with you today."

"Says the guy who's done nothing but take the piss out of me."

But he held out his fist for a tap and stepped a bit closer, half a head taller and twice as wide. Twice as soft, too.

Ryan tapped his fist. It felt more like a welcome than a goodbye.

As Ryan started to say, "See you ar—" someone knocked on the door, making him jump half out of his skin.

Since he was closest, Ryan reached for the handle, not needing to know which of the girls it was to start gloating.

"Guess I'm not the only one with a weak—"

Not one of the girls.

For one second, Lucas had exactly zero idea of what was happening. All he knew was that Ryan had opened the door and was now trying very hard to shut it again.

He failed.

Whoever was on the other side managed to force it open to launch themselves into Lucas's front hall.

Kellan.

"Get the fuck back here!"

So much for not waking his uncle.

Ryan had made for the stairs, but Kellan was on him, pulling him back down so the two of them toppled back into the hall in a heap of elbows and fists, crashing into the radiator with a clang.

Whatever fight he'd broken up last night was nothing compared to this: Kellan's punches caught the side of Ryan's head, each one short and savage enough to make Lucas wince.

He might have sworn not to get into any more fights, but it was better to break a promise than stand by and watch Kellan break Ryan's skull.

Hauling Kellan away was ten times harder than when it had been Ryan. He might not be all that big, but most of him was muscle, and he was intent on using all of it to inflict as much damage as he possibly could. Not just on Ryan, but on anything he could reach – by the time Lucas managed to push Kellan back towards the door and get between them, the hall was a warzone of a toppled vase of fake flowers, a cracked frame knocked from the wall and a scattering of the little figurines that had been lined up along the shelf above the radiator.

The hall filled with ragged breathing and animosity as Kellan glared past Lucas to where Ryan had pulled himself upright on the stairs.

"What's he doing here?" Kellan said, voice low and dangerous.

Lucas hadn't a clue where to start. This was not how he'd planned on having this conversation. Truth was, he'd not necessarily planned on having it at all – had hoped there might be some workaround that meant he got to stay in Kellan's good graces until after Ryan was forgiven and the whole thing was forgotten.

He'd underestimated the situation.

"Look. Me and Ryan have been out with some friends—"

"I'm your fucking friend, Big T. *Me*. Without me you wouldn't have any mates at all." Kellan's anger landed as hard as one of those punches.

Remember where your loyalties lie…

"Look," Lucas said. "Hear him out. It's not what you think."

Lucas had never had someone put enough faith in him to know what betrayal looked like, but that's what he was seeing in Kellan. The widening of his eyes and the slight, shocked gape that came a second before his face transformed into nothing but snarl and savagery.

"You knew?"

"No – I didn't—"

As Kellan lunged towards him, Ryan sprang up and whatever violence Kellan thought he could threaten against one of them faded at the prospect of taking on both.

"He didn't know anything till today," Ryan said. "And whatever you think, Kell, you don't either."

"I saw what was in that letter. Or did you think I couldn't read?"

"It happened after. I swear!" There was a plea in the way Ryan was saying it, the desperation of someone who'd never had anyone believe them. "I wouldn't do that. I *couldn't*."

Kellan's eyes narrowed like he might actually be listening, but then he curled his lip and shook his head.

"Do you think I'm that gullible? You slept with my girlfriend—"

"I slept with *Freya*. She's got a name," Ryan shot back. "And she wasn't your girlfriend when it happened. I *swear*."

Ryan trembled so hard with the need for his cousin to believe him that Lucas could feel it – judging by the cruel twist of his lips, Kellan could see it too. The best way to hurt Ryan wasn't with his fists, but with his faith.

"You're a fucking liar. I should have expected it. You always want whatever it is I've got. Why should my girlfriend be any different?"

Lucas planted an arm in front of Ryan to stop him taking any further steps towards Kellan.

"Freya's not a prize to fight over," he murmured. "Kellan, mate—"

"I'm not your mate," Kellan spat back. "Mates stick together."

"Mates can tell each other when they're out of order," Lucas said, calm coming along with the words. "But if you can't hear me say that, then I guess you're right. We aren't mates at all."

For a long moment, Lucas held Kellan's eye, hoping that there might still be a way back from this – that he could accept Ryan's explanation and let Lucas get away with sticking up for him. He didn't want to lose the first friend he'd made at Campion for the sake of someone else's pride.

"Well then. Fuck you." The words hit hard, spat through narrowed lips and accompanied with a look so cold that Lucas felt it spread to his own skin. A numbing of something that used to bring warmth.

When Kellan opened the door Lucas saw his rucksack on the front step – the one he'd left round Kellan's – and felt a fleeting twang of guilt that Kellan had cared enough to drop it off. Kellan kicked it on his way out, then turned to look back at where Lucas and Ryan remained in the hall.

"I'm done with both of you."

But as he sloped off down the front path, Lucas had a feeling it was he and Ryan who were finally done with Kellan Spencer.

WIN

The first any of them knew about Kellan's visit was when Sophie interrupted them by turning the radio down as Sunny belted out the chorus to "Starships", pointing out of the window and saying, "Er. Why is Kellan walking out of Lucas's front door?"

After that there'd been a flurry of concern as they hurried up the path, only to meet Ryan and Lucas at the door. Despite the fact that Ryan was the one bleeding (again), Sunny launched herself at Lucas and held him so tight that rather than prise her off him, Win suggested Lucas walk Sunny home while she dropped off the others.

"What the hell was all that about?" Sophie asked from the back, having relinquished the front seat.

"Really bad timing," Ryan said, looking utterly shattered as he collapsed back against the headrest.

"Are you going to be OK?" Win asked. "Or should we take shifts giving you round-the-clock protection?"

When Ryan let out a mirthless "Huh!" Win felt a tiny glow of pride at finally landing a joke on that one.

"Right now I'm just glad I don't have to avoid him in the exam hall like Lucas."

"Don't say the cursed word!" Sophie yelled from the back and Ryan grinned once more.

When they dropped him off, it almost felt like peace. The drive to Sophie's house was too short, and when Win pulled up at the bottom of her drive once more, neither seemed inclined to say goodbye.

Sophie had faded fast on the drive back from the sea. Several times, Win had glanced over to see her resting her head against the window, eyes closed. Shadowed crescents touched the tops of her cheeks and for all she was smiling, when she blinked, her lids only managed it halfway towards open.

"My mum's going to kill me," Sophie said, not making any move at all towards getting out. "At the very least I'm in for a lot of *Sophie Eleanor Charbonneau*-ing."

"See you only have that level – same as the *Winnie Su* level. But my parents have the option of going extra and pulling out my Chinese name. If they go full *Su Qiuyue* I know I'm never leaving the house till uni."

"And I bet you've never been *Su Qiuyue*-d once in your life." When Sophie said her name, she copied the sound perfectly.

"Once or twice – not nearly as often as Sunny gets *Xiaohui*-d." She saw Sophie's interested eyebrow twitch. "Although if you really want to wind her up, call her Amy. She *hates* it."

Sophie was chuckling, *"Amy?* You're kidding. She's so not an Amy."

Win held Sophie's gaze and thought about the way this had been happening with greater frequency since she'd shown her Freya's letter. Nerves rippled through her. This stuff was so much easier online, when she could analyse all the flirty messages in the safety of her own room and dissect a screengrab on a private chat.

"If I survive the *Sophie Eleanor Charbonneau*-ing, do

you think we could hang out again?" Sophie said.

"I think we could."

"Not just with the others…"

"I would definitely like not to have to hang out with my sister every time I see you."

"Or Ryan."

"Lucas is OK, but … then we're back to the Sunny problem."

"So. Just us."

"Just us."

Just. Us.

"I should go."

"Same."

There was one moment more of sharing a smile, a moment that unspooled every last bit of resolve that Win had wound round herself. That made her think that if – *if* – Sophie could like her as something more than a friend, then maybe Win wouldn't be waiting until university before she kissed someone else…

She watched as Sophie climbed out of the car and slumped up the drive, casting one last look over her shoulder before she put her key to the door and disappeared from view.

SOPHIE

Mum was in the hall before Sophie was through the door. Storm-dark expression, landline in one hand, mobile in the other. The two of them stood in silence, staring at each other as if prepared to duel. Then Mum let out a sob and pulled Sophie into a hug as desperate as the day she was diagnosed.

"I am *so* angry with you right now," she hissed into Sophie's scalp as she pressed a kiss on her hair. Sophie didn't have the heart to tell her that even that hurt. "You *cannot* do that to me. Not ever. I don't care how cross you are with me, you can't run away and leave me a *note*."

Oh God. She was just like Freya...

"I'm sorry," Sophie whispered, struggling to overcome the discomfort of having a phone jammed into her spine as her mum held her tight.

"That apology is far short of good enough, Sophie Eleanor." Mum gave her one last squeeze before releasing her, finally putting both phones down so she could tilt Sophie's face into the light that fell through the stairwell. "You look awful."

"Thanks a lot." She could have said the same of her mum, whose hair had been raked into a rough ponytail, eyes pink and puffy. She didn't, though. This was not an argument between equals.

"Have you eaten?"

Sophie nodded without elaborating. Fish and chips and an ice cream wouldn't please a woman who thought kale for breakfast was a treat.

"How's the pain?"

Almost overwhelmingly high. The ache in her left side had turned from insistent to agonising and a curtain of exhaustion threatened to draw her mind shut with every blink.

The look on her face was all the reply Mum needed.

"OK." Mum tucked her lips away and gave Sophie's arm the lightest touch. "We will have the conversation about consequences tomorrow – but they will be severe. Understand?"

"Understand."

"I don't think you do. I don't think you *can*." Any attempts at stern disappeared as she pulled Sophie in for another hug and a head kiss. "I was *beside* myself. I called your brother" – like Christopher would have been any help – "I called your friends' parents. I even called Anji Newmarch."

Sophie pulled back with a frown.

"You really must have been desperate," she said. Her mum and Freya's did *not* like each other.

"I know you think I'm clueless, but I *am* your mother. When Freya left, part of you went missing too." She stroked Sophie's face with the backs of her fingers, her smile as sad as Sophie's. "I worried you might have gone to Manchester to get it back."

This shook her. That Mum had thought this and Sophie had never even considered it. Not once. When she'd run, it hadn't been to Freya. It had been to Win and the others. But mostly Win.

Mum helped her up the stairs and along the landing,

leaving her daughter to slump onto her bed, bag still slung over her shoulders.

Sophie could change in a minute. Put on something comforting and lie down and rest. Wait to see if she could recover enough of herself to eat whatever vegetable-heavy tea Mum had left to prepare down in the kitchen.

It took her a moment to realise that her face was pressed into fresh bedding and the floor had been cleared of everything she'd let build up over the last few weeks. Clothes sat in a neatly folded pile on the window seat ready to be put away, jewellery hanging on the little hooks hammered into one of her picture frames. Even her make-up had been "tidied" away – a jumble of palettes and tubes and tubs swept haphazardly into an empty shoe box and put on the bedside table.

Next to her phone.

Sophie opened it up to find a message on there from Win.

Hopefully you'll live to see this…

Smiling, Sophie replied with a ghost emoji and *RIP me*.

There were other messages on there, but Sophie couldn't bring herself to read them. Not now.

Just as she'd managed to get as far as taking her bag off, her phone buzzed again, and she reached out for it. If Win wanted to chat, she could maybe find some dregs of energy for that…

Except it wasn't Win.

A text from an unknown number: *Hi*.

Frowning, Sophie wondered if it was Lucas or Ryan.

Although … a text was a bit of a presumption. A private message via Insta or Messenger, maybe… Then came another.

It's me. Freya.

Sophie felt like she'd swallowed her own heart.

New phone. New number.

Slowly, not sure she was ready, Sophie typed a reply: *Hey.*

I'm sorry I didn't reply to your messages. It's … well, there were Reasons. I've only just opened up my old phone. Saw your messages.

She'd sent Freya more than just texts. She'd sent emails, private messages through every channel imaginable. And Freya hadn't replied to them either. Maybe she'd got a new email, new accounts – maybe Freya hadn't just abandoned the old ones, but built herself anew.

She was still typing: *I never meant to hurt you. I'm sorry.*

Yesterday, that might have been enough. Today, though, Sophie was no longer so desperate to have Freya back that she could forgive all this on the strength of a couple of texts.

Freya had been her best friend. She was the first person Sophie wanted to share a joke with, whose messages she never skipped reading. She was the reason to go out on a night when Sophie wanted to stay in; a reason to stay home when she'd wanted to go out. School was better with her in it. *Life* was better with her in it.

Or it had been until she left.

After five months of pretending to everyone else that Freya was still her best friend, it came as a surprise to find that she'd stopped pretending to herself.

Her screen lit up, phone buzzing on her lap.

A call from the unknown number.

A call from Freya.

It was up to Sophie if she wanted to accept it.

A NOTE ABOUT SOPHIE

Sophie does a lot for someone with her condition. It's been a balancing act between writing a character with believable symptoms of lupus and one with enough energy for plot purposes. I took a lot of excellent advice from friends with chronic illnesses and Amy Frances Baker, who has written articles about her experience with lupus for *Glamour* and Lupus UK.

In the end, we have a character who is experiencing an improvement in her symptoms because of her medication, but is still vulnerable to severe pain, brain fog and the ever-present threat of fatigue. (Not to mention the side effects of her medication.) She's also been diagnosed very quickly; it's notoriously hard to get a diagnosis for lupus because of the wide range of symptoms that can present, but Sophie has one in under a year. Seven is the average.

While I'd urge you to have a look at www.lupusuk.org.uk, I'd also suggest you look up Spoon Theory as originally described by Christine Miserandino on her Facebook page. Some readers will already be familiar with Spoon Theory, but if you're not, please have a look – Miserandino has lupus and the post was written to convey her experience to others.

ACKNOWLEDGEMENTS

Welp. This hasn't been an easy one, but we got there in the end. Something that couldn't have happened without the relay of editorial work from Annalie Grainger and Gráinne Clear – when I say thank you, I mean "thank you for making the story better and for not actually murdering me when I was being as difficult to you as the book was being to me".

Thank you as ever to the editorial team at Walker, from copy edits by Jenny Bish to editorial overviews from Denise Johnstone-Burt. Thank you to Maria Soler Canton and Helen Crawford-White for another cracking cover and Anna Robinette for typesetting, and to all the production, sales, marketing and publicity staff who turn ideas into books and get them out there for people to read.

Thank you to Jane Finigan who continues to be the absolute perfect agent for me no matter what stage I'm at in the cycle.

This book needed a lot of eyes on it other than mine. I am eternally grateful to Claire Yau, who talked to me right at the start of the process, and to Wei Ming Kam who read it once it was the best I could get it and still saw ways to make it better. Both of you have had invaluable editorial input and said things to make me smile and also to make me hungry – thank you. Thank you also to Echo Wu who translated Win and Sunny's bilingual squabbles.

Thank you to the people who helped me more on so many aspects of Sophie's experience, but especially to Amy Frances Baker who pulled me up so brilliantly on so much. You helped turn a fictional character into something much better than I could have done alone. Thank you to Lupus UK and all the teenagers and young people who let me sit in one of your group sessions and shared some of your experiences with me. It gave me great insight into how different each person's experience of lupus can be and I hope I've done something good with what you gave.

Kim Warren, you were an absolute star and I'm very grateful for your extremely speedy read!

Oh dear God. I crowdsourced so much from Twitter, how the hell am I going to thank everyone properly? But if you answered one of my polls, if you tweeted me something and I said "Ooh great!" – honestly, I love you. You helped and I appreciate it, even if I didn't record your name properly.

To the people who put up with me IRL over the last million (?) years: thanks. Most heartfelt and sincerely to Lisa Williamson, who held me together on multiple occasions and also named half of Kellan Spencer. To Courtney Smyth who named the other half of Kellan Spencer and gave me the gift of your time and your energy and your insight. Thank you to Robin Stevens, who provided safe spaces for raging and sobbing and flailing. (And writing I guess?) To The Agency – Darran and Dave and Si-Pee and Ashley – there's been a lot of belief flowing from that source. And Alysia for always being my most fervent cheerleader.

And to my family. Thanks to my mum who let me grumble lots on the phone. (Maybe that'll stop now?) Thank you to my small one who showed support in the week of half term by never asking me anything other than "Is your book done yet?" To my big one, Pragmatic Dan. Dear God. I love you.

No thanks to the cats, you were no help at all.

Enjoyed **Every Little Piece of My Heart**?

We'd love to hear your thoughts.

🐦 #EveryLittlePiece
@WalkerBooksUK
@WalkerBooksYA
@NonPratt

📷 @WalkerBooksYA
@NonPratt